The Wild Road
To Key West

Michael Reisig

THE WILD ROAD TO KEY WEST
Copyright © 2017
Clear Creek Press/Michael Reisig (reisig@ipa.net)

All rights reserved. No part of this publication may be reproduced, stored in a retrieval system, or transmitted in any form, or by any other means, electronic, mechanical, photocopying, recording, or otherwise, without written permission from the publisher.

Paperback - 978-0-9990914-3-2
E-book - 978-0-9990914-2-5

Cover design by Powell Graphics
Cover design copyright © 2017 Clear Creek Press

Published by Clear Creek Press
P.O. Box 1081, Mena, AR 71953
1-479-394-4992

Once again, this book is dedicated to the lady of my life, Bonnie Lee. When I look back and see all the mistakes I would have made, the plethora of wrong turns I could have so easily taken, and all the challenges that would have been so much more formidable without her, I realize how kind Spirit has been in gifting me this single soul.

OTHER TITLES BY MICHAEL REISIG

The Road To Key West

Back On The Road To Key West

Along The Road To Key West

Somewhere On The Road To Key West

Down The Road To Key West

Beyond The Road To Key West

A Far Road To Key West

• • •

Caribbean Gold Book I — The Treasure of Tortuga

Caribbean Gold Book II — The Treasure of Time

Caribbean Gold Book III — The Treasure of Margarita

• • •

The Golden Persuader

The New Madrid Run

The Hawks of Kamalon

ACKNOWLEDGMENTS

One of those quotes that has always carried such weight with me is: "If it ain't broken, don't fix it." That is absolutely how I look at my editing team. Through the recent years, they have simply been irreplaceable.

Thanks so much, as always, to my beta readers: Virginia Williams, whose insight to plot and characters is so valuable; Tim Slaughter, who never fails to find something of great value to add or fix; and Kenneth Morris, whose encouragement always lends confidence to my uncertain ego.

Then there is my incredibly talented final editor and dear friend, Cris Wanzer. She takes what has been collected and sculpts it into a professional, accurate medium for publishing. I will say it again because it is so true. I don't know what I would do without her. (www.ManuscriptsToGo.com)

Finally, there is Donna Rich, who at the end makes a final clean sweep of it all and hands me back a book ready for print.

I would be remiss to not also mention my buddy, Dale Powell, whose artistic talent has provided me with such wonderful book covers.

I've said it before, but it's just as true this time: I owe the lion's share of my success to these people, and I am so grateful…

—Michael Reisig

PREFACE

Current scientific thought is that the earth was formed about 4.54 billion years ago. During that time, much of the planet was molten because of numerous collisions with other celestial bodies and continuous volcanic activity. As time passed, tectonic plates began to form and shift, grinding against each other with unimaginable force. Approximately one hundred miles below earth's fiery, fragmenting surface, temperatures above 1000 degrees Celsius and tremendous pressure over a period of one to three billion years began to compress and define particular strata in those molten depths. This process created what is now called "stability zones."

Eons passed and violent eruptions continued to occur deep within the planet's mantle, sending monstrous waves of magma surging up and spewing outward to relieve pressure in the birth of this new, impetuous child. During this time, two significant things were happening (particularly for those who would someday be women or miners): Volcanic eruptions passed through these stability zones — extreme pressure areas generally consisting of a rock type now known as kimberlite — on their journey to the surface. And, in the process, they dragged with them huge fragments of these zones, including newly formed gemstones.

Many scientists believe that during and after this same period, meteorites struck the earth on numerous occasions, recreating in various locations the same heat and pressure conditions that existed in early earth. The end result from all of this was the creation and the outward migration of a unique form of crystallized carbon to more accessible areas of the earth's surface.

We may call them a woman's best friend, but once you've pulled one from the gravel bed of a river, or carved one from the unforgiving rock of a rugged old mine, you'll damned well know the truth…

Diamonds are *everyone's* best friend.

It's a dangerous business, Frodo, going out your door. You step onto the road and if you don't keep your feet, there's no telling where you might be swept off to.

— J.R.R. Tolkien

PROLOGUE

Santa Elena de Uairén, Venezuela
November, 1987

The gunshot startled the room, even though those in the crowd, in their own wickedly perverse fashion, were waiting for it; expecting it. Hell, they would have been disappointed without the brutal finale at some point.

The man who had been holding the revolver barrel to his temple jerked, eyes flashing wide for a fraction of a second as his head snapped to the side from the impact of the round. A .32 caliber slug doesn't make a big mess, but that wasn't the intention. On the contrary, nobody wanted a serious mess. At some point, someone would have to clean it up. At some point...

And it took away from the game.

The dead man tumbled onto the weathered floorboards, gun slipping from his lifeless fingers amid the pandemonium of cheers from the winners and groans from the losers, who disgustedly tossed their useless markers to the floor. Two bouncers — large men of African ancestry, heavily muscled, and extensively tattooed — dragged the body away through the back door, while the bartender came around and quickly picked up the gun.

The winner (if that was the correct term) — a tall, gaunt-looking man with reddish colored skin, shoulder-length, tawny hair and keen gray eyes — stood and gathered his pile of winnings from the pit boss amid the cheers of the crowd. Given his hair and skin color, I wasn't sure whether the man was a native of the area, but he appeared to be one of their favorites. (If a group like this could have favorites at anything.) The place looked like a barroom scene from a movie by Sam Peckinpah on acid. Blood and booze stained the weathered floorboards. A couple of rusted fans jutted crookedly from the weathered ceiling, creaking out a weary refrain, barely moving the heavy cloud of smoke that hung above the room. And the customers (I'd seen better clientele in the drunk tank at Haiti's Port-au-Prince) were all armed with pistols, machetes, and deadly, thin knives in colorful scabbards at the base of their spines.

Someone intimated quietly that the winner showed up maybe once a week and played a game or two — that he had already survived a previous round of Russian roulette that night.

"*Cojones,*" the men in the crowd whispered to each other with a degree of respect and awe. These were tough men who had seen life at its ugliest — who had experienced the no-holds-barred existence in the streets of the miserable, mud-walled towns and the steaming, unforgiving jungles that surrounded them. They were all too familiar with the specter of death.

The quiet, gaunt man had just made as much as most of them would see in three months of work at the local farms or mines. But it took a certain kind of person to spin the cylinder of a revolver, put the barrel of the weapon to his temple, and pull the trigger.

Yeah, a certain kind of person...

Lost to the spectacle we were witnessing, snared by this moment of the bizarre and macabre, I glanced over at my buddy, Will Bell. His eyes registered the same shock and incredulousness as the bouncers dragged the dead man out and dumped his body in the back alley. Hell, Will and I weren't new to danger, and God knows we had pushed our luck to the very limits more times than I cared to count. But to walk into a place like this, sit down, barely get a drink in your belly, and wham! It was a bit much.

As the guitarist and the conga player in the corner tentatively began to perform again — a melodic, rambling canticle played by semi-talented fingers and hands wavering just above the harsh murmur of voices — Will looked at me and whispered a little shakily, "Kansas, I can tell you right now, I hope this isn't some sort of requirement to drink here, because I don't wanna play."

It had been a long road for us, from the comfort and relative safety of our homes in the Florida Keys to this hole in the wall in the middle of South America. Not a fun trip in a Cessna 182 Amphibian, packed with camping gear, supplies, a few well-hidden weapons, and a good deal of anxiety. Then there was the damned short landing strip, which was nothing more than a roughly bulldozed tract of red dirt cut from the constantly encroaching jungle. Several times along the way (from Key West, over Cuba to Jamaica, southeast to Aruba, down to Trinidad, then into Venezuela) I had asked myself if this was really a smart thing to be doing. Aside from the insistent little worm that kept wiggling in my stomach, we had no proof that there was really a problem with our old buddy, Shane O'Neal. For all we knew, he could be happily digging up precious stones in the daytime and drinking himself stupid in a bar somewhere at night. Maybe this was just an excuse to be on the road again.

I guess the truth was, we were adventure junkies. When I looked back at the last few years, it seemed that my buddy Will and I were most motivated by difficult but attractive women, wild challenges, and out-of-the-ordinary financial possibilities. Those were the things that scratched our itch. You could count out hundred-dollar bills in front of us and not really catch our attention. You had to sell us on a tale or an adventure that we could possibly survive and recount at the next bar. Or, you had to touch that strangely gallant part of us that only emerged when it came to our important circle of friends.

And maybe that's what this was all about.

One of our old buddies, the unshakeable Crazy Eddie, always said, "The truth is, average people collect things. But folks like us, we collect moments, and they get turned into stories, and when it's all said and done, the person with the most stories wins."

There was no argument that we loved stories. Life never seemed to be about what we had; it was always about the next experience. And this time, that search had led us into the Venezuelan jungle.

Will belted down the remainder of his drink, wiped his mouth with the back of his hand, and flagged down a waitress. A rugged-looking little thing wrapped in a faded, one-piece cotton shift waddled over — dark eyes, sable hair, and a pasted-on smile. We quickly ordered another round to blur the image of the dead guy's eyes as his head snapped back.

At that point, the tall man with the tawny, almost copper-colored hair (who had just won his life by default) got up and shuffled over to the bar. The bartender saw him coming and poured a heavy dose of tequila into a large shot glass, then pushed it over to him with a respectful nod. The fellow took a healthy swig and glanced around. Strangely, his eyes settled on us. Without breaking eye contact, he took his glass, moved in our direction, and stopped in front of us.

"Do you know a man named Shane O'Neal?" he asked in a strangely mellow voice.

Will and I glanced at each other, then turned back to the man. "Yeah," muttered my buddy cautiously. "Maybe we do."

The fellow nodded, his expression unaltered. "Your amigo, O'Neal, told me two men maybe were coming — one tall and thin, one short and muscled. Both with long hair bleached by the sun."

(That was a pretty damned accurate description of us. Although I never considered myself short — just not tall.)

"*La bruja de la selva* tell him," the man added.

"Who's *la bruja de la selva*?" I asked cautiously.

I knew the expression meant "the jungle witch." It didn't exactly lend any comfort. *A jungle witch...waiting for us?*

He offered a mirthless smile. "If you live long enough, you'll know." He paused and stared at us. "Now, we go. Maybe you can help your friend," he said, "before it's too late."

Will and I had met in college about ten years ago. Released from the bonds of education at graduation, we had cast off the garments of civilization and moved to the Florida Keys to start a diving business. From then on, life had become a continuous kaleidoscope of adventure — a conga line of bizarre people and strange situations nothing short of a Travis McGee novel.

We had met Captain Shane O'Neal at Sloppy Joe's in Key West several years ago. We ended up getting drunk together that night, and for some reason, a friendship blossomed. O'Neal was a tall fellow with a trim but muscled frame, Indian-dark hair, and green eyes. He loved the ocean with the same passion as Will and I, and we spent many a day diving and fishing off the Keys. Oddly enough, Captain O'Neal was one of the honchos with the South Florida DEA and he worked for the office in Key West. As we grew to know each other, we introduced him to a good friend of ours — a lady we held in high esteem (but whom neither of us could seem to win over) — and something magical happened. It was one of those rare, star-wrought miracles where two souls find each other and recognize a strange but remarkable connection. Shane and Julie were married less than six months later.

Captain O'Neal had served the DEA with distinction, working undercover on numerous major busts, but one night coming back from Jamaica, a sabotaged fuel line sent him and his Beechcraft plummeting into the ocean just off the Caicos Islands. He was rescued, but the injuries he suffered took him out of the field and put him behind a desk. That didn't sit well with a man like O'Neal. He retired early, about a year ago — fishing more, drinking more, and, as Julie said, "growing increasingly restless."

A guy like Shane needed a challenge and he began researching where the "jazz" was. Someplace that would still let a man take a chance or two, even if he did have a bit of a bum leg.

Our friend had witnessed firsthand a couple of our treasure-hunting interludes, and somewhere along the line the fever got the better of him. After his forced retirement and a good deal of research, he began to talk about Venezuela — about the fledgling gem-hunting industry there and the gold that hardy miners were digging out of the ground in the steaming jungles. Guyana, Venezuela, and Brazil were considered by most dreamers and schemers to be the hottest areas for newfound wealth, and Venezuela was the closest of those three.

But Will and I were wrapped up in an incredible Mayan treasure gig inside Guatemala at the time, and there was no way we could share his adventure. When we finally returned, we were mentally and physically exhausted. We needed a little hiatus — to just lock the doors, drink beer, and order pizza.

"It's just a burr under his saddle, Kansas," Will had assured me. "He'll get over it."

But he didn't.

One day shortly thereafter, Julie appeared at my door, gaunt and worried, eyes filled with uncertainty and angst. "He's gone," she said. "There was nothing I could do to stop him. He's headed into Venezuela with Jack Spur."

Jack Spur was a bit of a Keys rascal, not unlike ourselves, but I wasn't sure how well he'd do if and when the chips were really down.

That conversation had taken place the better part of a month ago. From phone calls, Julie knew they had made it to Venezuela and down into the jungle. But she hadn't heard a thing from Shane in nearly two weeks. She was worried.

And now, so were we.

"Okay, where in Venezuela?" I asked. "It's a good-sized country."

There was a pause, then Julie replied, as if recalling by rote, "He flew into Puerto La Cruz, on the coast, just east of Caracas, but he was headed far south, near the border of Brazil and Guyana. To a place called Santa Elena de Uairén." She exhaled softly. "He used the name so many times as he laid out his plans, it was difficult to forget." Julie brought up a finger in recollection. "Shane mentioned one other place — a serious hole in the wall, he said. Southwest of that." She paused for a moment. "I think it was called Icabaru." A soft, sad smile brushed her face. "He said it was such a rat hole, a dog wouldn't stop there to piss. Nothing but miners, bandits, and the ugliest hookers in the world. Or so he'd heard. But there were diamonds being found there..."

I pushed back my sun-bleached hair with the fingers of one hand, just a little uncomfortable with where this was going. "Ugly hookers and bandits. Terrific…"

"Yeah," Will replied. "But the diamonds part is definitely interesting." He looked at me, got that half-assed grin, those blue eyes of his gleaming, and held up an index finger. "I have never found a diamond…"

Obviously, that had pushed his buttons. I sighed, knowing that our latest R&R period was likely over…

CHAPTER ONE

Will looked over at me as we bounced along the rutted excuse for a road, winding our way upward into the dark-green mountain jungle. My tall, angular friend had his long blond hair tied back in a ponytail, and his eyes were narrowed to a squint. A fierce sun seared us as we held on in the open-cab Jeep Will had managed to rent in Santa Elena de Uairén.

"You know, don't you," he said, "that this is a lot more of a pipe dream than most of our crazy endeavors, right? And devoid of much reward."

I nodded and backhanded the sweat from my forehead, keeping the other hand on the vibrating steering wheel. "Yeah, no argument there. So, tell me again why we're trying to rescue Shane from his own pipe dream, huh?"

"Because he's a crazy gringo," muttered Arturio from the back seat. Arturio was the tawny-haired Russian rouletter we'd met at the bar.

We had learned that our guide was originally a resident of Caracas. When he was fourteen, his parents were killed in a robbery gone bad. From then on, he was on his own, scratching out a living with grit and audacity. At some point, he became too well known with the thieves and the police, so he drifted south, toward the jungle, in hopes that he might stumble onto an emerald or a diamond. He'd been living in Santa Elena de Uairén for the last year. He hated working full-time at anything, so sometimes he cheated locals at cards or robbed newcomers looking for gems. When all else failed, he played Russian roulette. "What's the worst that can happen?" he would say with that stoic shrug of his, thin arms extended, palms open.

"So how in the hell did you meet Shane?" Will asked, leaning around in the passenger's seat.

Arturio took a swig from the bottle of tequila he had wedged between his knees and eased out a hiss. "I try to rob him. He take my gun and break my nose. We make a deal — I show him around, no cheat him, he pay me son *dólares* and no break any more parts of my body."

Will chuckled. "That sounds like Shane." His grin faded. "So, how did this thing with you and us at the bar happen?"

The jungle con man shrugged again. "A week ago Shane tell me, 'you go back to Santa Elena an' wait for two white men to show up.' He give me descriptions. He say his wife say they may be coming. 'You bring 'em to me,' he say." He paused and exhaled. "So I do it." He eased out a sigh. "Besides, sonbody need to save that gringo fron hinself."

"How's that?" said Will.

Arturio took another hit of his tequila. "He is bold beyond common sense and he has dreams. He claims he sees de famous El Dorado or sonthing like it."

"And you believe him?" I asked over the noise of the engine and the road.

Arturio shrugged again. "I believe what I can touch. But there are rumors, very old tales of a place sonwhere in the jungle, and gold." Then he smiled. "But my friends tell me, 'is there one country in South America that don' have that tale?' Anyway, I work with him for now." He gazed at us and the glint of a smile touched his eyes. "I have played worse odds in my life."

We battered our way along the miserable road for most of the day until the sun started to meld with the tops of the trees and the shadows grew gaunt and ominous. About that time, the tiny village that Arturio had promised appeared almost magically through the twilight. Twenty years ago, before the concept of diamond and gold mining in Venezuela became more than a pipedream, the hamlet would have been a hole, hardly distinguishable from the jungle itself. Now, aside from the native huts of bamboo and fronds, there were a handful of slat-wood structures built off the ground (so that the things that crawled, stung, and bit the unsuspecting couldn't find their way into your sleeping mat). There was even a bar of sorts — a few bamboo tables and chairs on a deck just off the ground with a palm-frond roof. A few locals wandered to and fro — women in brightly colored cotton sarongs and shirtless men in loincloths or cotton *pantalones*. A handful of mongrel dogs lay about under the stilted houses or tied to trees. Some barked a few times at the newcomers, but it was too hot to work up much indignation.

We pulled in and parked. Arturio went to talk to the owner of the bar while Will and I guarded the few valuables we couldn't afford to lose (maps, guns, liquor, our U.S. Army field radio, and our food supply). He returned with a big, burly, bald-headed guy in tow — no shirt, blue jeans, and military jungle boots.

"We got place to stay, amigos," he announced. "Only fifty *dólares*, American."

Will and I looked at each other and I turned to the big guy. "I don't see anything here worth *buying* for fifty dollars. We'll sleep in the Jeep."

Arturio threw a quick glance at the landlord, realizing that their little ploy to scalp us hadn't flown. He gulped. "How about thirty?"

"How about twenty and a complimentary drink at the bar?" said Will.

There was a quick exchange of eyes and the landlord/bar owner nodded, not really happy with the deal but knowing he would have settled for fifteen.

We were shown to our accommodations — a twelve-by-twelve slatted wood shack on stilts with a small, open porch and a palm-frond roof, about seventy yards from the bar.

"At least the location is convenient," said Will with that wily grin of his.

There was a dark-gray dog — a mongrel with a white circle around one eye — who had parked himself in the shade at the top of the few stairs that joined the deck of our lodgings. If I were to guess, with his heavy chest and coloring, I would say he had a good deal of Shepherd in him — and probably something short-haired and smaller. The animal wasn't really large, but he was big enough to make a sensible man cautious. I normally wouldn't have paid much attention to him, except for the strangest of things. He had the battered remnants of a child's doll next to him — not just lying there, but tucked in close to him.

The dog looked up sleepily at us, but when he saw the landlord almost on him he instantly went into a defensive mode, sliding away from the big guy's kick before it could take a piece of his hide. The bald-headed landlord lost his balance when his boot touched nothing and he grabbed the weathered rail. His momentum and the rotten wood instantly melded into a bad combination. The old rail cracked and sent him tumbling off the three-foot-high porch. The dog scampered away like he was on fire. The fellow quickly stood, screaming obscenities at the animal and reaching for the pistol at his side, but before he could bring his sidearm to bear, the dog was gone. The doll was still on the deck.

I try to carry a broad empathy for most people in this world, but there are certain kinds of folks I can't abide. I can't stand liars because they're dangerous; they will always protect themselves first. I detest a man who will hit his lady because he's a bully, and nine times out of ten, a coward. And I can't tolerate a person who will hurt a dog — the creature God made to stand at a man's (and a woman's) side through thick and thin, asking little more than a bowl of food at the end of the day and a place at the hearth.

I knew this man, the owner of our little shack for the night. Yeah, I knew him well and my disdain for him raised the bile in my throat. I glanced at Will and our eyes touched with a brief but certain message. We'd encountered him before, many a time, and we instantly disliked the son of a bitch.

The introduction to our lodgings took all of two minutes. The single room had three "prison-style" mattresses on metal frames, a rickety table and a small chest of drawers. That was it. The outhouse was around back. The smell would lead us to it, the owner promised. There was no running water — a well with a hand pump and a faucet was out front. While we talked, I watched the dog circle out of the jungle on the far side of the clearing and cautiously work his way back into the compound.

We settled into our lodgings, bringing the valuable items in the truck inside, then changing into shirts that weren't caked with dust. When we headed out for dinner, I noticed that the doll on the deck was gone.

Regardless of the label, the rum was probably made in a drum out back. But the cans of Coke made it tolerable, and before long that night, the frond-covered, open-air bar took on a pleasant sparkle. I could just make out a few stars above the compound and somehow a bit of a breeze found us and backed off the mosquitoes. It wasn't Schooner Wharf in Key West, but with a little rum in me, I was beginning to look forward to a new adventure.

As we sat around our weathered plywood table, I noticed the dog that the landlord had run off had returned to our front porch. "Gutsy fellow," I muttered to myself. I looked over at Arturio. "So, what's the real scoop on our buddy Shane and this mining thing? How's he doing?"

Arturio did his shrug. "Who knows for sure? Nobody talks a lot about what they find in this business. That's a quick way to end up poor or dead, or both." Arturio paused and looked at us. "But the truth is, your friend is not the most simpatico gringo. He don't got a lot of 'easy' in his nature, and he is poking around for diamonds in an area controlled by a warlord named Santiago Talla." He paused and his eyes lost all sense of humor. "Señor Talla is not a good man to make angry."

"And what about this person, *la bruja de la selva* — the lady witch?" I asked. "You mentioned the name at the bar when we met. What is that all about?"

Again, our friend's eyes took on a strange glint — somewhere between intrigued and uneasy. He exhaled. "This is a strange thing," he said with an uncomfortable smile. "When you meet this person, and you probably will, I'll let you make your own decision."

While we were conversing, the cook/bartender offered to make us some dinner. Nothing fancy — some pork from a wild hog they had killed earlier in the day, yams from his wife's garden, and some fried bananas for dessert. We gratefully agreed. After a long day, none of us wanted to cook, even if it came from a can.

Later, after having what turned out to be an acceptable dinner, and gathering a pleasant glow from the rum, I watched the dog we'd seen earlier pick something up in his mouth, slide off our porch and cautiously work his way over to us. When he got close enough, I realized he had the doll. My friends noticed it too.

"How strange," muttered Will as the animal planted himself on his haunches below us, released the doll gently to the ground and looked up at us with dark, intelligent eyes that offered a subtle entreaty. When that didn't get our immediate attention, the animal emitted a soft, insistent whine.

Will, a sucker for animals of all sorts, tore a bone loose from the meat on his plate and tossed it over the rail to the creature. The dog caught it in midair and in moments its large teeth had crushed it and the heavy gristle attached into kindling. In two gulps it was gone.

I couldn't help but follow suit. I tossed him the charred pork skin from my plate and again it disappeared in a gulp. But about that time, I saw the owner of the compound step out from his shack and head toward the smokehouse — probably to pick out dinner. I glanced back down to where the dog was, but he was gone. And so was the doll.

Will saw it too and muttered an analogy regarding the owner and his heritage.

I decided to change the subject and turned to my friend. "Okay buddy, you're the historian. What do you know about the El Dorado legend and this area? Strikes me that Shane is in the wrong place for that story."

Will was a remarkable historian. He possessed an almost photographic recall of the things he read. (At least those that interested him.) He took a pensive sip of his drink and eased back in his chair.

"Well, you're right and you're wrong, but I'll start with some distant history and move forward."

I ordered us another round of drinks and Will began.

"First off, let's go way back to Christopher Columbus, who

sailed along the eastern coast of what is now Venezuela, in 1498 — his only voyage that reached South America. It was Columbus that discovered the Pearl Islands of Cubaqua — especially Isla Margarita, off the northeast coast of Venezuela. As usual, it didn't take long for the Spanish to kill off the resistance, enslave the indigenous people, and begin harvesting the resources. Those incredibly valuable pearls became the most important source of income for the Spanish empire between 1508 and 1531." He paused and sighed bitterly. "By that time, the pearl oysters and the indigenous populations had been devastated.

"The second Spanish expedition sailed the length of South America's northern coast, and the captain of those ships gave the Venezuela area its name because the coastline reminded him of Venice," he continued. "By 1522, Spain had permanent settlements, much to the disappointment of the locals. There were several groups of indigenous peoples, mostly agriculturalists and hunters, all of whom eventually met with the same fate as the Pearl Islands residents — conquest, disease, and annihilation."

Will took a sip of his drink. "The truth was, the Spanish were quite comfortable with killing anyone who got in their way, including their fellow explorers from other countries. And therein lies a tale, as they say…

"During this era, the Dutch, English, Germans, and French were all actively seeking the spoils of the New World," my friend continued. "And the area called Little Venice, oddly enough, became the most significant part of the German colonization of the Americas. From 1528 to 1546 the Augsburg-based Welser banking family obtained the colonial rights for the province of Venezuela in return for debts owed by Charles I of Spain. Curiously enough, the primary motivation for the Germans was the search for the legendary golden city of El Dorado."

That brought me up in my seat. "El Dorado, huh?"

Will nodded. "Yeah, quite the coincidence, huh? Anyway, the idea was first entertained by Ambrosius Ehinger, the German who founded Maracaibo in 1529. He had evidently heard rumors, via some of the Indians, about a city deep in the jungle. After the deaths of Ehinger and his successor, a potentate named Phillip Von Hutten — who was, unfortunately, more interested in exploring than governing — took over. While he was off in the interior looking for golden cities, the Spanish stepped in and claimed the right to appoint a new governor in Venezuela. It was basically a bloodless coup." Will grimaced slightly. "Well, almost bloodless. On Hutten's return, the new Spanish governor, who didn't want any resistance to his new position, had Hutten and his second in command, Bartholomeus Welser, executed. Most of the remaining Germans loaded their ships and headed home. Shortly afterward, the Germans' charter for Venezuela was revoked and the country became a Spanish possession."

Will took a sip of his drink. "Now, before you start getting fidgety, here's where the story gets interesting. Some historians say that upon their return to Maracaibo — and before their execution — both Hutten and Welser claimed to have found, if not El Dorado, at least a place of unique wealth in gold and precious stones…"

"Hmmm," I muttered, as I watched Arturio's gray eyes light up. Both he and I slid our chairs in closer as Will glanced around conspiratorially, then continued.

"In fact, it is said that they spoke of emeralds, and of brilliantly clear stones that the natives had somehow learned to polish. They said the remarkably hard, shiny stones could cut jade, and that the indigenous peoples, many of whom they claimed had oddly shaped heads, wore them and the emeralds 'cradled' in golden bracelets or mounted in leather collars around their necks."

That got everyone's attention.

"Last but not least, there was mention that this particular city, if you will, was built into a geographically unique gorge, with only one entrance in or out." Will paused and took another drink. "The fly in the ointment turned out to be a river crossing and a swift current where, on their return, Hutten and Welser lost their last two horses and almost all of the artifacts they had collected, including what gems they possessed. Carvajal, the Spanish governor, had his hands full with uprisings of indigenous peoples and encroachments by the tenacious Dutch and English. When Welser and Hutten claimed they had been captured by the natives and barely escaped with their lives —and possessed none of the remarkable stones they spoke of — he concluded it was probably the ravings of jungle-ravaged madmen, or that both of the explorers had concocted this story to preserve their lives."

Will sighed and shook his head. "At any rate, the tale didn't fly and the German explorers were hanged. In the end, the viceroyalties of New Spain showed more interest in the gold and silver mines of the Aztecs and the Incas, and the entire transaction involving the deceased Hutten and Welser, and the possibility of a satellite El Dorado, became little more than an obscure footnote in South American history."

Will paused for a moment and exhaled. "One last thing that probably has no bearing on anything — it is mentioned that there was an outbreak of smallpox in the capital shortly after Hutten and Welser returned, and the governor blamed this on the expedition as well." He held out his hands. "All this can be found in the archives in Spain, although not easily. I spent a month in those archives about five years ago. I gotta tell you, it was an enlightening experience. Those Spaniards may have been bastards, but they were meticulous record-keepers."

I shook my head, slightly amazed at the width and depth of my buddy's knowledge. "So, we're talking about a tribe of some sort, maybe even a small city, possibly sheathed in a series of natural walls, huh?"

Will shrugged. "Possibly."

"If this really exists," I said, "and that's a big if — why hasn't someone found it in the last four or five hundred years?"

Arturio answered. "Amigo, de jungle can grow over and hide a Jeep like yours in a year. Besides, nobody but Indians and lizards live in those deep jungles, until the white man find gold and diamonds there." He took another shot of tequila. "But I tell you this: What you say is not unheard of here. Many believe that there could be a place like this you speak of. Strangely enough, the monks of the monastery in the hills above Santa Elena de Uairén carry an interest in this."

"There is another line of thought here too...and not necessarily a nice one," Will added. "This was a time when smallpox and other equally virulent diseases were constantly being transferred to New World occupants by European explorers. If a single man in Hutten's entourage carried a strain of one of those diseases, the whole tribe could well have been annihilated after they left. It happened time after time in the New World."

"Well thanks for that enlightening dissertation," I said dryly. "But still, what we might be looking for is an odd natural formation, like a rock wall or a canyon somewhere."

"Ooohh, so now we're looking for it, huh?" grated Will sarcastically. "Does the name Shane O'Neal strike any bells with you? You know, the friend of ours who never came home and might be in trouble?"

I nodded, holding up a hand, duly chastised. "Yeah, yeah, I know. I was just saying..."

The moon was sliding into the treetops. The heat of the day had abated and a soft breeze was rustling the roof of the jungle. Night birds were issuing their final calls before roosting, and the drinks had settled what little anxiety we were dealing with at this point.

Will looked over at us. "I don't know about you guys, but I'm ready for some shut-eye. It's been a long few days getting ready for this, and I'm betting tomorrow is going to be even more...*interesting.*"

As we rose from the table, I went over to pay the "chef." In the process, I asked him about the dog and the doll. His eyes softened a little and a small, almost sad smile turned the corners of his mouth.

"He is just a mongrel now. He has no home." He shrugged. "I feed him some things when I can." He drew a breath. "Six months ago, an Indian family — *Guajiros* — came through here on their way to the diamond territory. The dog was with them. They had a little girl and the dog never left her side. You see the girl, you see the dog. Unfortunately, one night while she slept, a viper bite her,

The Wild Road to Key West

and a day later, she die." He pointed out across the compound to a hillside and a small wooden cross. "She was buried there." He shook his head sadly. "The family leave the next day, but the dog would not go. He would not leave her." He shook his head again. "I know it is strange past truth, but after three days of lying on her grave, the animal finally took the doll and returned to the compound. He was almost dead from dehydration, but finally, I got him to eat and drink." He sighed, looking over at the creature on our porch. "Normally, I would not have bothered — it is just a dog. But I was touched. He has carried that doll around with him ever since."

"Damn!" muttered Will as we headed back toward our little shack. "That's like one of the stories in *Reader's Digest*."

I nodded, truly touched by such incredible loyalty.

When we arrived at our lodgings, there was the dog, curled up on the deck by the steps, the doll by his side. As soon as he heard us he went on alert, rising slightly, tense and ready.

"It's okay, big guy," I whispered in Spanish. "We're on your side. Easy, boy, easy…"

Strangely enough, the animal gradually relaxed and let us pass by him. But his eyes never left us. I realized then that he was a bright, discerning creature, born into the wrong place at the wrong time. I could say that about many a person I'd known. I don't know why, but as my two friends cautiously worked their way around the dog to the door, I stopped and slowly squatted, reaching out carefully with one hand while offering a few soft, encouraging words. At first, there was a heavy rumble in the animal's chest and he tensed and cautiously sniffed my hand. I knew I could be risking fingers, but I continued, gently touching the creature's shoulder, still speaking softly.

"Don' be too stupid, amigo," whispered Arturio tensely from behind me. "Fingers no grow back…"

He was right, I knew, but I just had a feeling about this animal. Gradually, I began to stroke his flank, still speaking in a soft and gentle fashion. He tensed, but he didn't move. I continued, and in a few moments, I felt the creature relax and the caution in his eyes waned. Carefully, I removed a small package of scraps I had collected after dinner and laid it next to him. Then I eased back, considering that sufficient victory for the night. When I closed the door to our lodgings, the dog was still watching me.

The following day, a little after sunrise, we were already loading the last of our gear. Will had just checked the fluids and closed the hood to the Jeep, and Arturio was opening the doors of the cab. The dog, who hadn't left the porch overnight, was watching us intently. He had actually jumped in the back of the Jeep for a moment, then quickly scrambled out.

About that time I saw the owner of the compound headed our way. He glanced at the dog on the porch and made a beeline for him. I was just coming out of the shack with a duffle bag full of tools. As the big guy started up the stairs, that vehement arrogance masking his features, the dog began to back up, but this time (maybe buoyed by our presence), he refused to give up all his ground. He didn't run. He stood there behind me, holding the doll in his mouth, rolling the dice on his life.

As I watched this take place, I realized that this man was the epitome of a bully — he was angry and he wanted to hurt this creature simply because it had chosen not to be afraid of him this time. I don't usually pick fights because there's a standard rule in life: big guys can bluff their way out of an altercation and use their size to intimidate. They only have to actually fight about thirty percent of the time. But a smaller man almost always has to "ride the bull" to earn respect. While I had spent much of my adult life in a gym and was very capable when it came to mixing it up, I always did my best to avoid altercations. Will and I generally used the "confuse and disable" act, but this was one of those times that I just couldn't help myself. This was for every man he had cowered, for every brutal punch he had delivered with pleasure, and for every animal that had suffered his torture and neglect. This was for the ones who wouldn't or couldn't fight back...

I moved over to the top of the steps just as the man started up them — his position below me on the stairs, aligning our heights. I smiled and thrust the heavy bag of tools into his chest. "Here, hold this," I said.

The guy reacted just like ninety percent of people would in this situation. He instinctively reached out and grabbed the bag with both hands. At that moment I stepped in and hammered him with a straight right, with everything my powerful shoulders and arms could muster — center point, right on the nose.

I don't know how many of you have seen a man hit by surprise squarely on the nose. There is generally only one reaction — a complete collapse. The pain is immense, eyes begin to water instantly, and knees often buckle as hands instinctively rise to protect the damaged area, leaving the injured person completely open for a second assault.

I heard the bridge of his nose crack when I hit him. As he dropped the bag and collapsed to his knees, I caught him with a front kick in the throat. I knew it was brutal overkill, but I didn't want him getting up. As the man lay there gurgling and gasping for air through his damaged larynx, blood pouring from his nose, I picked up our tool bag, hopped over my battered victim, and tossed the bag in the back of the vehicle while yelling to my friends, "Time to go, gentlemen! Get in the damned Jeep. Now!

They didn't need a second invitation. Will had the engine revving in seconds. At that moment, I looked over at the dog. I dropped down the back gate to the Jeep. "Com'on boy," I said as gently as I could muster, given my blood pressure at the moment. "Com'on guy, it's time to go!"

The animal stood there on the deck at the top of the steps, trembling slightly, the doll still in his jaws, his dark eyes frightened and uncertain. The landlord, lying at the base of the stairs, coughed out some blood and tried to rise. I turned and kicked him in the head. He got quiet again.

"Com'on boy," I called as gently as I could, holding out my hand to the trembling animal. "You gotta come now…"

I could see some of the people who worked at the compound headed our way, coming out of the cafe/bar. I had no idea how this was going to fall.

"We gotta go, Kansas!" yelled Will. "Let's get out of here!"

"Com'on guy," I pleaded. "Please…"

The people behind us were yelling now.

At that moment, it was as if the dam of uncertainty broke and the dog took a few tentative steps forward, still trembling. I strode over the landlord, took a step up the stairs, and reached over, grabbing a handful of the animal's hair at the scruff of his neck and pulling him into my arms. I threw us both into the back of the Jeep and yelled at Will, "Go!"

My friend didn't need any encouragement. In moments we were a trail of dust and a memory.

About five miles down the road Will stopped and let the dog and me into the back cab of the Jeep. The animal's flanks were still trembling, but after a few seconds, I was pleased to see him settle down on the seat next to me. As we drove along the rugged road, my hand on the sleek, short fur of his back, he looked up at me with those shining dark eyes and gently set the doll in my lap. Then he laid his head on my leg and eased out a sigh. It damned near brought tears to my eyes.

CHAPTER TWO

Santiago Talla sat in a high-backed wicker chair on the veranda of his ranch home just on the fringes of the Venezuelan jungle outside the small town of Icabaru. He also had a home in Caracas and kept a yacht in Trinidad. Obviously, there were places he'd rather be than in the middle of the South American jungle, but this was where the diamonds and the emeralds were, and he was a "hands-on" type of boss. He often laughed when he used that expression, saying, "You do your job for me, you get to keep your hands on. You cheat me or steal from me, you get to have hands off…" And indeed there was more than one audacious thief, and even a greedy dredge boss or two, who failed to listen to those words and greatly missed the ability to pick up a fork at dinner.

Talla was a tall man — a composite of Castilian Spanish and indigenous Warao Indian. He was dressed in American blue jeans, calfskin cowboy boots, and a leather vest over a long-sleeved, light cotton shirt — very Western for a Venezuelan diamond lord. He had a thick mane of black hair that he swept back like a fifties rock star. A heavy, dark mustache perched atop his downturned mouth created the image of a perpetually arrogant soul. But his heavy build and his hard, bright-black eyes warned anyone who might have mistaken the image of haughtiness for incompetence.

It had been a long journey to where he was.

His actual father, the product of a wealthy Spanish family, had been a gem cutter in Caracas. He had come to South America forty years earlier, when the emerald fields were just being discovered. Santiago's mother, an indigenous Indian servant, caught the attention of the man, and from that tryst he was conceived. His mother had fallen in love with her *jefe*, but her attentions were little more than cheap entertainment for the lord of the house. When he found out she was pregnant, he dismissed her — threw her out on the street with a handful of pesos, not enough money to last out the month. Santiago was twelve when his mother died of a disease he couldn't even pronounce — an "old woman" at the age of thirty.

Santiago never forgot, but to stay alive he was forced to work the streets as a thief and a beggar. Nonetheless, he wasn't a person easily put down. His mother had made him attend school, and oddly enough, he became a voracious reader. In what could only be considered profoundly odd, Santiago found himself fascinated by the Old West in America — cowboys and ranching, and the famous gunslingers.

By the time he turned seventeen, Santiago had taken his mother's last name and was a man in every way. He had gone from a street urchin, stealing food to survive and sleeping in alleys, to a street boss for the local *mafioso*. His skinny young frame had filled out with muscle, and his dark hair fell to his shoulders. His bosses trusted him and the women loved him.

But most importantly, Santiago had never forgotten the man who abandoned him and his mother, and the hate inside him still sizzled. He had watched and waited, and one day he caught the gem cutter outside his safety net, making a delivery of cut stones. The man had barely exited his taxi and moved across the sidewalk when the large youngster stepped up behind him, put a knife to his back, and forcefully ushered him into an alley. Santiago whispered his mother's name in the frightened man's ear, holding him with an iron grip. There was a moment of confusion, then suddenly he saw the recognition and fear in the gem cutter's eyes.

That was what Santiago wanted. He shoved the fellow against the dirty brick wall and plunged the knife into his back again and again, and as the man dropped to his knees, Santiago took his bag of gems and reminded him again why he was dying.

Unfortunately, the gem cutter was better connected than Santiago realized, and a fairly serious police investigation ensued. The people he worked for said it was time for him to leave. He had heard about the emeralds, gold, and occasional diamonds being found in the jungle rivers of southern Venezuela. It represented more of a challenge than the streets of Caracas, but the returns were much greater. He convinced one of his friends to go with him, then he packed up what few belongings he had (including the gems he'd stolen, which he quickly negotiated into cash). They bought a four-wheel-drive truck and headed south, Santiago purchasing some mining equipment and supplies along the way. If those other *idiotas* could do it, surely he could too.

Santiago Talla was a hard individual, but he had no idea of the hell that was the ground level of Venezuela's gem mining industry — the steaming jungles and perpetually muddy rivers, the snakes and spiders, the filthy dredging, digging, and miserable sluice work. But Santiago was lucky as well as persistent. He hired a trio of savvy natives to help, and three weeks into his first operation along the Tareni River, they hit a handful of small emeralds. It was incredible luck. The old-timers around them shook their heads with unconcealed envy, and the coconut telegraph passed the word. The good news was, they were now players in a tough, dangerous game. The bad news was, he and his partner never slept at the same time ever again.

They invested their money in better equipment and hired additional crew (Santiago's native blood had ingratiated him with the local Indians), and it wasn't a month later that they hit another cache of emeralds. They weren't rich by American standards, but they were kings in Venezuela. However, not every story of discovered wealth has a happy ending. (In truth, not very many at all.) Santiago and his partner began to disagree on where to search, who to hire, and how much money to reinvest in the business. Two weeks later, his partner had an unfortunate accident. According to Santiago, he had been drinking, fell into the river, and drowned…

For the Caracas gangster-cum-jungle-gem entrepreneur, this was a dandy piece of luck, because neither of them had families and their contract was written for simple survivorship. If one died, the other received his percentage.

Over the next few years, Santiago expanded into gold and diamond mining and his holdings grew. So did his reputation. Gradually, he morphed from successful miner to jungle capitalist, to a warlord of sorts, who virtually seemed to own certain segments of rivers bearing gold and gems. If you wanted to work those rivers, you needed his permission. Those who ignored his requirements inevitably seemed to meet with "accidents." And, in the process, he carved out his dream of an American-style ranch in the jungle.

His personality was probably most defined by an interview with a reporter for one of the big magazines in Venezuela. Toward the end of the interview, the man asked him how much money he needed before he would consider retirement. Santiago, his hard, black eyes gleaming, replied, "Señor, there is no such thing as 'enough money.'"

Santiago Talla sat there in his wicker chair on the veranda of his attractive, ranch-style home, his cowboy-booted feet resting on the porch rail, his Colt .45 revolver in his holster. He took another draw on his *cigarillo* and huffed out heavily, the blue smoke catching the breeze and drifting across the mahogany porch. There were two damned gringos working a find on the Botatha River — in an area everyone knew he controlled. He had sent three of his men down that way to convince the Americans they needed to play by the rules. His men came back badly beaten, tied over the saddles of their mules, and in desperate need of water. (The remarkable thing about a mule is that it always knows its way home, although it often takes its time.)

"These people are beginning to annoy me," he said quietly, taking another drag of his cigarette. "They have no sense of boundaries..." Santiago stood up and clapped his hands. Instantly, two men appeared — one had been on his side of the walk-around porch, the other on the far side.

CHAPTER THREE

It took another day for us to pass through the low mountains and into the midlands, where the rivers poured through, carrying with them the bounty of time and geological alteration. Arturio seemed anxious for us to move along, but as we got closer to our destination, he became more wary, eyes carefully watching the battered roadway ahead of us.

"I would suggest that you have those weapons of yours loaded and ready," he said as we bounced along. "We are entering de land where morality decreases and mortality increases."

We had brought along one semi-automatic 9mm pistol each, with shoulder holsters and several boxes of ammunition. In addition, we carried a short-barreled 9mm rifle. It was just too tough to sneak much more than that through Customs in several countries on the way down and into Venezuela. Fortunately, our buddy, Crazy Eddie, had shown us how to remove the interior side panels of our plane and create clever hideaways.

Our latest addition, the dog, seemed content just to be away from his last residence. The farther we traveled, the more relaxed he became. I also noticed that while he showed attention to my friends, he began to display the first signs of affection with me — staying by my side as we took breaks from the Jeep and cautiously snuggling up to my legs as we traveled. However, he still made absolutely certain that the doll was never too far from him.

During some of this time, Will buried himself in topography maps of the region — particularly areas that might have correlated to the exploration by the Germans Hutten and Welser. Mostly, he was guessing, but at one point, he cocked his head oddly and muttered, "Now this is interesting. In much of the area we're coming into, the topography and the sediment lend themselves to gorges and canyons along the rivers, much like the area described by Welser and Hutten. If we can find our buddy in one piece, it might be worth our time to come back and check some of this out by air."

By afternoon we were starting to see signs of civilization — Indian villages along the winding river that began to appear to the south of us — and we would pass through an occasional rough-and-tumble mining town, like something out of the Old West.

Finally, we came into one of those towns, perhaps a touch more upscale — there were two or three bars/bordellos (the important things in life), a mining supply company, a general/tack store, a stable, an assessor, and an undertaker who also served as the barber. It reminded me greatly of an old Western town in perhaps the late 1800s.

Arturio muttered, "Welcome to Icabaru."

I also noticed a small airstrip about a half mile outside of town. I glanced at Will. He shook his head, a touch of ire crossing his countenance.

I turned to Arturio. "Why the hell didn't you tell me this place had an airstrip? We could have saved a lot of time!"

Our friend did that shrug of his. "The strip is new. I no think about it. Santiago use it to get his precious stones out of the jungle and back into Caracas." He paused and glanced over at the dog curled up by me on the back seat. A small, intuitive smile touched the corners of his mouth. "Who knows? Maybe there was something you needed to pick up on the way, amigo."

I glanced down at the dog. Will picked up on it instantly. We had experienced so many nearly unexplainable, practically impossible things during the last few years, we'd come to possess a wider view of the impossible.

"Who knows?" I replied. "Maybe we needed a dog."

"It's a possibility," muttered Will. "But I think if he's gonna hang out with us, he needs a name."

I thought about that for a moment. "How about Shadow? With that dark-gray coat and the way he moves, that seems just about right."

My partner nodded. "Sounds good to me. Shadow it is."

Arturio brought us back to reality. "We're only about half a day from your amigo's camp. We might want to pick up some extra food supplies — a bag or two of rice, maybe some dried beef and some fruit — mangoes, papayas, bananas..." He exhaled heavily. "You got enough ammunition for those *pistolas* of yours?"

"We have to hope so," I muttered, glancing at Will, reality starting to set in with both of us.

In almost every adventure there is generally a point where it goes from being an exciting exploit to a hard reality. We had just reached that point. We were going into a godforsaken jungle where there was no authority and no laws, other than the ones made by the strongest and the most dangerous. We not only had to save our friend from himself, we had to keep ourselves alive while doing it, and then try to get everyone out in one piece.

"One other thing," said Arturio cautiously. "This is where you get to meet *la bruja de la selva.*"

"Is that really necessary?" Will asked. "We've got our hands full as it is. Do we have to add some old hag to the brew, who is probably going to want us to pay her dearly for reading our palms?"

Arturio's countenance changed slightly and his gray eyes took on a strange glimmer. "She say, 'You got to turn over rocks. Real treasures are never on the surface.'" He exhaled softly, pushing back his long, copper-colored hair with the fingers of one hand. "Be patient. This is a woman even the tribal shamans listen to." He glanced around. "We guenna need to bring a gift. Son' mangoes. She likes mangoes."

"She likes soft stuff because she doesn't have any teeth, right?" muttered Will.

Fifteen minutes later, we had purchased a half-dozen ripe mangoes from an Indian street vendor and had driven along the rutted but passable road that led out of town, through fields of corn and sugarcane, to the edge of the jungle. We came to a small shack built with scrap lumber, but not done haphazardly. The roof was tin and the windows actually had glass panes.

Will turned off the Jeep and we got out. Strangely enough, Shadow, usually the first one out, hesitated, then eased himself from the Jeep but wouldn't go any further. He parked himself by the back bumper.

"Let me go first," said Arturio, reaching out for the bag of mangoes. "To make sure this is acceptable."

Will and I turned to each other, beginning to feel more and more like this was some sort of scam, but it was a little late to be backing out.

"In for a penny, in for a pound," I muttered, as I handed our friend the bag.

We stood by the Jeep while Arturio went up the rough stone walkway and knocked on the door. It opened and he went in. A few seconds later, he came to the doorway and waved at us.

"I wish I had some garlic to wear around my neck," whispered Will nervously as we moved away from the Jeep.

Shadow cautiously followed us, with his doll.

Arturio ushered us in, but Shadow chose to stay outside. That made me a little nervous. I garnered a quick look at the place. The front room was filled with Indian artifacts, urns, jars, native tapestries, strange flowers, strings of dried roots, and gloom. The light from the one open window cast a murky beam across it all. From our position, we couldn't get a good look at the person inside. She stood in the shadows of the back wall.

Gradually, *la bruja de la selva* slid from obscurity. There was a slight intake of breath from both of us.

"Not exactly what I expected," whispered Will, definitely surprised.

"But I'm not that disappointed," I muttered.

She stood in front of us dressed in a simple Indian cotton shift and leather sandals, her long black hair sliding off her shoulders and falling to her waist. She was about five foot four and her skin was a supple bronze — not quite Indian dark, and not "a drink in your hand, Hawaiian Tropic bronze" either. More like someone who lived and worked in the sun. She wasn't what you would call exceptionally attractive — her figure was a couple of Hershey bars past slim, but she possessed the strangest copper eyes, and her lips were remarkably full and seductive. All in all, for a witch, she was a pretty acceptable package.

But then, we hadn't known that many witches...

Arturio introduced us with a considerable deference in his voice, explaining apparently what she already knew. Without much ceremony, she moved closer and spoke, her voice soft but strong, like the timbre of an old river that has run its course for centuries.

"Your friend is a strong man but the old scar he carries has wounded his pride and made him foolish." She paused. "He has angered *El Jaguar*, and the man is going to kill him and his partner. I have seen it."

"Nobody is going to kill my friend," I growled, more harshly than I intended. "We're going to get him out of there. But we need to know where he and his friend are."

She exhaled heavily. "I can try to help you, but this I know. You and your people have little time. A darkness chases Señor O'Neal. He has left his camp, and this I know — you will never find him on your own." She drew an uneasy breath. "I have seen through the veil since Arturio first came to me. For you to have any chance of success, I must go with you."

"I don't think that's a great idea," Will said, holding up his hands, palms out. "Prior history says we don't do that very well, and this could be messy." He paused. "Why would you do this, anyway?"

A strange smile touched her lips. "Maybe because I am bored," she said with a sensual shift of her shoulders.

The air stilled for a moment. It wasn't the answer we were expecting.

She paused and her countenance changed. "A whole village can seek a gem," she said quietly, "but the gods choose who will find it. Like it or not, you will need my help."

At that point, Arturio spoke. "The woman makes a valid point, señors. We could wander in that jungle for weeks. And your friends don' have weeks..."

"I can contact the peoples in that area," the woman said. "They may be able to find your friends — to hide them for a while."

"How would you possibly get to them?" Will asked hesitantly. "I mean, are you gonna do some magic thought transference or…" He glanced over at two large animal-hide drums in the corner of the room. "Or call them on the drums?"

Her mouth turned down in disdain, but there was a glitter of amusement in her eyes. She pointed to the corner of the room, where a Vietnam-vintage, two-way radio sat. "No, *idiota*, I will call them."

The normally taciturn Arturio chortled, putting a hand to his mouth.

I couldn't help but chuckle. I turned to Will. "I know this isn't the best of arrangements, but Arturio's right. We need someone who knows where they're going." I shifted back to our *bruja*. "What do we call you?"

A strange smile touched those petulant lips. "It has been a while since someone asked me that," she whispered. Those incredible copper eyes softened slightly and she stared at us for a moment. "When I was young, they call me Passi," she replied, and again those eyes mellowed with recollection. "From the passion flower in the jungle, *Passiflora*." She straightened up and pushed a strand of lustrous hair from her face. Even as freaked out as I was, it was a damned sensuous thing. "We must move along. Come back in an hour," she said.

As we stepped outside, I paused and nudged Will. Shadow was back in the Jeep, waiting for us. But we noticed he had left the doll at the *bruja*'s door…

The sun was just slipping into the jungle as Shane O'Neal tied a handkerchief just above his knee to stop the bleeding from the wound in his calf, then he checked the magazine on his M1 Carbine. (Half full or half empty, depending on your opinion of life.) He had managed to give his pursuers the slip, but Jack Spur hadn't been as lucky. He'd caught a round in the back during their running firefight. His friend was dead before he hit the ground. If that wasn't enough, come nightfall, he would have to worry about more than just Santiago Talla's henchmen. The jungle was not a kind place after dark.

They had come for him and his partner just before sunset — four men with Russian-made AK47s. They weren't expecting the gringo to be too savvy when it came to perimeter protection. The assassins had no idea they were dealing with a Vietnam-vintage soldier/DEA officer. The leading two walked into his monofilament line connected to the slightly loosened pin of a grenade. Then there were just two. O'Neal got one of those, but he took a through-and-through in the leg in the process. The last one skedaddled. Unfortunately, he was the one with the radio...

An hour later, as the sun slipped beneath the horizon, O'Neal sat with his back against an outcropping of sandstone. He took a swig of water from his canteen, watching a large, black scorpion a few feet from him dissecting a lizard it had captured and stung. The ex-DEA officer should have been paying more attention, but he was tired. He hadn't slept much for a day or so since he'd spotted the first sortie of Santiago Talla's henchmen coming for him and his friend.

He never even heard the person who crept up behind him. Suddenly, there was a crushing pain in the back of his head and everything went dark.

CHAPTER FOUR

"What do you mean, 'they ambushed you'?" grated Santiago, his furious demeanor forcing the man against the porch railing, almost pushing him over it in the process.

The terrified henchman held out his arms in a pleading defense. "They had grenade booby traps and automatic weapons! I killed one of them, but the other — "

Santiago angrily waved off the excuses, turning his back to the man and huffing bitterly. Then suddenly, he swung back around, shaking a finger at him. "I want this man! I want him here. No one gets away with this! Get three more men and a tracker. Enlist some of your natives if you have to. Go back, now! Find him! I don't care if you hurt him, but I want him breathing when he arrives here, you understand?"

Shane O'Neal awoke in the pitch dark of a foul-smelling hut of some sort. He began to remember...

As he had regained consciousness, they'd tied his hands and feet over a pole, then carried him along like a luckless jungle deer. After an hour of miserable, jarring pain from his tightly bound wrists and injured leg, he had begun to appreciate being knocked out for the first half of the journey. As the pale-white, full moon finally rose to its zenith, they came to a village, where his captors unceremoniously dumped him in a hut. The language was a native dialect bastardized with Spanish. O'Neal spoke passable Spanish — there was no such thing as a DEA officer in South Florida who didn't. He picked up some of the conversation. It sounded like they were waiting for someone to take him away. Not damned comfortable news... He began working on his bonds.

Not fifteen minutes later, he heard a vehicle pull up. The engine shut down and there was a hushed conversation too far away for him to make out anything. The door to the hut swung open. He pulled back reflexively against the rough bamboo. All he could make out were a couple of shadows at the entrance silhouetted by a distant campfire. The taller one spoke. "Man, you look like hell!"

The other chimed in. "If you've found any diamonds, you're gonna owe us big time."

A smile of relief broke across O'Neal's weary face. "Kansas and Will! Son of a bitch!" Then he shuffled himself around and that image turned to seriously confused. "How? How in God's name have you ended up here?" He paused. "Not that I'm not glad as hell to see you. But how?"

I shrugged. "It's a long story. But the short of it is, you can thank your wife. She contacted us and gave us the info we needed to find you. The rest was just pure freakin' luck."

"Well, maybe not all luck," said Will as he knelt and cut our friend's bonds.

While we helped Shane out of the hut, Arturio and Passi came over and I introduced them. At that moment, Shadow moved up in between them, curious but cautious. Shane stiffened slightly.

"Don't worry," Will said. "He's on our side."

A few minutes later we were sitting by the fire. Shane looked as if he'd lost at least twenty pounds, his face was gaunt and weathered, and he had a nasty hole in his calf. Passi gave him a handful of crushed leaves to chew before she started to examine the wound, and within minutes he became comfortable and talkative.

"We ought to bring some of those home for Crazy Eddie," Will whispered. "Make a nice Christmas present."

The members of the small tribe were gathered at a respectful distance around us, the firelight reflecting off of their reddish skin and black eyes. The chief had explained, proudly pointing to the radio antenna extending up and out of the smoke hole in his hut, that *la bruja de la selva* had contacted him earlier. When they heard the explosions of weapons just before sunset, he and a few of his men set out to investigate. They, of course, found Shane, bleeding into the dirt and staring myopically at a scorpion on the ground. So, they did the only sensible thing…

This whole affair was a huge coup for us. As impossible as it seemed, we had found our friend, alive. The bad news was, the round he had taken in the leg appeared to have nicked his tibia bone. Passi removed a tiny piece of bone from the wound while cleaning and dressing it. Most likely, Shane needed surgery. We had to get him home quickly, before the damage to the bone became irreversible — and before this Santiago guy he and Passi were so unhappy with could make our stay permanent. If we had to deal with him, I wanted it to be on our terms.

"So, I guess the big question is, did you find any stones?" said Will as we sat around the last glowing embers of the fire.

Our native friends began to retire and only a couple of night guards remained at the edge of the light.

"Not much," muttered Shane with a bit of a frown. "A couple small emeralds and two diamonds of fairly poor quality." But then he brightened. "But they're out there, man. Tomorrow is gonna be someone's lucky day!"

"I like that," I said. "A gambler's epitaph — 'Tomorrow is going to be someone's lucky day.'"

"Unfortunately, buddy, it's not going to be yours," said Will. "Especially if this Santino guy finds you."

"Santiago," I said, correcting him.

"I know," he replied with a smile, holding up a forefinger. "'Always mispronounce your enemy's name. It takes away their energy' — as a Jamaican shaman we know once said."

"Rufus," I muttered with a reminiscent grin. "Rufus from Key West."

"Ya, mon," my partner replied with a smile.

I turned back to Shane. "And in case you don't remember, you've got a wife on the other side of the world who is absolutely freaking out."

Our friend exhaled heavily. "Yeah, I know, I know. I gotta make that right. And the last thing I need is another mucked-up leg." He looked at Will and me, the firelight etching the lines in his face. "I get it. I get it. We're going home."

The Wild Road to Key West

The following day, a handful of Indians escorted us out to where we had left our vehicle. A few hours later, we were back at the *bruja's* cottage. She took some time to clean Shane's wound once more, adding a special poultice to it and a fresh dressing. As she was kneeling in front of our friend, tying off his bandage, she spoke without looking up. "Lost friends are not the only thing you search for."

It wasn't a question. It was a statement.

We glanced at each other. Arturio's eyebrows did a little nervous bounce.

"You seek a lost place, and like most of your people, you seek its wealth, not its value," Passi continued as she tightened the last knot, then looked up at us, her eyes filled with a distant light. "You regard most what can be changed into coin, and you care less for the hearts of ancient people." She paused, her eyes cold. "But the shadowed walls there tell such a story, and it's a shame that man can't know..."

Passi exhaled heavily, her copper eyes losing their coldness and growing distant again. "Many years before it happened, their priests saw the coming of the pale invaders, so they fled their villages near the big waters. Deep in the interior, the people found a place they thought would be safe. And it was there that the 'miracle from the skies' occurred." She paused. "They might have been safe. But in the end, it was their kindness to strangers that killed them."

There was no good answer to any of this. We stood like statues, understanding about half of what she said regarding the nature of man and the destructive character of greed, yet having no concept of the remainder, about strangers, kindness, and malady.

Passi rose and stared at us, then sighed. "After all this time, it lies untouched." She drew a breath, then let it out slowly with a cold resignation. "All things, good and bad, are only a matter of time..." Again she sighed, resigned, as if coming to a decision. "Perhaps you are the ones...and perhaps I am doing you no favor. There is rarely a good ending in the search for riches you did not earn. But maybe..." She shrugged. "While I am not able to 'see' this place, I know that it exists. I have waited, as did my mother before me. But is the world ready for what lies hidden? It's not the wealth or the knowledge, but the truth that may be hard to abide." The young *bruja* shook her head slightly, as if to clear it. "But I suppose if not now, then when?"

Once again she stared at us. "It is not your fate today. But you will return, and when you do, we will search for the river 'that disappears' together."

We left the attractive but enigmatic Passi standing at the front of her cottage — her long, dark hair glistening in the morning sunlight, those bright copper orbs staring at us with a knowledge beyond our understanding. Aside from the fact that she was a most intriguing package, there was something about her that pushed a handful of my buttons. Perhaps it was that diamond-hard intensity...or maybe those exotic pointed breasts.

Will looked over at me and caught me in rapture. "Forget it," he muttered. "She's got the hots for me. I could see it in her eyes." He bounced his eyebrows in that whimsical Groucho Marx fashion. "When we come back, it's going to be every man for himself."

Thanks to fate, timing, or the will of the gods, we had just missed the manhunt for Shane that Santiago Talla organized. We were headed out on the main road on the eastern side of Icabaru while Santiago's men searched the jungle and the river to the west, where the firefight had taken place. His people questioned the natives who had helped us, but the jungle tribesmen just cocked their heads, glanced at each other, and scratched their loincloth-covered genitals, apparently witless.

"White men? What white men?"

As Santiago's people drove away, the Indians grinned at each other and went back to their business. After so many years of confrontation with Europeans and the Spanish, they had learned that survival often depended on knowing nothing. They had "ignorant" down to a science.

This journey was coming to a close, but I felt certain this was more than a one-act play.

Two days later, we were back in Santa Elena de Uairén, standing on the edge of the dirt runway by our aircraft. Will and I had filled our airplane's tanks upon our original landing, nearly a week ago — a standard policy of old adventurers. You never know when you might have to leave someplace in a hurry.

Less than an hour after arriving in Santa Elena, we were loading the airplane. Shane was in quite a bit of pain and he needed a real doctor posthaste. Arturio and I eased him into the back seat while Will began a preflight run-up on our 182 (battery switch on, flaps set, ailerons good, oil good, mixture rich, carb heat cold, throttle open slightly, primer in and locked).

When I asked Arturio if he wanted to come with us, he thought about it for a moment, then shook his head. Our new friend held out his hands, making a half-turn as he glanced about, then came back to us. "This is my place, amigos. I know it well and I am safe here." He grinned and dropped a shoulder in resignation. "As safe as a person can be who plays roulette in jungle bars." He offered a smile again. "Besides, I have feeling you guena be back pretty soon." Arturio glanced at the main street of town in the distance, and the bar where we had met, then turned back to us again. "I return your rental for you. You know where to find me, amigos. I give you a few weeks."

I reached into my pocket and handed him some hundred-dollar bills. "Take this. It'll keep you away from Russian roulette until we return."

He hesitated only as long as politeness required, then took them. "*Buenos, mis amigos,*" he whispered with that cocky smile of his. "It has been…entertaining…but now I need a drink and a woman."

At that moment I glanced at Shadow, who sat beside me next to the plane, those dark eyes uncertain and somewhat frightened. Will was just about ready to turn the engine over. I was sure the dog would bolt when that happened. I moved over, knelt, and scratched him behind the ears, then reached down and grabbed him. Before he had a chance to resist too much, Will pulled the front passenger seat forward and I stepped up onto the float of our amphibian, tossing the dog onto the back seat with Shane. I expected resistance — I thought for certain Shadow would try to escape, but Shane grabbed him, stroking the animal and speaking softly, and somehow, the dog quieted.

"Thanks to the gods for small victories," muttered Will, equally surprised.

With a last wave to Arturio, who had already backed away, I jumped into the co-pilot's seat and closed my door. Will turned the old girl over and she responded with a throaty roar as he pushed the throttle forward. We rolled to the threshold, did a run-up, then bounced down that old, dusty runway, kicking up a cloud of smoke like the Lone Ranger and Tonto.

"Hi-ho Silver!" yelled Will, as we disobeyed gravity and broke our bonds with the earth — old souls still constantly in search of the horizon, perennially pursuing those ancient elixirs of danger and excitement.

"The Lone Ranger and Tonto got nothing on us!" I cried, lost to the exhilaration of adventure and survival one more time.

"You got that right, Tonto," replied Will with a sarcastic grin as he eased off the flaps.

I shook my head and held up a forefinger. "How many times do I have to tell you? Me, the Lone Ranger. You, Tonto."

We flew into Caracas and got Shane to a doctor at the University Hospital there. After surgery and two days of recovery, he was in a cast from his knee down, but was well enough to travel. The consensus was that Shane would recover full mobility and the bone injury would heal, but it would be a while before he played any basketball.

Eighteen hours later, we had traversed the Caribbean, fueling three times, Will and I eating and sleeping in our seats and trading off at the controls when we saw the other falling asleep.

Key West Customs wasn't happy about a dog without papers, but thank God Shane knew one of the officers on duty that day.

The fellow agreed to a short, 24-hour quarantine providing the animal received an immediate rabies shot. We called a local veterinarian and left Shadow at his facility, promising to be back the following day for what, for all intents and purposes, had become my dog.

Will went out to the tarmac and the aircraft tie-downs to make sure his Cessna 310 was still accounted for and unmolested. He liked that airplane. It wasn't so much a possession as it was a friend. It had seen us through a number of situations.

From the airport, Will caught a taxi to his live-aboard shrimp boat on Stock Island. Shane and I got back into my floatplane and flew to Big Pine Key, landing in Newfound Harbor Channel and taxiing up onto the concrete slip at my stilt/canal home. I can tell you now, there was a deep, collective sigh when that propeller stopped. It was another adventure to be chalked up, for sure, but I was damned glad it was over.

I took Shane home to his very grateful wife, and after a tearful reunion and a brief explanation/recollection of our trip, I returned home. Ten minutes later, I was sitting on my deck, watching the sun sink into the back-country islands — reds, blues, and grays melting into the horizon as the last of that brilliant orb pasted the darkening sky with ribbons of fire. I took another hit of my beer, eased back into my seat, and closed my eyes…

Fifteen hundred miles south of the Keys, Señor Santiago Talla stood on his front porch in sullen anger, smoking another of his *cigarillos*. The gringo had escaped his net. Worse yet, it appeared that there had been two other gringos who had helped him slip away. Then there was the *bruja*, Passi. He knew they had met with her. He exhaled slowly, calming himself, and smiled. He was a patient man. All in good time.

On the plus side, one of his people — a distasteful man who owned lodgings on the road from Santa Elena to Icabaru — was able to identify two white men and their strange-looking accomplice, who had stayed at his camp just two days before all this. They had left for Icabaru the next day. Talla sent a man to track their trail backward and found they had arrived in Santa Elena three days before, in a private airplane. A floatplane.

Santiago had one of his people locate the fellow who owned the dirt strip and he got a name — Kansas Stamps, from a place called Big Pine Key in Florida. Through his anger, he smiled. Revenge was a dish best served cold.

CHAPTER FIVE

I awoke in the middle of the night, still sprawled out in my lawn chair. I got up, drank the rest of my beer, and stumbled into the bedroom. By seven the following morning, I was reviving myself with a long shower and a large cup of coffee. There's nothing like an expedition into the Third World to remind you of how good we have it in America.

I found the keys to my new Chevy pickup (a gift to myself for surviving our last adventure in Guatemala), then grabbed some breakfast at Island Jim's on the northern end of Big Pine. Island Jim's was a one-room, hibiscus-encased, screened eatery of about a dozen tables, owned by Shelly Jane, a woman possessed of remarkable culinary talent and mild schizophrenia.

Shelly kept a chalkboard on the wall with the specials of the day, a saying by some famous person, and what her name was this week. She also possessed a short, plastic baseball bat that she used without discretion on customers who burped loudly, insulted her food, or complained about the timeliness of its delivery. We all loved Shelly because she added dimension to our lives. It's the characters you meet that make the stories you remember, and the very best you can hope for is to be one of those characters.

But today I wasn't staying long. I had to get into Key West and pick up my dog.

When he saw me, Shadow broke into an anxious whine, tail hammering the sides of the metal wire cage in a staccato rhythm. I got him out, put his new collar on him (with his registration tag from the vet), and attached a leash. On the way down to Key West, I had stopped at Murray's Mart on Summerland Key and purchased these, along with dog bowls and food. Shadow wasn't altogether happy about the collar and the leash, but I swear I could sense the wheels turning in his head. He'd do whatever it took to get out of that prison. The vet, before releasing him, mentioned that Shadow had taken a low caliber bullet to the shoulder at some point in his life. "It was a 'through-and-through' wound that healed well," the vet explained. "But you never know how that will affect an animal."

After settling with the vet, we were on our way home — me and my dog...

I spent the first part of the day hanging out in my hammock, then I did a once-over of my 22-foot Aquasport to make sure she was still seaworthy. Finally, I drank a couple of beers, vacuumed the house and dusted the rare, black glass bottles displayed throughout my home — artifacts from our adventures, some of which dated back as far as 300 years. They were Spanish, Dutch, English, and early American, their hues, shapes, and original contents distinguishing their origins. Those old bottles were one of the few legacies that often survived a tropical sun, terrible storms, and the brutal indifference of man. They didn't really need dusting. I just liked touching them, while trying to imagine the bawdy souls who had held them last. Each one, I was certain, had a story.

The whole time, Shadow lived up to his name. After wolfing down a couple cans of dog food, he was never more than a few feet from me. Inquisitive, curious, and somewhat cautious, he was taking stock of his new world. I had discovered long ago that the expression, "It's just a dog," is most commonly used by people who just barely qualify as humans. Intelligent animals are hardly any different than their human counterparts in their curiosity, trust, and love, and they often eclipse their counterparts when it comes to loyalty and courage. It's the latitude you give an animal to "be more" that makes them what they are.

After a good night's sleep, Will had taken stock of his live-aboard shrimp boat. Everything was still in place, and all his special "cubbyholes" where he kept money, or artifacts that held special emphasis, were still secure. His most personally valuable artifact was a golden Mayan necklace with a three-inch, solid-gold medallion. Embedded in the center of that medallion was a 9mm slug — the parting gift from a renegade Bahamian policeman about a year ago. The medallion had saved my friend's life.

After he was satisfied that all was well, Will went out to purchase groceries and a newspaper. By afternoon he had grilled a couple of hamburgers, read *The Key West Citizen* from the front page to the last, swept the deck, checked and started his engine and generators, and was sliding well toward lackadaisical.

My phone rang. It was a little after five in the afternoon. I picked it up. "Hello?"

"I'm bored as hell," said Will. "There's nothing else I can clean around here and the snappers aren't biting off the docks. I think we're due for a night on the town — to celebrate journeys to strange places and survival."

I paused, thinking about it. He was probably right.

"Besides, it's 'two for the price of one' at Crazy Eddie's new bar until ten o'clock," my friend added. "I saw it in the paper."

Crazy Eddie, being an integral part of our very exclusive "Hole in the Coral Wall Gang," would be hot to hear about this latest adventure. After all, there was a damned good chance (according to history and a witch named Passi) that somewhere in the Venezuelan jungle there might just be a place whose people once possessed a fortune in gems and gold. It was the kind of story that really got Eddie's juices flowing. In truth, it stirred our juices as well, but I wasn't ready to go anywhere right now.

Eddie was in his mid-40s, tan, tall and gangly, and rarely seen in anything other than khaki shorts, fruit-juicy shirts, and weathered leather sandals. He had a short beard; long, sun-bleached hair; a thin, slightly bent nose (the consequence of a disagreement somewhere in the past); and he wore a black patch over one eye (the result of failing to duck quickly enough). While almost all of us flew airplanes, Eddie was probably considered our primary pilot. He had an older but well-maintained Grumman Goose and that boy could make it do tricks like a dog dancing for a bone. Actually, it was his third Goose. He'd had at least two shot out from underneath him — and us — on previous exploits.

Having been with us on our last adventure into Guatemala (and the recovery of a Mayan treasure as well as a World War II Nazi gold cache), he needed money about as much as Midas. But like Eddie always said, "The real treasure is in the tale. Gold? Hell, I got gold already, but you can never have enough barroom stories."

Actually, there were a couple other full-time members of our little Hole in the Coral Wall Gang — ex Special Forces soldier and pilot, William J. Cody (Cody Joe to his friends), and the legendary 7th Cavalry helicopter pilot, Captain Travis Christian—both bona fide hunters of old, shiny things. More than once they had earned their membership, and our friendship, in remarkable acts of sacrifice and courage. But they were definitely more about the game than the money. On top of it all, Cody Joe was a purely handsome dude — long blond hair, blue eyes, and freaking movie-star, women-peeing-in-their-pants good looking.

Travis Christian didn't miss much in the women-killing category either. Six-three, green eyes, dark hair...and he had a military reputation that preceded him damned near everywhere he went. The boys on the forward bases in Vietnam claimed he and his helicopter had saved more lives than penicillin. He rarely went into a bar anywhere that some ex-grunt didn't come over and slap money down on the bar top for his drinks that night.

There were other peripheral members, but those were the ones who had their names carved in the top of Eddie's bar.

But tonight, Will and I decided this would be just a simple foray into town — just us. A celebration of survival, timing and luck, one more time. Besides, our friends were way too much competition for average guys.

I had to leave Shadow at home. He wasn't happy about that, but he'd have to get used to it occasionally. It was a cool, breezy evening, with almost no mosquitoes, so I tied him to a piling under the stilt house. I was afraid to leave him inside without me yet — didn't want to come home to the remains of my living room.

Looking forward to a bawdy evening in Key West, I failed to notice the big Lincoln Town Car that picked up my tail as I turned

The Wild Road to Key West

out onto U.S. 1 on Big Pine Key and headed south.

I met Will at his live-aboard shrimp boat. We drank a beer each and watched the sun slip into the horizon from the roof of the craft's forecastle. Then we took his Mustang into town. We would have enjoyed ourselves less had we known that the dark car that had followed me from Big Pine had also tailed us into Key West. Two heavy Latinos got out and became our shadows.

Sloppy Joe's was way too crowded (a whole lot of tourists trying to be Conchs, failing to understand that "sloppy drunk" is not necessarily "Conch" until the end of the night). So, we slid down a few blocks to Eddie's new place, Crazy Eddie's Bar and Swill, just off Caroline Street. I eased out a breath as we entered, and I saw a smile twist the corners of Will's mouth. Eddie's place was probably the epitome of a cool, Key West bar. Ceiling fans churned the thick, smoke-filled air above batteries of heavy wooden tables that loosely surrounded a huge back bar. Off to one side was an area reserved for our friend's traditional "crab races." The long tables left ample space for the crabs to race, with lots of room around them for the betting customers. Wide windows faced the street and provided a free show for those inside and outside. Bartenders and waitresses, as high as they could afford to be, scurried about splashing liquid, sliding bottles, and clanging registers. From a small stage near the bar, a three-piece group with a guitar, bass, and a conga pounded out sensuous, driving rhythms, and the place virtually writhed to the tempos. It was kind of like coming home.

We grabbed a couple of seats at a table near one of the windows so we could watch the slideshow on the sidewalk — everything your mother told you to stay away from, and then some. The smell of pot pervaded the air. Women and men of all sizes and shapes promenaded along the sidewalk, gaudily or partially clad, or both. Panhandlers sat at corners with outstretched tambourines, the street traffic moved at a crawl, and the last of the evening light cast weird shadows across it all. It was like something from a Hunter S. Thompson book.

Eddie greeted us like family, bought our first couple of drinks, and turned us loose. We stayed there for about an hour, then headed out into the night, bouncing from bar to bar, searching for the girls of our dreams.

We met a couple ladies who pushed our buttons, but lost them to a brace of football players from Florida State University. Shortly thereafter, we found a couple of *touristas* who caught our attention, but after about a half hour of conversation, we realized they really liked each other more than they were ever going to like us. *C'est la vie…*

We were just leaving the Green Parrot when we heard a deep, heavily accented Jamaican voice rumble behind us.

"Hello! Hello, mons! My old friends, Willmon and Texas."

We stopped in our tracks and without even turning, I smiled and spoke over my shoulder, "It's *Kansas*, Rufus. *Kansas*."

Will and I came about in unison and there was our old Jamaican buddy. Sometimes mentor, sometimes guardian, but always our friend, Rufus, the psychic Rastaman, had connections to places that most of us have never seen.

"What are you doing here?" I said. "The last I heard, you were back in Jamaica."

He shrugged those big shoulders. "Da gods, dey bore easily, and sometimes dey move us around strictly for entertainment — like chess. We call it coincidence, but it just da gods adjusting da rabbit ears on da television of life."

Rufus was an incredible character who, without question, marched to a different drum. Our buddy claimed to be the progeny of an ancient race, and was gifted with the eerie disposition of oftentimes knowing what was going to happen well before it happened. He had saved our asses a number of times. It was never smart to ignore one of his appearances.

Nothing had changed with our friend, who was dressed in his standard Bob Marley T-shirt (very possibly the one I saw him in last), threadbare dock shorts, and weathered leather sandals. He was ageless, timeless — chocolate skin, long curling dreadlocks falling to his shoulders, a wide mouth with broad white teeth that always welcomed an easy smile, and startling gray eyes (which sometimes changed color to suit his mood).

Rufus eased out a heavy breath and shook his head, staring at us with a wry smile. "You been travelin' again, huh?"

It wasn't really a question. I glanced at Will, whose eyebrows did that little nervous bounce. (Rufus rarely showed up without having some celestial message or task for us.) I came back to our big friend. "Yeah…" I replied cautiously. "Did a little trip down to Venezuela. A friend had a problem."

Rufus nodded thoughtfully. "Da tides, mon, dey always pushin' dat flotsam an' jetsam one way or da other..." He paused. "Did you find anything interesting?"

There was no point in lying to Rufus. If you did, he would just make you look like a fool later on when he told you what you knew. I glanced at Will and got the eye bounce again. I cleared my throat. "Well, yes and no. There's a story…about an Indian tribe, way back when, that might have had interesting hobbies and jewelry. But it's possible the Spanish may have found them first, while in the process of 'finding' other tribes…"

Rufus interrupted. "Let me guess, mon. Dey come to dem natives, beat 'em up, take away dere gods, steal dere possessions and land, and den… give 'em Jesus." He held up a big finger and waved it. "Who, strangely enough, was always sayin', 'Thou shalt not steal.'" Our friend shook his head. "I find dat a little contrary."

Will nodded, struck by Rufus's insight. "Yeah. It's amazing how many excuses man can find to justify the compromises of his integrity."

That earned him a smile from Rufus, and I was thinking I should have said it.

Rufus stared at us for a moment with those huge brown eyes slipping into serious, then sighed. "Listen, mons, da new tide may be carryin' some flotsam and jetsam your way. So you better be watchin' behind you already." He paused and his eyes darkened. "Every dream got a price, mons. Everybody wanna be a diamond, but not many willing to be cut. It's a decision you gotta make." He held up a finger again. "An' remember, if and when you get to da place you be looking for, den your search begins for da place you gotta find..."

As I was trying to weigh that last statement, a car behind us backfired. Will and I snapped around like jittery meercats, but there was nothing to be seen — just the escaping ghost of exhaust smoke. When we turned back around, our old friend was gone. We were left with nothing but the new moon peeking through rustling palm branches above us.

My friend whispered to me almost reverently, "Did you hear that? He mentioned diamonds!"

I sighed. "Well, he mentioned *a diamond*, and metaphorically, the price you pay to be one or find one, I think... And he said something about two places that were, apparently, somewhere near each other...and connected somehow."

"Could be serious clues," Will said.

I offered a shrug. "Or he could just be messing with our heads. It wouldn't be the first time..."

As we headed for our car, the dark sedan down the street pulled out of its parking place and crept forward, passing us.

CHAPTER SIX

Running into Rufus and hearing his predictions broke the spell of the evening, and the alcohol had failed to take us where we wanted to go. We grabbed a couple Cuban sandwiches at Coco's Cantina, then decided to call it a night. Will dropped me off at his boat and I headed home.

When I pulled up under my stilt house, I immediately noticed that the dog was gone. I got out of my truck and cautiously checked the rope, which was still tied to one of the pilings. It had been chewed through. *So much for that plan.* I called for Shadow, but not too loudly. I was at the end of the canal, where it opened into Newfound Harbor Channel, but I didn't want to wake my neighbors down the waterway. No response.

I was about to call again when two men stepped out from behind my downstairs storage room. From the light of the moon, I could see that one was refrigerator-heavy and muscled, with a shaved head and a black mustache. The other was tall with long dark hair. Both were wearing Cuban *guayabera* shirts and loose cotton slacks. At that point, I noticed a dark sedan parked almost into the mangroves on the far side of the road.

The tall one pulled a knife. "You got a friend — big gringo, dark hair, shot in da leg probably. He make a friend of ours not so happy. Where is he?"

His Frigidaire partner straightened up and smiled in anticipation of what was to come, whether I answered correctly or not. It wasn't pretty.

"You tell us, den we don' gotta go find your friend on da boat..."

I instinctively blanched. Will! They knew where he was too. Quickly, I glanced around, trying to find something — *anything* — to defend myself with. If I could get to the canal, I was home free. Neither of them looked like Olympic swimmers, and if they had guns, they would have shown them by now.

Earlier in the day, I had taken some of my fishing gear from

43

the shed next to me — a tackle box, two of my light trolling rods and reels, and an ice chest. The rods still had heavy, treble-hooked Rapala lures affixed to their lines at the tips of each rod. I snatched up one of them, as if I was going to cast, locked the star drag on the spool, and backed up a step.

The guy with the knife grinned confidently. "What chu gonna do, amigo? Fish us to death?"

His big partner was still chuckling maliciously when I whipped the rod around and buried those big treble hooks on the lure into the tall guy's neck and jerked. The guy screamed like a crippled monkey, hands at his throat, knife gone — all thoughts of hurting me completely erased as I jerked the line tight again.

However, in my enthusiasm, I forgot about the big guy, who had now produced a weapon of his own — an old-fashioned barber razor, its curved blade gleaming under the light of the moon. Perfect for shaving real close, or cutting throats...

I jerked the rod tip again, just to keep the tall guy on his best manners. He shrieked and fell to his knees, one hand still clutching the line. I had skewered his fingers on one hand with my last snap of the rod tip as he grabbed the lure, so now he was in a real mess. But the refrigerator was coming at me — no hesitation, no compassion, his eyes excited and hard.

I remember thinking the guy was really fast for being that big as I instinctively stepped back and stumbled over the tackle box, sprawling out on the concrete floor. The man stepped in, slapped away my outstretched hand and grabbed me by the hair, pulling my head back and exposing my neck. I'm pretty sure I remember screaming as the blade started its downward arc.

But at that moment, out of the corner of my eye, I saw the gray flash of something hurtling across the floor, then going airborne — claws and fangs, and with a guttural growl that rose into a roar.

Shadow hit the man from the side, burying his fangs in the nape of my assailant's neck and ripping, using the weight of his heavy body to knock his opponent down and away from me. Man and beast tumbled across the cool, hard ground, Shadow's fangs ripping at the man's neck but not finding the jugular. Refrigerator Man managed to knock the dog away as he stumbled to his feet, blood running down his chest. He grabbed his friend, who had managed to break the monofilament line but still had one of Rapala's finest dangling from his neck, and they stumbled away into the darkness.

I sat there, my back against a concrete piling, gulping in air as I listened to a car start and roar away into the night. Suddenly, Shadow was against me, nuzzling me, breathing heavily, his flanks still trembling from the encounter. I ran my hands through the thick fur at his throat and pulled him into me. "Good boy," I whispered intensely. "Damned good boy..."

The best part of this recent development was that Shadow and I were still alive. The bad news was, somebody had some serious issues with us. I grabbed my dog, shoved him into the truck, and moments later, we were headed toward Key West.

"I can't believe this!" groaned Will as we sat at the table in the galley of his shrimper. "Why is it we can't seem to go anywhere without pissing somebody off?"

I took a slug of beer and nodded. "Good question. It's a talent of some sort. But we'll have to worry about it later. Right now, we've got to warn Shane that he's got problems."

Will was already reaching for his landline. Ten minutes later, we were headed out of Stock Island and taking a right onto U.S. 1.

Captain Shane O'Neal sat on the couch in his living room, his leg with the cast extended out on an ottoman, his face a mask of anger and concern. In a normal situation, he would have gone to his special wall safe, picked out the weapons of choice, and "fixed" this. But with a cast on his leg and his wife there with him, there was no good way to play this. He had no idea when to expect them, or how many of "them" there were. It came down to a decision — to stand and fight or run.

Our buddy, Travis Christian, would have been perfect for this, but we had leaned on him heavily to save our bacon in an extraordinary fiasco in Guatemala last year. Besides, he was out of the country visiting the English girl who had caught his attention so completely about eighteen months ago. He deserved some time off. He wouldn't be back for another week to ten days.

Cody Joe, Travis's most remarkable counterpart, was still living on his sailboat in front of Christmas Tree Island off Key West. He had just recently broken up with the lady he had met during our Mexican/Pancho Villa gold gig, also a while back. He would probably bite just to have something to take his mind off his present situation; and Crazy Eddie was, of course, always ready and willing. That's why they called him Crazy Eddie — well that, and probably a dozen other peculiarities bordering on lightly restrained insanity.

But the idea of a serious confrontation really wasn't my approach of choice. Will and I had always preferred to confuse and bedazzle. Unfortunately, that didn't appear to be an option and I didn't want to live constantly looking over my shoulder.

I glanced around at my friends in O'Neal's living room. "Here's how I see this. I think that Shane and his wife are going to have to take a vacation until we wrap this up."

Shane threw his hands out. "Whoa, wait a minute! I'm not running from these bastards!"

"This isn't just about you," I replied. "You've got your wife to consider. You think they're going to leave her alive after they deal with you?"

That took the wind from his sails.

I exhaled harshly. "Apparently, you've pissed off this Santiago dude in a seriously righteous fashion, as Eddie would say, and now we're on that list too."

Will corrected me. "Not *we, you*. You're the one on that list. I haven't beat up any of their people."

I huffed out a breath. "Yeah, well, before they slit my throat I'm gonna make sure they know the whole thing was your idea."

"Hmmm," my buddy muttered, his lips turning up in a touch of a grin.

I got serious. "To tell you the truth, I'm not quite sure how to

get out of this one. You got any suggestions?"
  Will thought for a moment and his eyes took on a strange glint. Not nice, but clever. "What's the last thing this Santiago guy would expect from you and me right now?" he asked.
  I shrugged. "Hell, I don't know. I'm not a mind reader. But you're gonna tell me, aren't you?"
  Will nodded. "Let's go back to Venezuela."
  I drew back. "Dude, you drank too much of that bad, 'south of the border' water. You're having delusions of lunacy." I shook my head. "That's where the people are who want to kill us!"
  "Exactly," said my partner. "Where's the last place in the world they'd be looking for us?" He leaned in conspiratorially. "We get Shane and his wife on the next flight to Hawaii." Will looked over at our DEA friend. "I know you've got some false IDs. Everyone in your business does, and with just a phone call, your people will put something together for your wife. You two can just disappear for a while...and have a good time while you're at it."
  Then Will turned to me. "You know damned well you want to go back. The words of that hot-looking *bruja* are burning in your ears. There's some sort of remarkable find there — probably something sparkly, different, and seriously valuable. And for some damned reason, she wants us to find it. I've been over my topographical map of the area she spoke of. There are a couple rivers — one in particular that feeds into a small lake, where we could land Eddie's Goose."
  "You're basing all this on a brief, stoic conversation we had with a self-proclaimed witch," I said.
  Will nodded. "Yeah, I know. But first off, I love the idea of Santiago running himself weary trying to find us here while we're in his own back yard." Will held up his hands. "I'm not saying we *have* to, but it also gives us a damned good shot at taking him out of the game if we *decide* to." My friend paused, drew a breath, and continued. "But most of all, what if there is a lost city back there in that jungle? I mean, there are cool things, and then there are *really* cool things..." My friend tilted his head slightly and got that

weird grin of his. "Talk about a barroom story..."
 I had to take a moment to digest this. A storm was coming in, and I could hear a fresh wind rattling the wind chimes on the deck. Finally, I exhaled, somewhat defeated. I looked up at my friend. "I hate it when you make sense. I guess we'll need to talk with a buddy of ours who owns a bar and a plane..."

CHAPTER SEVEN

It took Crazy Eddie about thirty seconds to decide. We were sitting at a table in the back of his bar.

"Hell yes, dudes!" he cried, slapping his palm on the tabletop hard enough to make me flinch. "Freakin' righteous! I been bored shitless for the last few months!" He calmed down then, unconsciously adjusting his black eye patch, his one good eye gleaming like a diamond as he leaned into us. "A city of solid gold, huh, man?" He pulled back and grinned. "Ooohh, yeah!"

Will waved him down. "We never said it was a solid-gold city, but the inference is that there might be gold there, and stones." My buddy smiled. "Pretty stones. Valuable stones."

Eddie shrugged, holding out his hands, palms up. "Okay, okay. Who cares? That works. Eddie just needs to get into his bird and groove to the celestial movement of adventure again. You dig?"

We couldn't help but smile. Eddie was simply one of a kind. He wasn't as dangerous as Travis or Cody, but he could make that airplane of his do things that would scare an astronaut. And I guaran-damn-tee you, when the chips were down, I wanted that dude on my side.

It had taken Shane and Julie less than three hours to be headed for the airport in Miami. Shane made one call to the DEA and they had new passports waiting for them at Eastern Airlines. Someone would pick up their car at the airport parking lot. He wasn't happy about it, but our friend knew this was the best thing. Shane would stay in touch with his old office, and when all of this had been resolved, they'd come home. Besides, they'd always wanted to see Hawaii…

That afternoon we were sitting in the cockpit of William J. Cody's sailboat on the other side of Christmas Tree Island, off Key West. We'd known Cody Joe for a number of years, but he never seemed to change at all. He was only about five foot seven, but there was an aura about him that said the percentages were against you in a confrontation. And they were — he was a martial arts expert in karate and aikido and he "dabbled" in other styles that I had a hard time pronouncing.

The sun was just reaching for the green water, a battery of puffy-white cumulus clouds drifting into it, their rims turning gold for the effort. A vee of pelicans made their way toward the shoreline like falling shadows in the sky.

Cody took a sip of his drink. "So, tell me about it," he said. "I know you've got something going on."

Will and I glanced at each other. My buddy spoke. "We've got a little situation. It involves the possibility of shiny stones and some gold — a lost treasure."

"That's the good news," Cody said, not looking up.

"But there's a bad guy that we may have to deal with in the process."

"Isn't there always?" Cody replied, taking another sip of his drink.

Twenty-four hours later, we were lifting off out of Key West, the heavy hum of the big radial engines in Eddie's Goose offering a rich orchestra of vibration and sound. Eddie sat there, the tarred end of a joint hanging from his lips as he pushed in the throttles and adjusted his mixtures, the ball cap he claimed Jimmy Buffett had given him askew on his head, his one eye gleaming with excitement. Eddie was back in his element — living for the moment, looking for shiny things, and riding on the edge of life. Will was flying second seat. Cody and I were sitting behind the cockpit partition. Shadow was curled up apprehensively at my feet — not altogether happy about this flying thing, but adjusting. Our gear was stored center and aft for correct weight and balance numbers.

We also had an admirable collection of things that go boom. I noticed that Shadow had an immediate reaction to the sight of weapons. His hair bristled and he backed down into a crouch, a slight rumble emanating from that big chest. It wasn't so much fear as it was a distinct enmity. There was a part of me that said I wouldn't want to be a person holding a weapon that threatened that dog or his friends.

Speaking of destructive items, just before we left the Keys, Eddie had visited Bobby Branch, a buddy of his on Cudjoe Key. Branch had done a year in Vietnam, at which time he worked in the arms depot at Da Nang. In the process, he had broken down and shipped a huge variety of weapons back to his girlfriend in the States. He lost the girlfriend, but he still had the weapons, which he sort of "rented out" for special occasions. Actually, through the years he had developed somewhat of a small weapons black market. He had a special this month on stick dynamite and AT4 anti-tank/vehicle weapons — basically, nothing more than smallish, forty-inch metal tubes that fired a finned, extra powerful rocket grenade accurately up to two hundred yards. Indiscriminately dangerous. Eddie took one. In addition, he took a few sticks of dynamite. Like he said, with eyebrows bouncing, "You never know…" Eddie had cubbyholes in that airplane that a ferret couldn't find. We were good on "bang."

We also realized that with this plan — taking Eddie's Goose from Santa Elena to Icabaru, and landing in a local river we'd plotted out — we'd have no transportation from our point of debarkation. So, I had visited the local Yamaha dealer in Key West and purchased three Yamaha XT250 dirt bikes with ramped-up engines and shocks, extra-large gas tanks, a couple of large saddlebags, and frame-mounted foot pegs for a second rider. These weren't luxurious traveling machines, but they would get us over the rough stuff, they were good on fuel, and they were as tough as a boot-camp drill instructor. Shadow would have to hoof it behind us, but we weren't looking at traveling fast, nor would those old jungle logging roads allow us to.

Once again, we bounced from Key West, over Cuba to Jamaica, southeast to Aruba, down to Trinidad, then into Venezuela. Finally, at the end of the second day, just as the sun was biting a piece out of the western jungle, we dropped down in a full-flaps landing onto the little strip in Santa Elena de Uairén.

There were no Customs people. Hell, we were in the middle of the jungle — the closest we came to Customs was a dark little Venezuelan guy with a fuzzy Afro, his hand out, saying he would watch our plane for thirty, American.

"We guard it wid our lives," he said with a bucktoothed smile, brushing down his dirty T-shirt self-consciously with his right hand.

"We?" I asked, eyebrows up. "You got a mouse in your pocket?"

He shook his head and pointed to the large rubber tree shadows by the airstrip. Suddenly, a dark shape emerged from the gloom. A big, dark shape — something like a gorilla on steroids, with dirty white *pantalones*, arms like pythons, and a straw hat. The gorilla waved.

"Me and him," the little guy said, the wisp of a smile lifting the corners of his mouth.

It was a good act. I don't know if it was planned, but it was a good act and we bought it. Ten minutes later, we had grabbed the items we couldn't afford to lose, locked the Goose, and the only taxi in town was dropping us off at the place where I had rented our Jeep the last time. We rented it again. (The car-rental business is slow in the middle of the hellish Venezuelan jungle.) From there, we found a guesthouse that looked like it might have been built about the time the Spanish arrived, but the rats had eaten most of the roaches, so it was acceptable.

Now, we needed to find our buddy Arturio, who had proven to be so handy and capable during the last trip. Knowing Arturio's inclinations, the best place to start was the local bar.

I left Shadow in the Jeep. It was a relatively cool evening and he made himself comfortable in the open back. No one would bother anything with him sitting there. Our furry companion was becoming very possessive of us.

Nothing had changed in the bar, except perhaps a few new bloodstains on the floor. It still looked like a twisted Mel Brooks barroom scene. One of the two rusted ceiling fans jutting from the ceiling had died, the same heavy cloud of smoke drifted just below the roof beams like mountain clouds, and the same odor of booze, sweat, excitement, and death hung in the air.

It is said that timing is a toy of the gods. Sometimes they're in a good mood and you are blessed with the impossible, and sometimes they're pissed off and you catch the brunt of it.

The four of us had no sooner walked through the door than we heard the report of a pistol. I flinched like a frightened buck, I admit it. I could barely bring myself to look. This was just the way the gods would do it — spare our friend once, only to kill him in front of us later.

"Oohh shit," Will muttered, and at that point, I couldn't help but steal a glimpse. There across the room was a man spread out on the floor, arms splayed out, blood oozing from a head wound. But it wasn't Arturio. I eased out a sigh of relief as the big African bouncers dragged the body out the back door into the alley. But my relief was short-lived.

As we stood there like statues, the losers tossed their tickets and someone splashed a bucket of water on the old floor planks. The winners collected their money, and in moments, the fervor of the crowd was rising again, like the surge of a hurricane's first crest. There were two more gamblers ready to risk their lives.

I glanced up. There was Arturio!

"Holy freaking Christ!" I cried, grabbing Will by the arm. "There's our boy!"

The rules were clear. This was a tough society. Once you committed to a game, you played or you never showed your face in Santa Elena de Uairén again. If you did, the penalty was "accidental death," delivered by the coroner.

As we stumbled to a table in the back of the room, Arturio and his competitor sat down in their chairs, the .32 revolver between them. Will grabbed my arm hard enough to make me flinch. "We gotta stop him, man. We gotta stop him!"

I agreed, but I wasn't sure what the penalty would be for interrupting a game of Russian roulette in a place where bets were flowing and life was cheaper than a New York hamster.

The cards were drawn from a ragged deck and Arturio's

opponent was forced to the pistol first. The man hardly hesitated. Eyes like distant fires, he picked up the gun, spun the cylinder, put the barrel to his temple, and pulled the trigger.

I hate to say it, but I was damned unhappy to hear nothing but the click of the hammer on an empty chamber. The crowd responded with cheers and moans, depending on where they'd bet their money.

Now, it was Arturio's turn.

As our friend reached for the gun, he saw us in the crowd. There was a moment of recognition and he nodded to us, but it was eclipsed by a strange sense of precognition. His gray eyes faded to acceptance and he smiled sadly as he spun the cylinder and brought the gun up, still staring at us...

I was out of my chair before I actually knew I was out of my chair. Flying across the bloodstained floor, I caught my friend's hand just as he was pulling the trigger and we tumbled backward as the weapon discharged. My senses were so wired, the report was like a cannon as we careened across the floor.

There was a roar of disappointment across the crowd as we lay there, tangled on the bloodstained floorboards. But the first thing I saw was the strange smile on Arturio's face in front of me. He was still alive.

"Good to see you again, amigo," he whispered.

Cody was already up and backing off those who were most disappointed. Will was right behind him, trying to quell the natives, hands out, promising to pay double to the winners and the losers. It took a moment for this to sink in, but it seemed to have a calming effect, especially when he pulled out a handful of bills and slapped them on the bar.

As we clambered to our feet, Arturio looked at me strangely. "You got son' pretty amazing timing, amigo. Maybe you be a *brujo...*"

"Yeah," I growled. "And maybe you be an idiot."

CHAPTER EIGHT

By sunrise the following morning, we were preparing for a second foray into the wilderness. Somewhere before us in the Venezuelan jungle lay the possibility of a lost city, with the likelihood of a bit of gold and maybe a handful of brilliant stones. Who knew? It was possible. But first off, there was an attractive witch to meet with again…

The "security" we had hired the night before had done a surprisingly admirable job — although we hadn't left anything in the aircraft we couldn't live without. After paying them, we were transferring our gear from the plane to the Jeep when I noticed what appeared to be two monks coming down a road that led up into the mountain behind us. It was an odd thing. Their dress and demeanor were right out of the 1700s. They were attired in brown robes with a light rope belt at the waist. Their heads were partially shaved in tonsure style (the typical bald spot on the back top of the crown shaved and a fringe of hair around it.) Their feet were bound with leather sandals and each wore a cloak with an attached hood, or "habit," as it's called. Both carried a strand of wooden beads with a cross attached to their weathered rope belts.

"That's not something I would have expected to see here," I remarked, somewhat surprised.

Arturio shrugged. "Actually, amigo, we have one of the oldest monasteries in de Caribbean Basin here."

"Yeah," said our historian, Will, nodding. "He's right. The first group of Franciscan monks arrived in Mexico in 1523. In the early 1600s, one of the friars — Fray Alonso de Molina — established a monastery on Roatán and began sending their followers to all points south in the Caribbean Basin." He paused. "I remember that now, from my research. But I wouldn't have expected any of the monasteries to still be in operation."

Arturio smiled. "Amigos, you should know that religion, like politics, don' surrender any foothold easily." Our friend paused for a moment. "Everyone here searches for wealth." He nodded at the monks. "They, too, in their own way. The monks bless the miners and the searchers, and they are often rewarded if good fortune finds its way to their people." Arturio offered a sarcastic grin. "It is much easier to splash a little holy water on a miner than it is to dig in the hole next to him. But you can be sure, if the miner is fortunate, some credit and wealth is given to God — and to the Very Reverend Abbot of the monastery."

Before departing, we grabbed an almost acceptable breakfast at the only real restaurant in town — scrambled eggs and day-old rice. In the process, I made sure Shadow had a good breakfast as well. It was going to be a long day.

During our meal, Eddie explained that he had found a small river close to Icabaru with a road nearby. It was a really old logging road and it wouldn't be fun, but the dirt bikes could easily make the distance to the *bruja*'s home. We had to accept the fact that we might have to deal with Santiago, but if we could slip around him, we needed to meet with Passi. We needed the insight she could offer us.

"Let's not lose sight of the mission," Cody said, glancing around at all of us, but his eyes slowing as they came to me. "I don't like the idea any better than you, but I don't think this Santiago guy is going to be happy until he's had a piece of the people who bit him on the ass. Guys like him stay in power only because they're more ruthless and vengeful than the people below them."

I eased out a nervous sigh. "I know, I know. But I still say we need to keep a really low profile and find the *bruja* first. She gave us a couple of cryptic hints the last time we saw her, but she knows, or she 'sees,' more than she's telling about some sort of lost city. Besides, right now no one knows we're here. If we go after Santiago first and we botch it, we'll never have a shot at what's out there in that jungle."

An hour later, after a thorough preflight check (we were going into the depths of the Venezuelan jungle — no Flight Based Operators, no 7-Elevens, and not a single tarred airstrip for several hundred miles), we settled into our seats and exhaled almost in unison.

Eddie took a half-smoked joint from his ashtray, put it between his lips, and lit it. Blowing out a bluish cloud at the top of the cockpit, he offered it to Cody, who was flying co-pilot. Our friend smiled but declined with a wave of his hand. Eddie let the joint hang out the side of his mouth as he pulled down the bill of his Jimmy Buffett ball cap and grinned. "Hang on dudes!" he yelled, taking a quick glance back at Will, me, and Shadow. "Into the lands of Mordor!"

A moment later, our crusty pilot had the throttles to the wall and we were rumbling down that potholed dirt strip, then lifting into a pale-blue, cloudless sky. Below us, the emerald jungle tumbled recklessly across thousands of miles, cleaved by the fingers of a hundred muddy green rivers. In the distance, I saw an eagle rising on a thermal. I had to smile. I couldn't help it. I glanced over at Will. He was staring out of his window with the same rapturous grin. I reached down and stroked the thick fur of my new friend, who rarely left my side now. Shadow had proven to be a fine companion. He appeared to have adjusted to this concept of flying far easier than I had expected, and had already shown he wasn't squeamish about defending what was his.

"Once more, into the fray..." I whispered with a cautious smile.

It took our remarkable pilot less than an hour to find the river of choice for a landing. We tried to stay well away from Icabaru and the residence of the area warlord. If we were going to come for him, we wanted it to be a "stone-cold surprise," as Cody put it. After a couple of passes, Eddie spotted a battered but apparently passable road coming off a fording spot on a twisting, muddy river, obviously used by the area natives. "That's the place, amigos," he shouted over the engines as he set up for a straight-in approach toward a mangrove-covered beach that accessed the road.

Half an hour later, we had our three cross-country motorcycles and the balance of our equipment unloaded — a couple small tents, sleeping bags, some basic medical supplies, a couple of pans, several bags of freeze-dried food, and, of course, the "instruments of destruction" Eddie had gotten from his buddy, Bobby Branch, on Cudjoe Key.

Everyone carried a weapon of choice — Will and I liked 9mm Walthers (so we could exchange ammo if necessary), Cody carried a Colt .45 at his belt, as well as his trademark weapon — a vintage Thompson machine gun (both using interchangeable ammo). Eddie, with only one good eye, didn't want to bother with aiming. His gun of choice was a semi-automatic Mossberg 12-gauge shotgun. Each of us carried as much ammo as our conscience required. Arturio carried a long-bladed knife at the base of his spine. His argument was, "If I can't stop you with my knife, señor, I should be in another bar…"

The truth was, Will and I, and even Eddie, were not cowboys when it came to guns, but we damned sure didn't want to go into this without them. Cody was a professional — very dangerous when the chips were down. He and his buddy, Travis, could cut a path through anything short of a Panzer tank assault.

Truth was, Cody wasn't quite as stoic as Travis. With his long blond hair and movie-star looks, he could be flamboyant at times. But unlike so many handsome men, he had never become smug or arrogant, and rarely used his looks to his personal advantage — other than to get laid occasionally. Because, as our more crass buddy Crazy Eddie would say, "When all the tallies have been made and they're putting you in the ground, the roll in the hay you passed up is the roll in the hay you didn't get."

We thanked God for the logging road, or we could never have pulled this off, but we scorned the devil for making it such a miserable course. The road had really become nothing more than an overgrown path, which even our cross-country bikes had a tough time negotiating. Eddie rode behind me on my bike, Arturio rode behind Will, and Cody led the group on his bike. We weren't moving so fast that Shadow couldn't keep up comfortably.

We stopped once for a short break and a drink of water. As soon as I was off the bike, Shadow was at my side, mimicking his name, his ears up and his eyes alert.

Cody watched this and smiled. "That's a fine dog," he said with a warm smile. "I've known a lot of fascinating women in my life, but I'd trade most of them for a dog like that."

Will, his back against a tree, nodded. "If you eliminate gambling, electronics, and sex, you'll discover that almost all of your greatest pleasures are shared with your dog."

That brought a chuckle from the group.

Five minutes later, we were back on the trail. Eddie's map and his instinctive dead-reckoning kept us on course, and by the end of the day, we were coming into the western outskirts of Icabaru.

Somehow, we managed to find that small, weathered house on the edge of the jungle just as the sun was setting.

Passi met us at the door. She was dressed in a soft cotton shift adorned with flowers of the jungle. It was simple, as always, but it clung to her full figure, and the sensual, casual way she moved once again caught our attention.

We introduced her to Eddie and Cody, and the *bruja*'s eyes did the inevitable once-over with Cody. We'd seen it before. It wasn't a surprise.

We settled into her small den and explained what had happened with us stateside — the attack on me, and, of course, Santiago's obvious attempt to get our friend, Shane.

She eased back in her chair and sighed angrily, then glanced around at us. "You will be forced to make a decision at some point, but for now, the past is the past. Move forward."

"Yeah," I muttered. "Easy for you to say. But we're like babes in the woods here..."

Passi stared at us for a moment, then spoke quietly. "For some reason that I don't understand, the gods have chosen you... A monument of kindness, greed, and knowledge has lain hidden for hundreds of years." She glanced around at us. "I offered a small oblation to the dark and the light, and I was given a vision."

There was a stillness that swallowed the room.

Passi continued, almost in a whisper. "I have seen it — the City of the Stars. It is where the river stops."

Will and I turned to each other for a quick glance. My buddy's eyebrows did that quizzical little bounce.

"The city was built into a small, low canyon, but the walls have long since been covered by jungle," she began softly. "A river runs into the narrow mouth of the canyon and continues into the walls at the far side, where it drops down into a subterranean cavern that carries it out into the depths of the jungle, only to rise up and begin again, miles away." She paused and looked around at us. "This I see in the mists when I close my eyes." She sighed. "If you wish to find the lost city, find the river that stops in the jungle."

I'd been puzzled for quite some time over something that Passi had said when we first met, so I asked, "When we were first here, you said the people who originally founded this city moved from the coast to the interior to avoid the coming invaders — the Spanish, I assume." I paused. "Then they found someplace safe, where the 'miracle from the skies' occurred." I paused. "What was that all about? Do you understand that statement?"

The young *bruja* sighed, somewhere between sadness and bitterness. "You ask for an oracle and I am just a woman," she muttered. Then slowly she brought her head up. "I can only see so far into the mists, but I understand this. There was an...*encounter*... of some sort, and it offered a wider understanding of life to these people."

Will and I glanced at each other again, speculation running rampant.

"You mean like other people?" said Will. "Like a different race?"

The *bruja* shrugged. "I cannot see it, but yes, something like that. But most of all, it changed how they saw things. It gave them a greater understanding of nature and this planet in relation to others."

Before Passi could continue, Will added, "But you said their kindness killed them — the people of the city. How is that possible?"

"This I can see," she whispered sadly. "It was much later, long after the miracle from the skies." Passi drew a ragged breath. "The people of this city had survived on obscurity. Hundreds of years before, their priests had foreseen the coming of the pale foreigners and they had fled into the deepest jungles to establish a safe place." She paused. "But eventually, it wasn't far enough. At some point, a small party of foreigners from the shores of the great water found them. It had been so long since the oracle and the people took in the nearly starving strangers, feeding them, offering them presents of the sparkling stones that they found in the rivers and mountains."

I glanced at Will. His eyes widened and the corner of his mouth lifted slightly.

Passi exhaled, then continued. "When the strangers left, I think life went back to normal for a while. But then the people began to fall sick, with sores on their bodies and an evil inside them that stopped their breath. One by one they faded, then in groups, and in the end, there was nothing left but the carrion birds..." Her eyes glistened with sadness and recollection. "They offered kindness, and in return, they were given sickness and the city died."

There was no good answer to any of this. We sat like statues, understanding well what she said regarding the nature of man and the destructive character of Europe's early explorers, as well as the diseases they brought...yet having no concept of the remainder, about the strangers and the miracle from the skies.

Passi rose and stared at us for a moment, then walked to the window and looked out at the jungle. She sighed, still staring outside. "After all this time, it lies concealed, untouched — the City of the Stars." She sighed softly with a sad resignation and turned to us, her eyes in a distant place. "All things, good and bad, are only a matter of time..."

As it was, we now had a definitive clue. But there was still a lot of jungle out there. Remarkably enough, Icabaru had only just received phone lines in the last month — two phones. We drove into town and waited in line for an hour to use one. My friend placed a collect call to a buddy in the Keys, then had him go to his live-aboard and find his notes from the Spanish archives. It took the better part of the morning, waiting for the guy to find what we needed, then having him read the document carefully before calling us back. But shortly after lunch, Will had the information.

Unbeknownst to us, while we were gone, the *bruja* placed a call of her own, on her two-way radio...

"In my notes from the Spanish archives, the section that detailed the story of Welser and his journey into the interior only consisted of a page or so, but it divulged a couple of valuable facts," Will explained. "The explorers apparently traveled southeast out of Maracaibo into what is now called El Caura — the heart of the Venezuelan jungle — for almost a month, using rivers and Indian guides whenever possible. But most importantly, they portaged around a 'magnificent waterfall' the day before coming to the City of the Stars."

When we returned to Passi's home to tell her what we had learned, we found her dressed for jungle travel: khaki pants and shirt, canvas boots, and a light travel bag at her side.

"Whoa shit," Will muttered. "I think we got some wires crossed here. We didn't say anything about you coming."

"It doesn't matter what you said," our feisty friend replied. "You would have nothing without me. Do you think I am going to leave you to find the dream that I have seen?"

It was a tough argument...

A half hour later we were on our bikes, scrambling down the same battered trail on which we had found our way to Icabaru and Passi. We were headed back toward Eddie's airplane, our crusty pilot already on edge, muttering about the possibilities of "jungle rapscallions" breaking into his Goose.

Passi had chosen to ride behind Cody on his bike.

"Some things never change..." muttered Will.

CHAPTER NINE

By the grace of God, no one had found Eddie's plane while we were gone. (The truth was, there were few people in that area who had ever seen an aircraft up close. They were probably terrified of it.) We set up camp in and around it. The consensus was, we'd spend the night there, then, the following day, Eddie would begin to run sorties in the direction from which we believed the Spanish explorers had originally come, from Maracaibo. We had two landmarks — a river that suddenly stopped and became subterraneous, and a large waterfall which might not still be there after 400 years. It was basically as Eddie had described it. Two needles in a haystack.

The following morning we were up just after dawn, unenthusiastically forcing down some Vietnam-vintage C-rations that Eddie had procured. The food hardly mattered; it wasn't high on our list of priorities. Fifteen minutes later, Eddie had done his preflight, the camp was secured, and we loaded aboard.

I noticed that during the night Passi's and Cody's sleeping bags seemed to have ended up together, just at the edge of camp. I glanced at Will, who threw out his hands, palms up. "I don't care. I still think she has the hots for me. Yesterday afternoon, when we went to get wood for the fire, she became…really inviting." He grinned. "I didn't resist...much." My friend shook his head. "I don't know if she's a witch, but she's got some damned bewitching parts…"

It was a strange thing. One moment she seemed to be aloof and enigmatic, and the next, sexual and inviting. It seemed like maybe she was playing the odds with all of us. Well, with most of us. I hadn't had my turn…

After a thorough preflight, Eddie swung his big bird around and took her into the river. Cody pulled up the wheels and locked them. Our pilot set twenty degrees of flaps and slowly pushed his throttles forward. In seconds there was the sound of water slapping the hull as the old girl picked up speed, then the familiar, reassuring sound of silence as we broke the laws of nature and lifted out over the jungle and into the sky.

Hour after hour, the ocean of green and brown below us crested in rolling waves, then flattened into snaking, muddy rivers as we cut out quadrants on the map, then scratched them off in disappointment. I often turned to Passi, in the window seat across from me, looking for a sign; a modicum of hope. But those strange copper eyes remained unyielding. By midafternoon, Eddie had burned through almost a quarter of his standard wing tanks and we had nothing to show for it — no waterfalls, no greenery-covered canyons. We decided to turn to the east and set a course for our camp.

I could see the disappointment in the eyes of my companions. I was about to offer some droll statement of encouragement when Will, in his typical, indomitable fashion, eased out a sigh and threw up his hands, looking around at all of us.

"So, we screwed the chicken today," he cried. "So what? What did you expect? That there would be freakin' billboards sticking up out of that freakin' sweaty labyrinth down there, saying 'Bring your buckets! This way to the City of Diamonds!'"

That broke the quiet despondence like the shattering of a mirror. Even Cody was laughing. Shadow looked around and pulled back under my seat, convinced we'd all gone mad.

Late that afternoon, after the usual dinner banter, Eddie explained that we could do this two-quadrant routine maybe two more times before having to refuel. We would probably have to go back to Santa Elena. Although there was a small strip at Icabaru, he doubted they could give us the fuel we needed, and most of all, there was no point in Santiago knowing we were there. If we were going to mix it up with him, it had to be on our timing and on our terms.

The following day, we were back in the air just a little after dawn. The rising sun turned the treetops to gold and the sluggish river glistened softly. Hordes of colorful waterbirds took to the shallows, their long wings arching out in tumultuous, ungainly landings as they settled into their favorite feeding grounds. This time the course we had chosen was farther southeast of Maracaibo, at what I considered the range limit for conquistador exploration from the northern and eastern coasts of Venezuela. When we came to the Orinoco River, which splits Venezuela from east to west, I had Eddie stay with the river, running west, and we began to look for tributaries that might simply stop in the jungle.

Sometimes the Gods, they get bored, and they throw you a bone...

Just after eleven o'clock, Cody perked up and pointed to the southwest. There was definitely a break in the river ahead, where a tributary slid south.

"We've got nothing to lose," said Eddie, as he gently rolled a wing and we took up the course.

Gradually, the winding waterway drove deeper into an absolute no man's land of dark jungle and forest. The terrain below was tough and unforgiving, and anything that lived there had absolutely no sense of kindness. Life was all about surviving another day.

We stayed with the river for the better part of an hour, Eddie dropping down and reducing power to give us more time to observe. But in truth, we had all begun to realize how nearly impossible the task was that we had set for ourselves. I even heard the indomitable Eddie mumble something about chasing wild geese with his Goose.

I admit I had become discouraged, especially from my position in the cabin. I had taken a moment for a drink of water from my canteen, and had just poured some water into Shadow's bowl near my seat, when I heard Cody mutter, "I'll be damned!"

"And you probably will be," Will groused, beginning to lose some of his enthusiasm as well.

"No!" said Cody adamantly. "Ahead, thirty degrees off your starboard wingtip. There's a waterfall!"

Eddie drew up in his seat and stared out as we all came back to life, moving toward the cockpit en masse. Shadow felt the surge in activity and whined anxiously.

The river suddenly swung to the right and tumbled down a hundred-foot waterfall. To the cheers of our delight, Eddie brought us down to about 500 feet and we skimmed along the top of the jungle, staying with the river as it snaked ahead. About fifteen minutes later, when the excitement of finding the waterfall was beginning to wane, the river disappeared. It simply... disappeared. One minute it was there, flowing peacefully below and ahead of us; the next it rolled tumultuously into a slanted cavern in the dense green labyrinth and was gone.

"Whoa shit..." whispered Will, almost reverently. "That's a good trick."

Eddie took some readings so we could find it again. Then he swung around in a wide circle and brought us at it once more. The whole thing got better. This time, because we were looking for them, we could see the faintest outlines of the jungle-covered, horseshoe canyon walls that the river flowed into. We had found it!

We all crowded into the cockpit, shouting and cheering as Eddie made one more pass. We had found the canyon that protected the "City of the Stars."

Strangely enough, the only one who didn't appear to be ecstatic was our *bruja*, Passi. I caught her when she didn't think anyone else was watching. There was an excitement in those copper eyes, no question, but there was a shadow of uneasiness as well...

"Okay, okay, dudes!" yelled Eddie, holding up a hand. "I got a fix on this. It's been groovy, but we gotta split." He could see the disappointment in our eyes. "We've been out a lot longer than I expected today," he explained. "I want enough gas to slide back to Santa Elena without pulling at the short hairs."

That evening, as we talked in the firelight, the daylight quietly edged away and the conversation slipped from the speculation of wealth to the necessity of revenge.

"We're gonna have to come back to what we came here for," said Cody, glancing around at all of us. The inference left an uncomfortable silence. Our friend exhaled. "We've got a buddy who will never be able to enjoy a good night's sleep for the rest of his life, which will be short if Santiago Talla has his way."

Again things remained quiet. Then Will, who was known for clever escapades rather than violent confrontations, sighed heavily. "We've got to get him. We've got to take Santiago out."

"Damned right we do," I added as I reached down and rubbed Shadow's fur. "I've already had a taste of his revenge and I don't want to live waiting for the next."

There was a pause and Cody nodded. "It's got to be done before we begin to search for anything valuable..." There was a moment of heavy silence. "We won't have time afterward..."

While this conversation was taking place, I noticed that Passi was unusually quiet, carefully observing us as we made our decisions. I turned to her. "How do you feel about this? About the choices we're making?"

She glanced around at the others, then turned to stare at me. "We all come to a place in life where we must balance the cost of our soul against the dreams that we've recklessly chosen." She sighed and there was a strange look in her eyes. "I have made my choices as well, perhaps just as carelessly. I think the die is cast — for all of us."

It was certainly an enigmatic answer. Actually, it made me somewhat uncomfortable. But that night, after the camp had succumbed to sleep and the half-moon was well up and casting soft trellises of light through the jungle, I heard something off to my left. I had chosen a sleep nook in the huge nodes of a rubber tree at the edge of the firelight, and had been moments from dozing off when I felt a hand touch my shoulder. I started, but another soft hand gently covered my mouth. I could smell her then — that earthy essence of passionflower and heat — as she silently slid into my sleeping blanket.

"Passi..." I whispered as her naked body slipped in against mine. "Wha —"

But that hand covered my mouth again. "Do not always question what the gods give you," she whispered, as her hand found my shorts and gently pushed them down...and her mouth found mine.

Just before dawn, as the morning mists were weaving in and out of the foliage, I felt her starting to move away, back toward her own sleeping mat. "Passi..." I whispered hesitantly.

"Simply accept," she murmured, then she smiled impishly. "*Brujas* are cursed with such fierce libidos."

And then she was gone.

Later that morning, as we organized for our assault on Santiago, Will nudged me when no one else was watching.

"I'm not certain, but I think you became a member of 'the *bruja* club' last night," he whispered. "I don't know if I'm happy about that."

"A gentleman never tells," I replied.

"Oh, bullshit," my friend muttered. "Everybody tells someone."

CHAPTER TEN

To kill a man, you must first decide how. That's where Cody came in. He went to his "special" duffle bag and pulled out a two-piece, scoped .22 caliber Ruger rifle with a silencer, a box of hollow-point CCI Stinger ammunition, and a box of standard 1050 fps (feet per second) ammunition. With the velocity of the CCI Stinger ammo, the silencer was a moot point because the speed of the bullet would break the sound barrier and make a "crack" regardless. But you got a much more devastating hit. The standard 1050 fps ammo didn't have a great punch, but it was very quiet. With that, it could be a "whack-'n'-go" as Eddie said. The shooter didn't have to give up his position to make the kill. The rest of us carried our weapons of choice (pistols by and large, with the exception of Eddie and his 12-gauge shotgun.)

Passi refused to be part of this and we reluctantly respected her wishes, though it would have been nice to have possessed her special insight.

Shane, who was now safely out of the country, had told us that Santiago Talla had a ranch on the west side of town. He had cleared 300 acres of jungle and managed what appeared to be a successful operation, modeled after early American ranching operations.

"The damned guy thinks he's some sort of American-style cowboy," Shane had explained. "He wears a six-gun in a gunfighter-style holster, and they tell me he practices his fast draw and shooting style all the time. It's strange as hell, but that doesn't make him less dangerous, just more psychotic."

We headed back to Icabaru on our bikes, leaving our sensuous witch to watch the camp.

It took us about a half hour to make the trek from the river, where Eddie's bird was, to Santiago's big ranch home. It wasn't hard to find. The first person we stopped gave us directions. The property where the house was located had been fenced off and there was a guard at the gate. I let Cody out about a hundred yards around the bend, well before the gate. We waited five minutes, then drove around. By the time we got there, we found Cody sitting on the bench out in front of the sentry shack.

"The guard?" I asked, afraid of the answer.

Cody shrugged with a half smile. "He's resting..."

At this point, we drove the car in another hundred yards, still out of sight of the house, and parked. Cody put his rifle together and selected two magazines. One magazine was loaded totally with CCI Stinger ammo; the other had three rounds of the quieter but less powerful 1050 fps ammunition at the top, then Stingers for the remaining rounds.

We all checked our weapons one more time. I left Shadow with Eddie and Arturio, who were covering our rear. This was it. Showtime.

As we prepared to move in, I turned to Will. Serious gunfighting was something we generally tried to avoid. I could see he was pretty antsy around the edges. I'd seen him take incredible chances in many a situation, but he wasn't all that comfortable with guns. Nonetheless, he was a brave son of a bitch. Today he had chosen to serve as the distraction while Cody did his thing. No one was better at distractions than Will, once he got going...but this was "head in the lion's mouth," purely dangerous stuff.

"Remember," I said to my partner, "you're not dead until you see the devil."

He couldn't help but find a small grin. "How do you know that? Do you swear on the virginity of your sister?"

"Humph," Eddie muttered as he slid another shell into the side port of his shotgun. "I've met his sister. That ship has sailed, dudes." He held a hand out, palm up. "I mean, like, a mythical creature at best."

That drew a smile from everyone who knew my sister, who had probably deflowered more men than Cleopatra.

Will's only weapons in this gig were a half bottle of Venezuela's Santa Teresa Rum, and his ability to act like a belligerent drunk. His job was simple — draw Santiago Talla out to the front of the porch so Cody could take his shot.

The Wild Road to Key West

Five minutes later, as the two veranda guards sat complacently playing dominos, a man came walking (actually, wobbling) into the compound parking area in front of the house, across from the main entrance. He wore a baggy pair of cotton *pantalones* and a slightly stained shirt. Will appeared so innocuous, everyone watching thought he was one of the hacienda workers, and no one else really paid much attention — until the gangly fellow with the battered straw hat pulled to a shaky stop and drew himself up.

"Chu run over my only goat!" Will cried in Spanish, shaking his bottle of rum at Santiago, who was standing in the shade of the covered deck smoking a *cigarillo*. "Now I got no goat, no cheese, no milk," the belligerent stranger continued.

Will did this kind of thing so well — a combination of huge *cojones* and terrific acting.

"My wife is crazy mad like thunder, and she say I no sleep in her bed until I fix this. So I'ne here to get a goat fron you, or I'ne gonna challenge you to a duel."

This drew Santiago from his contemplation and his good *cigarillo*.

Will spun around dizzily, stumbling slightly, barely keeping his balance. Now aimed in the wrong direction, he swung back around and jerked to a stop. "Chu gonna get me a goat, or chu gwenna fight me like a man?"

"How did this idiot get past the guard at the gate?" muttered Santiago incredulously, not happy, but slightly taken by Will's remarkable performance. Talla took another step forward and put a hand out, grasping one of the wooden pillars at the front of the veranda, the morning sunlight making his oiled black hair glisten. "You are a damned crazy idiot. You know that?" he exclaimed, half in anger and half in disbelief. "Go home, now! Or I have you shot!"

While all this was taking place, Cody had climbed up and settled into the nook of an old lignum-vitae tree at the perimeter of the compound, less than a hundred yards from Santiago, with a clear shot. He had decided to go with a quick "double tap" of the low-velocity CCI rounds because there would be virtually no sound. Then he'd hit the Venezuelan gangster once more. He would have preferred the last shot to be to the head, but that would have been messy and it would have completely blown Will's cover. Will needed the confusion for a better chance of escape.

Will had just made a reference to Talla's family and river leeches. The bandit exhaled angrily and was pulling a pistol from his belt when he suddenly jerked up and stumbled backward (as the first two rounds struck him in the chest almost simultaneously). There was no sound. No one could understand why their boss had suddenly stumbled back and grasped the back of a chair with one hand, the other going to his chest. Santiago dropped to his knees, a thoroughly surprised look on his face. Then he jerked again and fell face down on the wood planking of the deck.

Crazy Will, in the center of the compound, was still vehemently complaining that if no one was going to fight him, he now wanted *two* goats — and another bottle of rum.

While everyone was focused on Santiago lying on the floor of the veranda and gasping, I and my trusty motorcycle came screaming through the entrance of the compound, cutting a path through the open parking area and screeching to a stop in front of Will. My buddy needed no encouragement. He clambered onto the back and we were gone like a greyhound on crack. There were a couple of people who came to their senses and got off a few rounds, but Cody and his accurate little .22 rifle knocked down two men and drove the remainder into hiding.

It was damned near like stirring up an ant's nest. All of a sudden people were yelling and shooting at anything that moved. Two of Santiago's men had grabbed him and dragged him into the house, but with Cody's marksmanship, I figured that was a waste of time. Will and I burst out of the gate we'd entered earlier, sped down the dirt road, and found Arturio and Eddie waiting anxiously at the small guard post. In mere seconds, Cody came stumbling out of the underbrush, rifle over his shoulder, and threw himself onto his bike.

"Go! Go!" he yelled.
And we did, like a pack of scalded cats.

The arrival back at our camp was a combination of elation and somber acceptance. None of us felt good about what we had done. Taking a person's life is never easy, and if you reach the point that it does come easy, you've lost an important part of yourself. But we had made the world safer for a good friend and his wife, and for us, and that made the whole package a little easier to swallow.

Passi reacted strangely when she heard the news. "Are you sure he's dead?" she asked carefully, the disclosure apparently taking a moment to set in.

"He took at least two to the chest," replied Cody. "I'm pretty sure, but then, we were busy…"

That seemed to settle her. She exhaled and began gathering her things as we started packing the remainder of the camp back into the plane. If we left anything of any real value, it would probably be gone when we returned.

As we were loading, I noticed Arturio watching Passi. Studying her might have been a better expression.

"What's the problem, dude?" I asked quietly as we returned from the aircraft for another load.

Arturio shrugged. "Ahh, *nada,* amigo." Then he slowly blew out a breath. "It's jus, you know, I don' ever remember a 'good' *bruja.* It takes son' getting used to. Especially such a friendly one…" He paused and grinned. "She's crazy about me, you know."

I shook my head. "Here's a newsflash, amigo. She's crazy about all of us."

CHAPTER ELEVEN

The sun was nearing its apex and the suffocating heat crawled over the Venezuelan jungle like the devil's breath. The strange, suntanned creature — unruly dark hair falling well past his shoulders, clothes in tatters — absentmindedly scratched one of the burn scars on his left arm. He studied the lizard as it worked its way across an outcropping below him, just before the jungle began in earnest. The iguana...*a nice, fat, tasty crawler*...was still cautiously moving toward the snare when suddenly a small, black-collared hawk swept down and snatched it off the rock like the devil's own messenger. The smallish soul who was observing exhaled harshly, his fingers twitching, black eyes staring upwards, his face a mask of desperate anger.

"*Cabrón!*" he whispered harshly. "By da wicked teeth of da jungle beasties! The filthy little thief stealed our only dinner! It takes our tasty, sweet-fleshed wiggler! Again! We hates 'em! We hates 'em!"

Suddenly, the stranger heard a second voice, which spoke quietly; not happy, but somewhat soothing. "What is done is done. We find another lizard. They are not rare here."

So it was in this jungle — this nasty, green peril. Every day was a challenge. It had been a long time since the fellow could remember much else — the heat, the strange creatures, and the vicious winged wraiths of so many varieties. Normally, he and his companion did their best to stay above the peril in this strange world. At least, the day-to-day struggles kept him from remembering. It hurt his head when he tried to recall...

The sudden explosion of one engine...people crying and screaming in the old metal bird as it plummeted earthward...then the terror and jarring pain of impact...

He wasn't even certain how he had managed to get out. All the battered fellow knew for sure was when he regained consciousness, he was alone. Before him lay the shattered, scorched hull of an old DC3 and the air was suffused with the smell of burning metal and charred flesh. Adding insult to injury, the plane had crashed into the deep jungle, plowing into the base of a canyon wall and bringing part of the wall down on top of it. Given the deep jungle and the unusual crash site, the remains of the aircraft could hardly be seen from the sky.

He couldn't have known, but the searchers gave up after two weeks. That was considered to be the survival interval for a civilized person in the jungle.

The first month of his existence was a brutal amalgam of terror, confusion, and desperation. He had lost all memory of the past. He had no recollection beyond the crashing of the metal bird. He was a starving, skeletal wisp of his former self, drinking water from a river that disappeared into a cavern and eating wild fruit, lizards, and mice to stay alive. Looking back on it, the whole thing seemed impossible. And it was, at least until he found Safren. Or Safren found him. As time passed they discovered things in the odd, horseshoe canyon. Strange things and secrets…

"Come," said Safren's soft but firm voice. "We will try again, but only for a while. It will be dark soon and the Painted Faces will be out."

The small man remembered being caught out after dark one time and the Painted Faces had chased him, shrieking and howling, their poison arrows stabbing trees and bouncing off rocks around him. *"Cabrón!"* He cried like a child for ten minutes after reaching the safety of the canyon and the olden city. It seemed the Painted Faces considered that area to be sacred and haunted by spirits. And who knew? Maybe it was. It always made him uncomfortable there — old, gray ruins swallowed by twisty vines… But there were precious things among the ruins, too…

We likes the shiny things, he thought. *Pretty rocks and shiny stones and old broken bones. All togethers, all alones.*

The small person eased out a sigh and reached for his canvas knapsack — his only surviving possession. He had grabbed it and pressed it to him just as the plane crashed. As the fellow picked up the backpack, a small paperback book fell out. He quickly snatched it up and carefully brushed it off, then stuffed it away.

The old novel was dog-eared and the cover was torn, leaving only a few words of the title: *Lord of the Rings*...

We were in the air a little after noon. By and large, there was a communal sense of relief in the cabin. With Santiago gone, we wouldn't have to constantly look over our shoulders. Today, this time, we would set down on the river and move inland, into the horseshoe canyon and hopefully the ancient city. It wouldn't be easy — the jungle is never kind to strangers — but this was a gig no one wanted to miss.

After a couple hours of flight, Eddie finally broke the monotonous hum of the Goose's big radials. "Okay, amigos. There's the waterfall, twenty degrees off the starboard wing and a mile out. It's showtime! Man the windows and start watchin' for the horseshoe canyon."

In just minutes the relief of the canyon magically rose up on both sides, as well as in front of us, and the river tumbled into the open gorge in the jungle floor, then simply disappeared. Without knowing what we were looking for, it would have been impossible to discern the outline of the canyon through the tenacious green jungle below.

Eddie swung around and took us back a half mile. He didn't like the way the river plummeted with a roar into nothing. He wanted to set down well ahead of that.

"Watch for an eddy or a cove where we can tie up," he yelled at all of us. "We gotta get out of the slipstream on that river."

I could feel the excitement building — that same old heightening of blood pressure wrapped around a prickle of anticipation. I reached down and ran a hand through Shadow's thick fur and I heard the soft, contented rumble in his chest. It's amazing how quickly you can become attached to an animal — especially one that has saved your life. I couldn't help but recall what an old drunk in possession of a feisty Chihuahua at a Key West bar once said to me. "Man often shares the most profound and truthful moments in his life with his dog. Not simply because the dog can't tell anyone, but because he wouldn't..."

I glanced over at Will. He grinned and ran a hand nervously through his long blond hair, those blue eyes shining with tension and elation. This was what we did. This was what we lived for — the excitement and the story. Only the true adventurer understands the intoxication of a little danger. (However, I will admit that danger becomes less intoxicating in proportion to the amount you experience. Let's face it. Menace and peril are always more intriguing in their telling — with fermented beverages.)

Will turned to Passi, in the seat across from him, and took her hand. Their eyes touched and held — words spoken without sound. They were getting along well, it appeared. I could only assume he wasn't yet bothered by, or wasn't actually aware of, her propensity for late-night visits with his friends.

It was Cody, up front, who spotted a slight groove — a small inlet of sorts, on the eastern course of the waterway only a few hundred yards from the mouth of the huge cave that sucked in the river. There was probably enough beach to get the Goose in as well, but being a water bird with a pontoon hull, there was no point in taking chances. He pointed. Eddied nodded, dropped flaps and power, and suddenly we were falling in a sharp arc. Seconds later, our pilot bounced us in against the current and guided the old Goose into the perfect, small cove beside the river. Ten minutes later, we were standing on the mangrove-covered, rocky sand shoreline with the Goose securely tied off to several trees that jutted out of the sand just before the beach began.

We were in the center of the horseshoe canyon, which appeared to be less than a half mile square. In the distance, we could hear our river tumultuously disappearing into the underground gorge. We had all agreed as we came in that the jungle seemed to rise and fall in this area. Very possibly, there might have been structures here at one time.

The strange, sun-darkened creature with disheveled hair and tattered pants stared up at the metal bird as it descended toward the river, one skinny hand shading his eyes from the sun.

"Strangers," he muttered with the slightest lisp. "Evil interlopers!" He threw up his scrawny arms in anger and disgust. "Filthy little muggers and thuggers. They's come to steal it from us. But it's ours and we owns it!"

The odd, smallish fellow took a breath and exhaled shakily. "Okey-dokey, okey-dokey," he hissed, holding up a crooked forefinger. "We's gwena follow them! Yes, we will! Pilferers, plunderers, and scroungers!" He quickly snapped around, and suddenly there was his friend.

Safren nodded wordlessly.

After arming ourselves with weapons for the second time that day, we locked the cabin door to the Goose. No use taking any chances. We were just east of the entrance to the cavern that swallowed the river, and it appeared that the river moved with greater enthusiasm as it reached the throat of the subterranean entrance and tumbled down into the depths of the earth.

We had been trekking northeast for about a half hour, working our way through the tangled terrain of trees, vines, and brush, when Eddie called out. There, off to the side but well disguised by the robust flora, was a low building of grayish-white stone. It was weathered, but the stones, although mildewed and stained, were obviously well cut and fitted with care. The roof, probably built of wood and thatched, was gone. Just a few of the heaviest wooden rafters remained. Nonetheless, there it was — a building!

Slowly, like communal sleepwalkers, we edged over to the structure. I could already see another, captured by vines, and between them stood a huge Mayan-style relief statue. But the lines were smooth and gentle, not squared-off and fierce.

"My God," I whispered. "The city in the canyon?" I glanced around at my friends. "Could this be it? Could we have found it?"

"Slow down, Tonto," muttered Will, trying to keep his imagination (and mine) in check. "A couple of white stone buildings don't make a legend." Then he looked at me and got that half-assed grin, his eyebrows bouncing. "But it's a good start…"

We broke out our metal detectors and for the next half hour worked our way through the jungle, discovering structure after structure, all of which were made from carefully laid white stone. Will and I kept a careful eye on our compasses — most people have no idea how easy it is to get lost when you can't see the sun. Shadow stayed close most of the time, but he was a dog and couldn't help chasing a scent here and there.

We discovered numerous white stone statues, similar to the Mayan design, but again, carrying more rounded lines — softer and less warlike. We had just reached the back entrance to a large, apparently communal building when Eddie gave a low whistle. I looked over at him as he stood there, holding in his hand a 16th century Dutch, black glass rum bottle. He had just pulled it from a hole in the white rock wall. I gasped in disbelief. I don't know how many times Will and I had found bottles in the walls of old out-structures. It seemed to be a thing the people did in the old days (probably men) — hide a bottle in a wall somewhere outside the living quarters and go pinch on it throughout the day.

Nonetheless, here was the remarkable provenance we needed! This was proof of the encounter between two societies! Most of all, it fit the research knowledge that Will had acquired — that single piece of molded black glass said unequivocally that a Germanic/European expedition had made it to this city sometime during or after the 16th century!

We continued to run our detectors through the area for about a half hour without so much as a bleep, when suddenly Will stopped and ran the head of his machine over the spot in front of him once more. I looked over at him. (The truth is, when you're metal detecting with a friend, you're just as in tune with the sound of their machine as you are your own — it's the avarice and the sense of primal greed that treasure hunting brings out in people.) My friend ran the head over the spot once more and again it chimed.

He knelt and started digging with his spade. I became his shadow. In just moments he got a "clunk." Will dug around it, reached down, and pulled out something about six inches by two inches. He had barely started wiping off the object and the sun began to reflect off gold.

"Son of a bitch," I muttered in amazement and envy.

"Yeah, son of a bitch," Will muttered with pure competitive pleasure.

It was truly a gift from the gods — a small golden idol with a humanoid shape and perfect green emeralds for eyes. We were here! We were in the right place!

On the butte of a nearby ridge, just outside the walled city, a reddish-skinned Indian sat in the crook of a large ficus tree. With great curiosity, he watched the strange white people move about below. His dark, copper skin and the ocher and red paint on his face and body disguised him well. His people rarely went into the stone city. It was cursed. Their priests said it had been cursed a thousand moons ago, when the people died — all of them — in the changing of a moon. Or so the legend went. It had been taboo ever since, and the penalty for disobedience of the shamans and the gods was a quick death and a burning. Or at least, it used to be. Eventually, times changed...

Tabo and his son had come looking for wild bird eggs in the crevices of the ridges and deteriorating walls around the city when they had heard voices. They hunkered down on the vine-covered wall and watched as the strangely attired, pale-skinned people stumbled about, making enough noise for an entire village and shouting with occasional glee.

Tabo had been so taken by this remarkable event that he climbed a tree for a better view. Who were they? Could they be spirits? He failed to notice that his son, equally captured but possessed of the boldness of youth, had slipped down the ragged wall and moved into the jungle for a closer look at these most

The Wild Road to Key West

remarkable people.

Neither the man nor the boy could have known that a jaguar had been following them for the last half hour. The beast was aged, far past his prime, and was partially crippled in his right rear leg (from mating combat almost a year ago). He was no longer as quick as he was before, but he was still a formidable foe, and he was hungry... His green eyes followed the child with a hard, desperate stare, and slowly he moved off in a liquid slink, the only sound, a low rumble in his chest.

When Tabo realized that his son was gone, he called in a harsh whisper, "Caba! Caba! Where are you? Come here, now!"

But there was no response. The child, with brazen audacity, had moved down the hill and come up behind the strangers.

Tabo quickly followed his son's trail. It was easy. In his excitement, the boy was being careless. Still, none of the strangers had noticed the child or the cat.

The jaguar, with a cunning second to none in the animal world, had quickly slid up an old mahogany tree in the young man's path. As the child moved closer, the cat instinctively issued a deep, quiet growl. The growl morphed into a throaty hiss, and the big cat's cold, green eyes glittered with purpose as the young man moved toward him.

Shadow had just wandered off after an iguana. Although we had spread out in a radius of perhaps a hundred feet, Will and I were close enough to Cody to see an immediate change in him. He suddenly perked up, his eyes wary, head swiveling, his years of training and observation in Southeast Asia kicking in at the sound of the cat's growl. I started to speak but he silenced me with the sharp slash of a hand, his eyes hard now. We followed his gaze. It was then that we saw the child, hiding in the deep cover, and the tail of the cat drooping down out of the foliage above him.

Tabo was fifty feet behind his son on the barely discernable animal trail when he saw his Caba, crouched in the brush, watching the strange white people — and the big cat above him, flanks trembling, crouching for the leap. Terror gripped him and ripped at his entrails. Still, he stood and ran, bringing up his small bow and knocking an arrow as he moved, knowing he was outclassed, too late, and equally as dead as his son. But a man does what he has to do — death being a much kinder gift than a lifetime of recollection of fear and failure.

The cat's flanks rolled with a tremble and he leapt. The child caught the movement above him and screamed as the shadow of the animal fell over him, the creature's front legs outspread, claws extended.

Both Will and I were struggling to get our sidearms out when suddenly there was the ear-shattering rip of an automatic weapon. The jaguar shuddered in midair, its body losing purpose and falling. But it still struck the boy, sending both child and cat tumbling to the ground. Tabo cried out helplessly as he ran. Cody was still moving forward, trying to find another shot. Shadow came bursting out of the jungle on the far side, ears back, muzzle drawn back, exposing his fangs. I grabbed him and forced him to my side as the two men reached the jungle monster and his victim. But there was nothing left in the green eyes of the cat — only emptiness.

Ignorant to anything around him, Tabo grabbed his child and pulled him free from the creature's embrace, hugging him and checking him for wounds. It took a moment or two for him to be certain his son was unharmed. It took another moment for him to realize that it was the pale stranger with the loud device who had saved his son.

Tabo, his family, and his people had lived deep in the Venezuelan jungle since the beginning of their time. They were nothing more than a tiny dot in a giant expanse of nature.

Anything they couldn't understand — like small shiny things flying far above them — was simply attributed to the movements of the gods. Actually, some time ago, one of the shiny flying things had tumbled into their jungle, but it was ravaged beyond any understanding — burned and melted beyond comprehension, and they were afraid to go near it. But at least one magical creature had flown from the flames — of that, the Indian was certain...

Tabo and his people couldn't have known, but in the greater scheme of things, across and around our giant green-and-blue globe, there were a multitude of tribes and peoples who had never seen and had no understanding of the world beyond their small, functional radius of often only a few dozen miles. Sometimes these were the remnants of earlier, great cultures that had collapsed. Many of these were found in South America and its dense tropical rain forests, living day to day in primitive societies, close to nature, relying on each other, and with simple customs and simple gods — without the challenges of world wars, race wars, crooked politicians, contending religions, and the perpetual challenges of the human "race."

Perhaps they were the lucky ones...

Still clutching his wide-eyed son, Tabo stood and stared at us.

I stepped forward, having holstered my pistol, hand out, palm up. "You don't have to leave," I said in Spanish. "We come in peace."

That really sounded stupid, but it was the only thing I could think of. It made little impression. But as the man grasped his son and moved back, he suddenly stopped and stared at Cody. There was a moment of fragile stillness as the Indian slowly brought a clenched fist to his chest, his eyes holding respect and gratitude. Then the two figures melted into the jungle and were gone.

Will looked at me incredulously. "We come in peace?" he said, holding up his hand, middle fingers separated in the Star Trek Vulcan configuration. "Live long and prosper," he added with a grin.

"Yeah, yeah, I know," I huffed out. "It was all I could think of."

"The good news is, we've made contact with the natives," said Eddie. "And we've still got our scalps. That's a good sign."

The small, scarred, outcast creature had been following the strangers from the beginning of their entry into the jungle. He sat, hidden by a large palmetto tree, not a hundred yards away.

"They kill the snarlin' biter, the snarlin' biter," he hissed to himself. "Dangerous, greedy little stealers they are, but they'll not find much. Sneaky little seekers — wicked and tricksy!" The smallish fellow paused, calming himself. He held up a scrawny forefinger. "But nots the matter, sneaky thieves. Nots the matter. We already knows where the good stuff is…" He paused and whispered to the people standing together in the distant jungle. "Look your little fingers numb. It's all in the precious place of the mists, all that was hidden by those that are dead, and the dead hold it where the darkened river dies the falling death."

CHAPTER TWELVE

During this day of exploration we had worked our way east for a while, still finding ruins, but the more significant ruins seemed to be to the west, closer to where we had come in with the plane. So, after the sun struck its apex and began to fall at the horizon, we began our trek back toward the Goose. In the process, we discovered what must have been a large fairway made of cobblestones running through the center of the city. Numerous smaller stone roads branched off of it, but all of this was covered by several hundred years of jungle. We did, however, encounter a most interesting conundrum. In the eastern walls of the canyon that enclosed the city, we discovered a large cave. Actually, Will found it when he had excused himself for a call of nature. He told us about it and we had to have a look.

The cave was physically hewn out of the sandstone. It had a small entrance that led into a sizeable cavern, perhaps fifty feet by fifty feet, with a rounded dome maybe twenty feet high. As you came in, the first thing you noticed was how the far wall had been carved into a huge, panoramic curve, both width and height, much like a movie theater, sculpted and sanded perfectly smooth. There was also a flawless circular hole, perhaps a yard in diameter, about two feet above the entrance on the far side of the panoramic curve. Above that perfect hole (which helped supply light), was a battery of exotic symbols representing a language none of us were familiar with — not even Will or Passi. In fact, at the discovery of this, our knowledgeable witch was nearly in a trance.

"The old ones," she kept whispering. "From the stars..."

As we cautiously moved into the cavern, I saw them — two skeletons, one on each side of the room, each in a kneeling position. Their clothes were in tatters, but they had worn heavy loincloths of what could have been leather, and jaguar-skin capes, as well as thin, simple neckbands made of solid gold and embedded with diamonds and emeralds. But as incredible as all this was, there was something else — a profound conundrum.

Their heads (skulls at this point, for any flesh was long gone) were slightly oblong, offering slanting foreheads (as possessed by some of the ancient Central American and Egyptian cultures) that extended back to a rounded, almost conical shape. The shape was not so exaggerated as to be esoteric, but there was a significant difference from the standard human skull.

There was something about this place that murmured substance, esoteric intelligence, and eerie significance, and in the back of my mind I couldn't help but recall the words of our visionary shaman, Rufus, during our last visit in Key West: *"An' remember, if and when you get to da place you be looking for, den your search begins for da place you gotta find..."*

"All that we have seen today," I whispered, exhaling heavily, "was nothing more than a warm-up. This, I think, is the main act."

"You got that right," muttered Will. He took a deep breath and slowly gazed around. "When we have more time, we need to come back here. We need to come back..."

I glanced over at Passi again. Her eyes were wide and lost, and her breath quickened. I knew intrinsically that we had stumbled on something here, but there was a sense of guise that I couldn't shake. There was something in this room of import and essentiality, but the gods weren't going to give it to us today, and the sun was well across the sky. We had to go...

Eddie, the most pragmatic of us all, took another look around and sighed. "There's something here we're not seeing yet. I can feel it. But we're burning daylight. Don't want to be caught in this funky pad at night, dudes, for a number of reasons." He drew a breath. "There're rapscallions around here. Serious rapscallions."

There was little argument.

CHAPTER THIRTEEN

As the strangers filed out from the dimness of the cavern, several pairs of eyes were watching them from the cliffs above with considerable curiosity.

"The pale ones have found the ancient place," said Ama-ta to his friend, Tabo, as they sat quietly on the canyon ridge at the edge of the jungle. "We must tell the others..."

"But they saved Caba..." the younger man said. "They are the same as the crazy one who fell from the skies. He and the one he talks to have not harmed us."

"They hoard the yellow metal and bright stones of our ancestors, from the city of spirits," Ama-ta said.

"What does that matter?" his friend replied. "The yellow metal means little to us, and besides, how many shiny stones must we possess to be happy? Give me a warm woman and a healthy son any time over cold, shiny stones." Tabo sighed. "If it were not for the high priest's words about the evil that abides there, we would share the good soil and the soft river of that canyon."

"We are told it is cursed," Ama-ta replied, looking out at the small valley. "It has been cursed since memory..."

"I have been in that land," said Tabo quietly. "Many times..."

His friend swung around. "Your tongue is twisted! No one goes into the canyon of death and its city."

Tabo shook his head. "I have. Many times."

"And you have not suffered?"

"Just opposite," Tabo replied. "How do you think it is that my wife's cooking pot is always full? And the skins of adtas and mangas adorn my lodge? I don't know what might have been there before, but now, the land is rich and healthy and the river is filled with fish. Let us compromise. Gather two friends, and I will do the same, and I will take us into the walled city..."

"But the holy men —"

Tabo waved him off. "Our shaman, the aged Ganto, and his nodding cronies drown our questions with proverbs, and gleefully exercise punishments when we shy from 'the path.' Where is 'The Spirit of Everything' in that? Let us prove them wrong here, so that we might have the privilege of proving them wrong elsewhere, eh?" Tabo paused. "Besides, I have witnessed something that you should see — a white-skinned tribe with strange weapons..."

Not more than a hundred yards from the two Indians sat the aircraft crash survivor — a small, ravaged soul struggling to keep a finger on sanity. His eyes were locked on the new white strangers.

"*Cabrón!*" he hissed caustically. "They's found the strange cave... What's they got in their nasty little minds, those wicked tricksters?"

He sat there for a moment, huffing in anger and fear, staring at the ground. Then, suddenly, he straightened up, filled with animation again.

"We knows! We knows what they can't stand to lose. We's seen it with our own eyes."

The small, crouching man looked up to his left, his large eyes bouncing with glee.

"We've seen it, haven't we, Safren? Without it, they's be stuck in Mordor forever."

Safren didn't say anything. He just nodded and smiled.

About that same time, a privately owned, slightly overloaded Bell 206 helicopter was lifting off out of the tiny airport at Icabaru. The men on board, aside from being seriously vexed, had issues they intended to resolve. There are few things that incite a soul more than gold and revenge.

As the sun fell at the horizon, we began to work our way back toward the plane. Cody led with his trusty Thompson; Eddie, Arturio, and I were in the middle; and behind us, Will and Passi followed. There seemed to be the beginnings of a relationship forming with them, but with a lady as promiscuous as our little witch, it was hard to tell. A half hour later we were coming up on the little bay where the Goose was tied off. But something wasn't right...

"The plane's not in its moorings," whispered Eddie tensely as we worked our way along the mangrove animal trail. "Something's seriously bogus, dudes!" he muttered. "We should be able to see it by now."

He was right.

Without a word, Cody cut through the dense mangroves to our right with his machete. Will and I were right behind him.

"Son of a bitch!" I heard him cry out as we quickly doubled our efforts to reach the aircraft.

Seconds later, Eddie, gasping and out of breath, was at our side. The sight before us stole what little air we had left.

"Whoa shit!" muttered Will. "Whoa...shit!"

The Goose was nearing the center of the wide river, a hundred yards out in front of us, its mooring lines free and dragging in the greenish, dark water. From there, the news got worse.

We knew from our observation flights and a quick look in the mouth of the grotto as we'd set off for the interior, that the river descended into a huge, wide cave, plunging downward into a tumbling sixty-degree incline and disappearing into the bowels of the earth as the incline increased. Once that plane made it inside the cave, it was gone forever.

Eddie instinctively moved out into the water, starting to pull off his shirt. Then he stopped and turned, his face filled with helplessness. He held out his hands. "I never mentioned this, but..." He sighed. "I can't swim."

Cody stared at his friend incredulously. "You own an amphibian aircraft and you can't swim?"

Eddie shrugged. "I don't know why, dude. I just never

learned."

Some of us have stronger survivalist instincts than others. Mine are pretty high. Being stuck in this godforsaken jungle for the rest of my certain-to-be-short life wasn't on my bucket list. Besides, I was a good swimmer.

I don't even remember ripping off my boots and my shirt. I do remember yelling at Eddie to grab Shadow, so he didn't try to follow, and that I had barely hit the water when there was a splash behind me. I glanced around while treading water and there was Will, long blond hair already matted down around his face, his blue eyes shining with equal portions of excitement and fear.

"Did you think that I was gonna let you own a barroom story like this, just yourself?" he huffed.

I couldn't help but smile.

For the next five minutes, we chased the mooring lines on the plane, all the while wondering how two very well-tied ropes could have possibly come undone at the same time. And also wondering if these waters had crocodiles or piranha…

Finally, it was clear we were gaining. The old plane's big tail was twisting from side to side less than fifty yards from us, but the huge cavern where the river dropped into a tumbling waterfall was coming up fast. There's no incentive like survival, and somehow, while breathing in ragged gasps as the last half of the sun was sinking into the jungle horizon, I felt a hand bolstering me up and pushing me ahead to the plane's stern line buoy. My partner's voice grated out behind me, that sense of undeniable indomitability in his words.

"Remember buddy, you've already survived a hundred percent of the worst days of your life." He coughed and spit out a mouthful of river water, pushing me forward with the last of his strength. "Just grab the line and we're still batting a thousand."

Hand over hand we drew ourselves along, gradually reaching the tail, then swimming to the hatch door and pulling ourselves into the plane. I didn't like the fact that the door was somehow unlocked, but right now I wasn't up to questioning the mouths of gift horses. Besides, we were seriously running out of time. We were coming up on the mouth of the cavern, and the water, being compressed into the smaller opening, was beginning to pick up momentum. We pulled in the mooring lines and I threw myself into the pilot's seat. No time to argue that decision. Will dropped into the other and was immediately into the preflight procedure with me. (Both Will and I had several hours of flight time in Eddie's Goose — if you travel to strange places, you'd better have more than one person who knows how to fly your plane.) The roar of the upcoming underground waterfall was becoming a thunder in our ears.

Within seconds we had the big radials whirring. There was no time for the pleasantries of a standard preflight — we needed to stop this baby from going over the underground falls we were approaching. The plane was canted slightly. The starboard wing was grating on the rocky side of the cave and it was as dark as a witch's heart. I threw on the landing, interior, and in-flight lights, which helped, but also took away our breath when we realized how close we were to the waterfall. Mists rose up around us like a thick fog, and clouds of spray outlined by our lights cast a glowing luminescence, obscuring our view.

The thunder of the falls was growing into a living thing, the vibration shaking the aircraft — and then there were the falls themselves. They were no more than a hundred yards ahead. It was all incredible and terrifying at the same time. There was literally no way of taking off straight ahead, into a cave with no determinable width or depth. The only chance we had was to bring the plane about and attempt to build enough drag to take the bird out the way we'd come in.

As all of this was taking place and we were surging around, forcing our faltering aircraft to lunge forward toward the entrance of that giant cavern, I caught something. Just for a moment, a flash of the eye, I saw a small staircase hewn out of the rock on the inside of the cavern, starting a few yards inside the mouth of the cave and leading up somewhere into the interior. Will saw it too.

For the next couple of minutes, we concentrated mostly on not tearing off a wing on the jagged walls around us and building the momentum we needed to get out of this carnival ride from Hades. I finally got up enough speed to overcome the relentless current of the river and gradually, with the hull of the Goose skipping on the black surface, we broke contact with the water, lifted up a few feet, and soared out of the cavern like a bat from the gates of Hell.

We were back to our original mooring in minutes, where our friends waited. The sun was dying in reds and yellows on one side of the sky, and an orange moon was rising on the other. I was exhausted. As everyone gathered around us, all speaking at one time, my hands were still trembling from the marathon swim and the Batman-and-Robin takeoff and escape.

Will looked over at me. Passi stood next to him, holding his arm. "We should be writing some of this stuff down."

I grinned. "Why? Nobody would ever believe it."

CHAPTER FOURTEEN

Standing in the moonlit Venezuelan jungle, still alive and still in possession of our means of transportation home, we decided to approach this whole thing from a different angle. Whoever had cut the mooring lines (actually, they looked like they'd been chewed through), had also rummaged through the cabin, stealing packages of crackers and pull-top cans of meats and vegetables, eating some right in the airplane and scattering the food around like a hungry spider monkey.

"From now on, someone has to be with the airplane at all times," growled Cody. "We lose this bird and we could end up growing old here."

"If we got a chance to grow old," muttered Eddie.

With all the excitement, none of us had noticed the soft thumping of a black helicopter as it cut its way out of the darkening sky and landed a mile or so east of us — just inside the jungle-covered walls of the old city. Nor did we notice the creature with the glazed eyes, hidden behind a large outcropping of Spanish bayonets about seventy-five yards from us...

"They's magic tricksters, they are," said the small, emaciated man as he wrung his hands nervously. He jerked up, staring into the shadows behind him, head cocked, listening, his disheveled hair scattering across his shoulders. "Yes, yes. I know. I know. Theys was close to the place...and they saved the metal dragon." He bounced a closed fist against his scrawny temple. "Evil takers! Hateful stealers! Curse and crush them!" Then the creature calmed to a nervous entreaty. "Dids they find it? Dids they find it? Surely not. Surely not... Ooohhh, we's got a sore stomach from all the truths and maybes." He exhaled hard. "We's need to eat a rat...a juicy, fat rat...to settle our tummy..."

We all spent the night in Eddie's Goose, taking turns guarding the open hatch door. It was hot and the mosquitoes were unrelenting, but it was safe for the time being. Sunrise found us anxious to be on our way back to the City of the Stars. We refused to be run off by a small act of sabotage.

Unfortunately, as Cody had said, a couple of our people had to stay at the plane. We didn't need another "accident" or the possible loss of our only way home. There was definitely someone — or something — out there...

We drew lots — a half-dozen little twigs, long and short, that I clasped tightly in my hand. Arturio and Eddie lost. Eddie wasn't altogether disappointed with that. His desire to keep his Goose in one piece probably outweighed his curiosity regarding the cave.

As the morning sun was cresting the treetops, we began our trek back. I noticed that Cody had thrown the AT4 anti-tank weapon over his shoulder.

"Expecting trouble?" I asked.

"Not necessarily," replied Cody. "But if we find it, I want to annoy it badly..."

The truth was, we had found very little in the way of valuable artifacts (gold or precious stones) in the city itself, and certainly not enough to make this trip worthwhile if that was what this was about. But we had unearthed a strange conundrum at the cave. There was something in that room that captured the imagination and drew on the instinct of every one of us. We had all felt it, especially Passi, who had called it, "the Cave of the Stars." There was something there that we hadn't yet discovered — something that shouted for presence. It was the feeling of standing on the edge of transcendence and knowledge. I didn't know what it was, but I knew we had to find out.

As excited as we were to reach our destination, our forage through the outskirts of the lost city again drew our attention. We discovered numerous additional structures, some clearly containing astrological information. In addition, there were several remarkably unique statues that distinctly defined the physical characteristics of the people. We were like children in a strange and wonderful garden, studying and speculating, and in the process, we lost a few hours. It hardly mattered. As Will said, the cave we were seeking had been there for over 500 years. It wasn't going anywhere.

We'd been hiking for about an hour along an old animal trail that took us back into the actual city, Shadow continuously weaving in and out of the jungle around us, when Cody put up his hand. "We're getting close," he whispered. "About another quarter mile. Let's get quiet for now — no more talking."

No one argued. Cody had done this kind of thing more times than he cared to remember — when the game wasn't about gold or silver, but life itself. We quieted and began moving as noiselessly as possible. Less than ten minutes later, the jungle opened slightly, and there before us were the sandstone walls of the canyon and the small, insignificant orifice cut into the sandstone — our entrance to the remarkable cave in the City of the Stars.

With the early afternoon sun at our backs, we stepped into the room and turned on our flashlights. To our great relief, nothing had changed. The skeletal guardians with the strange skulls still sat on each side of the room. The remarkably smooth dome still rose above us, leading back toward the wall like an amphitheater. The faint smell of animal feces and the scattered bones of small creatures here and there only slightly diminished the aura of age and ancient knowledge that the room wore like a comfortable old cloak.

Without words, we slowly began to move around, examining the walls and the ancient guardians. While lost once more to this discovery, we were, at first, unaware of the incredible phenomenon that was taking place. Outside, the sun was slowly working itself across the far side of the sky, and as it did, the room was growing lighter. The sun was falling precisely into the large, perfectly circular hole in the wall above the entrance.

As the setting sun eased out of the afternoon sky and its brilliance touched that flawless opening, it began to light the entire back wall of the cave, which now, with the aid of the sunlight, appeared as if it might have been covered with a fine veneer of resin plaster of some sort and troweled smooth. But the dust of centuries had hidden what lay behind the veneer. I could see the faint outline, the indentation, of a hand in the center of the back wall — almost indiscernible until the brilliant sunlight touched and circled it. Beneath it, etched into the rock, was an elegant calligraphy of sorts, consisting of dots of different sizes, exotic slashes, and the most delicate, extraordinary curls of different sizes and depths. I was certain it was a language, but its beauty was profound. It was similar to old Arabic, yet it carried a sense of art and virtuosity as well as speech.

I don't know why, even to this day, but I walked over and, somewhat hesitantly, placed my hand in the practically imperceptible indentation. It was almost as if I couldn't help myself. There was a slight give, then I heard a muted snapping sound. A crack began to appear in the plaster, gradually running out from the hand in the wall toward the hard rock sides like a slow-motion lightning bolt. Then another appeared, splintering outward; and another, and another across the wall, like a mirror shattering from a center strike point. The resin-like plaster began to collapse in sheets, which shattered as they hit the floor and slowly exposed the most incredible revelation — a vision so remarkable that I found myself gasping. My friends around me, captured by this same spectacle, stood like statues, lost to the images that leapt out from behind the collapsing, hardened sheets. Arturio crossed himself while muttering a brief but adamant entreaty.

But beyond this incredible experience was an astrological revelation that stunned our senses. We would never have experienced this — no one could have witnessed it — had we not been there on the exact day of the year that produced the sunset in this particular place in the heavens and on the earth. Once a year...

The coincidence was beyond belief. But in truth, there was no coincidence in the design. It was created by and for someone who knew the formula — the day of the year and the time, only once annually, when the rotation of the earth was perfectly aligned with the sun.

But the revelations were not yet over.

Gradually, as the dust began to settle, we beheld the most remarkable vision. There, across the smooth back wall, was a rendition — a view, if you will — of our solar system and beyond. Like an ancient planetarium, the rock wall had been cut in a perfect, semi-circular fashion, extending into the roof almost to the point above our heads. There were thousands of small and large stars, all laid out in flawlessly accurate, 3-D perfection. All of the celestial bodies were represented by incredible diamonds and emeralds, as well as jade, amethyst, and topaz stones, ranging in size from ostrich eggs to pebbles. They were mounted into an ebony background and anchored around a solid-gold, foot-wide sun, which was an inch thick and embedded into the rock. It was brilliant, mind-boggling, and humbling at the same time. But most remarkable was the fact that it depicted a perspective of our solar system and the stars around us that few, if any, humans had ever physically seen. In fact, in order to capture and present this image, one would have to have been in space, far on the other side of our solar system.

I was suddenly reminded of a quote by the artist Michelangelo: "I saw an angel in the marble, and carved until I set him free."

Today, we had set the angel free.

We all knew the display represented millions and millions of dollars in precious stones, but what it represented in art, history, and mind-shattering revelation was simply beyond calculation. This could only have been created by a people with an intricate, advanced knowledge of our solar system and beyond.

I stood there, stunned.

Will stared for a moment, then walked over, reached up, and ran his hand across the wall and the glittering stars. He exhaled heavily, then turned to us. "It looks to me as if — and I know how impossible it sounds — this was created by someone with a greater astronomical perspective than the people of earth had at that time..."

"That's an interesting long shot," I said. "Give me a scenario…"

My friend shrugged slightly and paused. I could practically hear his mind whirring. He slowly held up a finger. "Perhaps," he whispered, "at some time, a long time ago, a group from another place, far away, may have landed here with, say, technical problems they couldn't resolve.

I cocked my head and stared at him. "You mean like space people, huh?"

He shrugged. "I know, Kansas, I know," he said, holding out his hands. "It's a stretch. But hear me out. Maybe it was just a landing party that came down and somehow became stranded. perhaps due to a catastrophe of some sort." He glanced around at all of us and continued. "In the process, they discovered a handful of primitive but fairly 'cordial' inhabitants after touchdown. They remained here, hoping for a rescue. But when that didn't happen, and months, then years passed, these humanoid explorers interacted, then interbred, with the indigenous peoples." Will sighed, struggling to grasp the very words he was saying, while Passi, lost to the vision above us, seemed almost comfortable with the concept.

I shook my head sadly. "Unfortunately, the folks of this isolated hamlet were probably discovered by European and/or Spanish explorers. The intruders might well have considered the strangely shaped heads of some of the populace nothing more than an anomaly. They had no reference; they had never even dreamed of an off-planet possibility. Their religions wouldn't have allowed such heresy."

Will nodded. "I would also suspect that any power sources the marooned explorers might have had eventually died. With little or no tools, the castaways were reduced to adopting the ways of the society into which they'd been cast."

At that point, Cody smiled grimly. "You'd be amazed how

quickly we revert when the power goes off." He looked at Will and me. "If I took your television away tomorrow, could you rebuild it?"

I offered an impotent chuckle. "Shit no. To me, it's just a magic box."

"Point made," Cody replied.

Will ran his hand across the wall again, almost wistfully. "Perhaps at the end, the 'people from the stars' decided to leave one distinctive testament that would clearly define the nature of who they were."

"This cave and the planetarium," whispered Passi, who had become so absorbed she was almost catatonic.

My buddy nodded. "Yeah, the planetarium. It was perfect in its subtlety. A less-advanced people discovering this would have considered it little more than a beautiful display. But a progressive race with a grasp of astronomy would understand instantly the off-world perspective of earth it represented." He sighed wistfully. "And the subtlety of the hand on the wall and the sun...it could barely be found throughout the whole year. But on one day each year — a day that must have carried some significance to their people — the sun would illuminate it, offering the key..." Will paused and drew a breath. "Unfortunately, the European explorers from the coast of South America — quite possibly the ill-fated Germans, Hutten and Welser — may have discovered these folks and transmitted one miserable, fatal gift before they departed with what gold or gems they were given."

"Disease," I muttered. "Probably smallpox, and apparently neither of the two races — the indigenous one or the one from a distant place — possessed the genetic fortitude to resist it. The residents and the visitors from the stars died. The city collapsed and the jungle swallowed it."

Will glanced around at us, his eyes narrowing. "What's gonna happen if and when somebody finds this? Somebody less ethical and seriously greedy? Not only would they steal the gems, they would steal something of incredible historical and social significance. We're talking about the discovery of humanoids with cranial designs that match the hierarchy of some of the most ancient civilizations, like the earliest Egyptians, Incas, and Mayans. This offers the possibility that the influences of these peoples might actually have had a common beginning."

"Perhaps we're overthinking this," I said, the realist in me struggling with the facts. "Maybe they weren't from a distant star at all. Maybe they were simply a race of people who challenged the seas of this planet and established themselves here and there, or...they could have been simply a more advanced segment of the Mayan or Incan cultures who made their way into the interior of this continent."

"That would be the easy answer," Will replied, nodding slowly. "But that doesn't explain away the planetarium and its unique perspective of this solar system." He sighed. "Yet, in truth, I suppose this knowledge could just as well have been delivered in the form of spiritual insight. Religious texts for Christianity, Buddhism, Judaism, and others offer experiences of intuitive visions to their followers that extend well beyond practical or common knowledge."

We fell silent for a moment, contemplating the possibilities and the uncertainties. We had uncovered one of the most remarkable finds in modern history — first, a physical wealth beyond belief; and second, a Tutankhamun-type of discovery that offered an alternative to man's knowledge and advancement.

The conundrum was, the enormous wealth represented here jeopardized this small planetarium's survival as an instrument of enlightenment. And as Eddie would say, "Dudes, when you mix historical finds and greed, the Huns are constantly at the gates of Alexandria..."

He was right. The question was, what would we do? For us, this wasn't about money; this was about recognition of an extraordinary find which revealed, without question, that somebody knew more about the structure of our solar system and the movement of the stars beyond it than we had previously considered. It was possible that this was nothing more than an advanced segment of the Mayan or Incan cultures who had settled here, but it was still an extraordinary find. If all the stars and planets that this "planetarium" held were made from quartz and gypsum, it would still be remarkable, but it was the damned diamonds, emeralds, and other precious stones that put a huge fly in the ointment.

The archaeological value of this find was what gave it such relevance. The moment people started pulling "stars" off the walls, it would become just a cave, and I was willing to bet dollars to donuts that ten days after the announcement of this find, there wouldn't be a stone left on that wall. Even worse than that — it was in the middle of the freaking Venezuelan jungle. There was no way to turn this into a tourist attraction that could be safely secured. I wouldn't give it a month before a handful of guys in ski masks and Uzis killed the attendants and made off with the "stars."

I turned to Will. "Get your camera out, buddy. We need a handful of photos…for posterity, if nothing else."

CHAPTER FIFTEEN

"Well, now we know what was drawing us back to the cave," I said as we stood outside the entrance, watching the sun bury itself in the top of the darkening jungle. After taking a battery of photos, we had decided to spend the night in the cave of precious stones. The South American jungle was no place to be hiking after dark.

Just into the jungle, about a hundred yards away, a small, thin figure sat on the limb of a large mahogany tree, tearing at the remains of a poorly cooked iguana and watching intently.
"Safren! They's in the olden cave! Aaarrrk, the hateful finders!" He caught himself speaking too loudly and suddenly crouched, drawing in against the trunk of the tree, an angry rumble in his chest as he glanced around. "Okays, okays," he whispered. "We's waits and sees what the beastly searchers does."
Safren didn't seem to care.

By ten o'clock, most of us were fairly worn out from the hike through the jungle and the excitement of the find. We were just laying out our bedrolls and Cody was saying that we needed to post a guard, when a man appeared at the mouth of the cave. He was holding an AK-47 and he burned a half a magazine into the sandstone at our feet, just to let us know he knew how to use it. Instinctively, I glanced around for my dog. Shadow had been by the door a few minutes ago, then he'd gone out into the jungle to share the darkness and the glow of the moon with other creatures like himself. He would often stay gone half the night. The truth was, given his brutal past, he was closer to wild than tame.
"Put your weapons down! Now!" the man demanded.
"What weapons?" muttered Will, holding his bedroll.
In seconds, three more men materialized. One of them was

impossibly familiar. Santiago Talla.

Dressed in cowboy boots, blue jeans, a khaki shirt, and sporting an American six-gun, the tall Venezuelan with the hard eyes glanced around at us, then stared at the extraordinary collage of precious stones for a moment. He turned back to us. "So...all the rumors and legends were true." He grinned without mirth. "Thank you, amigos, for making my job so much easier."

While his men held us at gunpoint, Talla casually walked over to the wall, drawing the long knife at his side. He wedged the point of the blade behind our solar system's moon (an incredible four-inch emerald) and pried. The gem popped out and danced across the dirt floor, its raw cuts grasping and reflecting the lamplight. I could see Will's eyes go wide as Santiago took a couple steps, reached down, and picked it up.

For God's sake, man!" my friend yelled. "This is an incredible archaeological treasure — something that could play into the very origins of man! It's not a freaking carnival sideshow!"

Santiago turned to Will and brought the knife up in a menacing fashion. "You don' shut up, amigo, nobody guena care about your origins. *Comprende?*"

"How could they possibly have found us?" snapped Will, staring at Passi, who had suddenly begun to move over toward Santiago, perfectly at ease.

We watched in disbelief as our lady friend slid up to the jungle gangster and put her arm around his waist.

"What the hell?" I cried.

She shrugged. "One takes advantage of all opportunities. I had to make a decision."

I exhaled hard. "But...how? How did he find us?"

This time, our *bruja* eased out a breath. "Santiago had given me a homing device that I was supposed to have put in your friend Shane's equipment, so they could find him, but I never had the chance. So, I brought it with me in my pack..."

"Why?" I asked incredulously. "Why did you do this? This whole charade? All the damned way back to Shane?"

"I was tired of being a poor witch," Passi muttered with an

indifferent shrug, piercing me with a remorseless stare. "All the visions in the world are worth nothing if you have no means of accessing them." She sighed heavily. "And then along came that amigo of yours, Shane, who kept telling me about his remarkable group of friends — adventurers who could accomplish nearly anything. What a perfect situation, s*i?*" Passi grinned. "You are good at finding old things. It is your job, no?" She drew a hand down her mobster friend's shoulder. "Santiago is good at getting what he wants."

Cody stared at the mobster. "I killed you..."

Santiago smiled. "Well, not exactly," he said, holding out a hand. "You *shot* me." He offered a second grin with a bit more sobriety. "I was wearing a bulletproof vest, thanks to my *bruja*, who called me on the radio that day and told me to wear it." He paused and touched his ribs, wincing slightly. "But I can tell you, *mi amigo*, it was a painful experience." He looked at Passi and bounced his eyebrows. "An' she told me to have my helicopter ready — to follow the beacon she put in de gringo's fat airplane." The tall brigand nodded somberly. "*Si*, it was a gamble, but then, all of life is a gamble. You must risk big to win big."

At this point, we realized Passi had been playing us the whole time. It was the treasure she wanted. The "concerned *bruja*" act had been smoke and mirrors.

"It's not that I am without 'the touch'," she said. "I could 'see' some of the area and I could sense a little of the history, but," she added bitterly, "I could not find the exact place. The gods hid it from me. But they could not hide it from your machines and your insight." She smiled and held out a hand. "You see? We make a good team."

"Screw you," said Will. Then he smiled rancorously. "Wait, I already did. Hell, I think we all did." He turned to Santiago. "She wasn't bad, for a lying bitch." He paused, dropping a shoulder, a hand out. "Well, truthfully, she wasn't that good. I'm glad she was free."

I saw Santiago flinch at that. Those words found a nerve.

Cody couldn't stand it. With that almost cynical delivery of his, he added, "Fairly nice tits, but a terrible lay. The woman's in a hurry all the time."

"Enough!" shouted Santiago, who was reaching for his gun.

I held up a hand. "You're gonna need us if you're going to understand what this is all about or get this out of here."

Passi moved closer to Santiago and placed her hand on his arm. "This is an extraordinary treasure; something unimaginable. Its true value is in its totality. We must have it all." She nodded. "He is right, we might need them to help us take this back…"

I thought I had won a round and bought us a little time…even though my gut was twisting with the revelation of how thoroughly we had been taken by this woman. Unfortunately, I hadn't counted on the viciousness of the Venezuelan gangster.

"I don' give a shit about their airplane or their help," Santiago grated in Spanish. "I want their blood in the dirt." He turned to two of his henchmen. "Take them out to the jungle and kill them. We will cut the stones from the wall tonight and leave in the morning." He paused, then huffed out, "A stone is a stone. I don't care where it comes from or what it means 'existentially.'"

"Big word for a cowboy idiot," I muttered.

Santiago swung around at me and reached for his gun, then for some reason thought better of it. Maybe he didn't want blood on the floor. He turned to two of his men — the two heavyset guys. That told me who the pilot was. Rotary pilots are rarely huge guys with sausages for fingers.

"Take them out into the jungle and kill them, now," Santiago growled. He pointed at the priceless skeletons on each side of the entrance and again spoke in Spanish to his men. "And when you get back, get those damned things out of here. I'm not sleeping with them."

I saw Will tense at that. In truth, between he and I, Will was probably the more scholarly — more of a preservationist. The rest of us seemed to always be competing for the "Harrison Ford" role of the gang.

"The loss of those would be incredible," my friend whispered harshly.

"Let's worry about the big picture," Cody muttered. "They're talking about shooting our asses."

In a matter of seconds, they had bound our hands and were leading us out of the cave to the moonlit periphery of the jungle.

"Stop here," said the big guy at the front as we entered the dark-green labyrinth. "No use getting lost in this damned jungle." He turned to us, all business now, a hard glaze to his eyes. "On your knees!" he shouted. "Now!"

There was no question. He had done this before.

I looked at Will and our eyes met. I couldn't believe it. It had happened so quickly. One minute we had just discovered a priceless treasure, and the next we were kneeling in an inconspicuous jungle in the middle of nowhere, about to be shot.

"Not at all how I imagined it..." I whispered to my friend. "I'll see you on the other side, buddy."

He offered a wan smile. "If you get to the bar ahead of me, save me a seat." Then he paused and exhaled softly. "You know, my friend, through it all, I will remember...our times..."

Cody was bracing for a final kamikaze rush, even with his hands tied. That was Cody...

The guy in front of us brought up his Uzi. I closed my eyes and waited...

But all I heard was a grunt or two. I slowly opened my eyes. Our executioners stood in front of us with the most surprised looks in their eyes, staring at the long-shafted, colorfully feathered arrows that protruded from their chests. In slow motion, they both dropped to their knees, then toppled onto the jungle floor.

We were still kneeling there, somewhere between amazement and disbelief, when a group of Indians stepped out of the dark labyrinth like graveyard wraiths — loincloths and shiny dark hair, yellow and red paint slashed across their cheeks and torsos.

I looked up and my eyes went wide. There was the fellow whose son Cody had saved from the jaguar. Quietly, without a word, he gazed at Cody and raised his fist to his heart. No words were necessary. The message was clear.

In moments they had us untied. We rose, brushing ourselves

off (the night jungle has a lot of creepy, crawling things you really don't want in your shorts). There was no conversation. I bent down to retie my boot, and I swear to God, I blinked and our rescuers were gone. Suddenly, we were left in the saffron glow of an old moon who had seen it all before…

    The enemy was down two. That left Santiago, his helicopter pilot, and the lying bitch…

CHAPTER SIXTEEN

As we began to move away toward the east side of the cave, I whistled. Not loud or piercing, but shrill enough for those remarkable ears out there. Seconds later, I saw a gray specter slide out of the jungle to our right and move fluidly toward us. Cody brought up one of the guns we'd taken from our executioners, but I touched his arm and shook my head. It was Shadow, slipping in, rubbing up against my leg and offering the softest of whines from the back of his throat.

The best thing we could do, as cold as it sounded, was to ambush Santiago and his pilot. I didn't want to have to kill Passi. I just wasn't comfortable with the idea. But she had damned well shown her colors and the woman had to be contained in some fashion.

We quietly moved in, working our way through the brush, the moon sweeping in and out of batteries of heavy stratus clouds and casting furtive shadows that doubled our anxiety. I could see the mouth of the cave and the glow of our lantern inside, creating a silhouette. We spread out. I had a pistol from one of the men our Indian friends had snuffed, and Will and Cody had taken their rifles.

A burst of automatic fire tore the leaves from the branches just above our heads. We all hit the ground. Cody rolled over to one side and got off a burst in the direction of the rounds.

Suddenly, it was quiet. We waited, easing out nervous breaths. No one could see much in the thick brush.

After about a minute, Cody hissed, "You guys move around to the left. I'll take the right. If it moves, shoot it."

A few minutes later, as we were closing in, we heard the engine of a helicopter firing up, probably a half mile from us. I realized then that Santiago was brighter than I'd thought. He must have had a periphery guard watching the whole thing.

"They were on their way back to the copter while we sat here, pinned down by one of the guards," snarled Cody. "You can bet he's long gone too." He sighed angrily. "He knows we won't pull those stones out of the wall, so you can damned well bet he'll be back, and soon…"

We had just made it to the cave when we heard the main rotor blades on the helicopter catching wind with that "humph, humph" sound they make at liftoff.

I realized then, with a sudden sense of panic, that Santiago would never have left us here with a means of transportation.

"The Goose!" I cried, pointing at our bags still lying in the corner. "Get out the walkie-talkie! The Goose!"

The only thing that saved Eddie and Arturio was the idea of fresh fish for dinner. They were about fifty yards down the shoreline with a couple of rods out, hoping to catch an exotic catfish, when I called. Eddie, smart fellow that he was, had the walkie-talkie with him. They had grabbed their weapons and slipped into the jungle just moments before the black helicopter came across the full night moon like a Halloween witch.

Santiago slid open the cabin door, grabbed the entry straps near the ceiling, leaned out, and pounded the Goose with his AK-47 as the pilot made two low passes.

Fortunately, Eddie and Arturio annoyed them enough with their rifles to keep this from being a total disaster. The Venezuelan gangster made another pass, but when his copter took a couple of hits, that was enough. No point in becoming a resident of this little hellhole.

Will, Cody, and I breathed a little easier to find most everything still intact inside the cave. Santiago had been caught off guard by our unexpected survival, and he hadn't had time to steal any more stones from the wall.

In a matter of a couple of hours, life had gone from very interesting and possibly very good, to what could only be called a Mexican standoff. While Santiago now knew of the incredible fortune in jewels, he couldn't come back for it in any legal fashion because he'd have to deal with the government. Any archaeological find legally belonged to the Federal Republic of

Venezuela. Santiago and his people wouldn't get a damned thing out of this approaching it straight-up.

But "legally" wasn't a word that Santiago dealt with much. He didn't give a rat's ass about the archaeological value in this situation. He just wanted the stones.

On the other hand, we couldn't just cut the jewels out of the wall and fly them to safety because we would have to dismantle an international treasure to do so. In the process, we'd lose the historical and cultural aspect of its value.

After contacting Eddie via our walkie-talkie, we were relieved to learn that our friends were safe. Neither Eddie or Arturio were injured, but the starboard engine of the Goose had taken a couple of hits and the fuselage was as vented as a colander. Worst of all, the radio had taken a round. It was apparent that we were now officially castaways. We had just joined a very exclusive club in this diminutive portion of Hell. Even more vexing was the fact that Santiago would have to come back, to finish us and get his jewels. He sure as hell wasn't leaving any witnesses to his extraordinary greed.

The small, emaciated man had watched with terror as the black dragonfly attacked the fat metal dragon on the water. A part of him understood that the water dragon had been wounded — one man had crawled inside the beast and it trembled as the blades on its arms twirled (Eddie was trying desperately to move the Goose, to get it in the air). The flames and fumes from its wings were foul and caustic. A couple of days earlier, when he had crept in on the beast to release its fetters so it could drift to a watery death inside the monster cavern, the creature had been sleeping. But this was fierce and terrible. One of the two beings, not unlike himself, fled into the jungle, throwing loud firesticks at the black dragonfly, but ultimately neither of them were able to save their dragon, which was now listing and smoking.

"Evil, evil beasties," he muttered fearfully as he crouched in the freshwater mangroves along the shore. "Fiery demons, Safren! Screeching Painted Faces!" he cried, shaking a half-eaten crayfish at the helicopter moving away in the distance. "Bind them all and blind them all! Steal their smoke and fire! Aaahhh!" He quieted then, exhaling harshly. "Hide we's must! Yes! Until theys flies away..."

The following morning, we sat around a cooking fire just outside the Goose with mugs of coffee in our hands and a damned tough situation facing us. Eddie had checked the engine that was hit. The carburetor was badly damaged. He shook his head, adjusting his black eye patch, sweat beading on his suntanned face. He pointed at the starboard engine.

"Even if I could get that little puppy to run again, it would be a limp at best. And that's the good news. The bad news is, to get her off this water, the ol' girl would have to be damned near empty — stripped of everything that ain't nailed down." He looked around at us. "No passengers."

I glanced around at my friends. "Hell, one of us gets out, he can come back for the rest."

Cody didn't hesitate. "Damned right," he said with a grin. "You get out and by the end of the day you can have a rescue helicopter out of Caracas headed our way."

Back at his hacienda, Santiago was in a black mood. Even Passi's attentions couldn't divert him. He wasn't sure which he wanted most — the stones on that wall or the heads of the gringos who had beaten him at his own game. One thing was certain: There was no way the gringos were flying their big plane out. He had seen bullets rip across the starboard engine cowling and he was fairly certain they had torn up the tail feathers on the big bird as well. He was already gathering a team for a military-style helicopter assault. Santiago Talla lived by one code: "Revenge above all."

By afternoon, we had run the plane up on the mangrove beach and rolled her on her side (simply by weight of numbers on one wing at a time), pumped/drained out the water, and had hot-patched the places where the bullets had punctured the hull. Will had found a couple rolls of duct tape (Eddie's favorite tool) and had managed to seal the breaches in the wings and the tail feathers. They wouldn't last that long, but with any luck, our pilot would be back to civilization before things started coming apart.

In the meantime, Crazy Eddie did his magic on the wounded engine. The man truly was a wizard, and inside a couple of hours, he had the old girl running again. She was coughing and complaining, but she was alive.

All the while, in the back of our minds we knew that this was a race against the clock. There was no question that Santiago was coming for us. If any of us were to survive, we had to get Eddie out of there.

It was midafternoon. We were cutting it close, trying a flight like this, with a beat-up, shot-up, poorly patched plane. So, as heavy, gray-and-white thunderheads formed on the western horizon and lightning cut slashes through their bulbous paunches, Eddie offered us all a brave wave from the hatch. Then he boarded his aircraft and fired her up. The port engine responded on cue. The starboard engine coughed and complained but seemed to be holding together. He moved the Goose out into the center of the river, pushing the old girl into the current. Then, with a quick preflight and little or no fanfare, he pulled up the wheels and shoved the throttles in.

As smoke belched from the exhausts on the starboard engine, she surged forward, both engines whining. No one breathed...no one moved. The big airplane began bouncing across the surface as she entered her takeoff ritual. Eddie's face was locked in a rigor of concentration and brazen hope as his battered lady started to come up on plane...and lifted off.

A few minutes later, my clenched hands began to relax. Eddie and his wonderful old bird were probably three miles out, and I was starting to risk a smile when there was a distant detonation accompanied by an immediate burst of smoke from the Goose. The old bird dropped a wing and started tumbling in the distant sky. Eddie was way too low for an easy engine-out recovery. I glanced at Will and the others. The fear in their eyes said it all.

The extraordinary Edward Jackson Moorehouse had just managed the slightest of smiles when the starboard engine quit with a bang. Now the overworked port engine was beginning to cough. Eddy knew he was going in. Practically standing on the left rudder to keep the asymmetrical thrust from forcing the aircraft over into a roll, he fought the bird's instinct to kill him. Even as stressed as he was, Eddie was the consummate pilot, taking in everything around him as he struggled with the dying craft. Suddenly, through it all, he smiled. "Son of a bitch..." he whispered.

Below, in the distance, he recognized a diamond mining operation. The river it was on (probably El Caroni, by his chart) had been diverted slightly and there was a *chupadora* — a mechanized mining barge on one bend. Eddie was cautiously setting a course for the diamond mining operation when his port engine suddenly shuddered and stopped as well. Everything went quiet. The only sound was the wind rushing in a slipstream around the cockpit.

Edward Jackson Moorehouse exhaled hard and a grim smile touched the corners of his lips. The gods weren't throwing any bones his way today. He wasn't going to make the river. Not even close...

Eddie's last thought, before the shadowy green labyrinth came rushing up and the jarring pain cast him into darkness, was for his friends. They were on their own.

We all stood there, numb, our senses bitch-slapped and what little hope we had possessed shattered by the gut-wrenching reality we had just witnessed. Moments later, a narrow plume of smoke rose out of the jungle in the distance. We could hardly bring ourselves to look at each other. This disaster not only staggered us emotionally — the loss of Eddie, down in the jungle somewhere, possibly dead — but it meant we were on our own against a ruthless, vengeful gangster who was, without a doubt, coming for us.

On the ridge of the canyon walls, probably half a mile away, Tabo and his friend Ama-ta sat, staring down toward the river. They had just observed what had taken place — the fall of the metal creature. They didn't understand the mechanics of any of this, but they were certain it was not a good thing.

Not a hundred yards on the other side of the camp, just into the mangroves, one other creature sat hunched and fretful, dark eyes glowering as he watched these new, audacious strangers who had invaded his refuge.

"Aarrrkk...falling dragons," he hissed under his breath.

He paused and glanced downstream, where the river plunged into the cavern. "Has theys found it? Did theys see it?" He shook his head. "No, no, we's don't think so... But we's hates them just for looking..."

CHAPTER SEVENTEEN

"Here's the way I see it," said Cody, as we all sat around our campsite by the river. "First off, I'm not ready to mourn Eddie. He's a resilient son of a bitch. But this much we know — he ain't coming to help us. Secondly, there's no doubt in my mind that Santiago *will be* coming for us and the gems in that cave." He eased out a breath. "We can hide in the interior and try to outlast these people until they get bored and go home. But if we do that, we have no advantage. They will carve the stones out of that wall and we will become the hunted, not the hunters." He paused and glanced around at us. "Or, we can be ready for them — make it miserable enough for them that they decide to give up and go home." His eyes got hard. "Those that are left…"

Shadow, sensing the heaviness in the air, moved in closer to me, placing his head against my knee. I reached around and ran my hand through the thick gray hair at his neck and received a rumble in his chest for my efforts.

"We all have guns and we picked up a few weapons from the two men that Santiago had ordered to kill us," Cody continued. "And we have a handful of dynamite and a grenade or two we got from Bobby Branch in the Keys. In addition, I have the AT4 anti-tank weapon from Branch." He grinned without humor. "That's only a 'one-shot' thing, but it's a mean little bugger."

"What we don't know is when or where to expect him," I said. "Santiago's got some skin in this game now, and his people know we can be dangerous. But I'm guessing that after that little nighttime fiasco, he's gonna come at us in the daytime, and given we're in the middle of hell here, he has to come in by air."

Cody held up a forefinger. "Here's one last thought. We can take a couple sticks of the dynamite we have and set them off at the top of the ridge above the cave.

I smiled as I remembered that the cave was actually cut into the base of one portion of the sandstone canyon walls. "We can bury that cave enough that it'll take a bulldozer to dig it out."

"I like that," said Will with a grin. "That'll really piss 'em off."

"It'll also preserve that incredible statement...for a while," I added.

In the end, we decided that at the first sign of an approach by Santiago, we would split up and use our walkie-talkies so we couldn't be cornered or surprised. Will and I were delegated the job of burying the cave (it seemed like the only safe alternative for securing the intellectual and physical treasure). But there was no point in doing that until we were certain that company was arriving.

Once we'd made the decision about the cave, Cody and Arturio set about planning a welcome party for Santiago by our camp. But the truth was, it was a pretty glum affair. It was damned near impossible to see a happy ending in this.

Will summed it up while we were packing the dynamite and fuses into a knapsack. He smiled grimly. "I always liked that movie, *The Alamo*. I just never thought I would find myself in one of the leading roles." He sighed and looked at me, a grim reality shading his eyes. "I'll tell you what I hope for when I'm dead and gone. I hope the people who knew me well, on occasion, will proudly raise a drink at Eddie's bar and say, 'Here's to Will Bell — a damned fine fellow.'"

I offered a nostalgic smile. "I think the best you can hope for when your name is mentioned at a bar is to hear those who barely knew you saying, 'Yeah, I knew him well. He was a good friend of mine.' That's the acid test for the footprint you leave in the sand."

Throughout the day we waited, watching and listening, but there was no sound of approaching helicopters, which was the only way Santiago could get to us, given the situation.

What we couldn't have known was, the gods had thrown us a small bone. One of Santiago's helicopters had developed a tail rotor problem, and it had set his little island attack back a day.

Because we had no way of knowing exactly how or where they would come in, there was no way to plan any sort of major

The Wild Road to Key West

defense. Probably the most significant weapons we had were Cody's AT-4 anti-tank weapon and the dynamite, but their values remained to be seen.

While we were planning, Arturio, who had been fairly quiet through all of this, excused himself. I figured it was a call of nature. We were just wrapping up our war plans when we heard a sudden, high-pitched shriek from the mangroves behind us, followed by a couple of choice Venezuelan phrases about illegitimacy and somebody's mother, voiced by Arturio. We all snapped up as the thick brush about fifty feet from us swayed and shook, and out came our South American buddy dragging a kicking, squealing creature that looked like the lead character out of a Stephen King movie. It had long, bedraggled hair, wide glazed eyes the size of quarters, and thin lips pulled back to display a mouthful of grayish teeth, all attached to a scrawny, sun-darkened, slightly scarred body that was naked but for a tattered pair of pants that would have embarrassed a Haitian orphan. Clutched in his right hand was a threadbare canvas knapsack.

The creature was screeching in Venezuelan Spanish, "Aaieee! Oooohhh! Don' hurt poor Slinka! Don't eat Slinka! Please!"

Will and I quickly rose and helped Arturio hold the squirming fellow, while trying to calm him down.

"No one es gonna eat you!" yelled Arturio. He kicked the guy's feet out from under him and forced him to sit down in the sand with his back against an old driftwood log.

As Will held the character, he winced from the body odor. "Trust me, man, the way you smell, nobody's gonna want to even touch you."

Arturio leaned over. "Listen," he muttered, still holding the diminutive fellow. "I see him whispering to someone else before I grab him, but there is no one else around." He rolled his eyes. "*Un poco loco*, I think…"

"Good chance," said Will. "Real good chance."

"As if we didn't already have enough baggage on this ride," muttered Cody.

It took fifteen minutes to get our "guest" to settle down.

Arturio was delegated the job of trying to find out what he was all about, because he understood the dialect. The rest of us dragged out our implements of war and prepared ourselves for what was coming. In the middle of all this, Shadow came over to check out our new addition, which freaked out this "Slinka" guy all over again. It took a full five minutes to convince him that the "snarly biter" wasn't going to eat him.

It turned out that our new "guest," who we estimated to be in his early twenties, spoke Spanish and even a smattering of English, but he was so far gone psych-wise, it was like trying to communicate with a frightened monkey. We had to tie his feet or he would have been gone in a blink.

He was thin as a rail and mentally barely touching the earth, so I decided to use the same technique I'd use on a wild animal — food. I found a bowl from our mess kit and opened a can of corned beef. At first, as I squatted down close to him, he drew back, but when he saw the food in the bowl, our relationship changed. He snatched it from me and quickly pulled away, wolfing it down with his fingers. I got out another can. When he had finished that, he held out the bowl cautiously. "More for Slinka?"

By the third round of corned beef, our new acquaintance was relaxing a little. He burped loudly and set down the bowl. I gave him a cup of water and he slurped that dry as well. He wasn't what I would call at ease, but he was curious now.

"Chur dragon..." he whispered carefully to me. "Fall from sky..." He suddenly got the strangest of looks, somewhere between terror and sorrow, and eased out a sigh. "Sometimes, in da back of my head, I see a dragon fall from da sky." Again he paused and blinked a couple of times, his eyes filled with confusion. "I think I was in da belly of a dragon once..."

It appeared that he had some recollection of being in an airplane. It seemed that he had been watching us for some time, and probably had seen Eddie's plane fall out of the sky.

Arturio glanced at me, then back to our new guest. "Yes," he replied in Spanish, realizing we were making some headway. "Our dragon fall from the sky."

"Painted Faces..." the creature replied. "Nasty, mean Painted Faces. They's small black dragon wound it. I saws it." He threw up his hands, suddenly becoming agitated again. *"Cabrón!* De catch you! Beat you! Eat you!"

I suddenly realized he was relating Santiago's people to the natives in the jungle, as one and the same. As agitated as he was, this was a good relationship switch. The small fellow was still cautious to the point of flight, but he was no longer viewing us as "Painted Faces" or enemies. But there was more to this...

While he thought we weren't looking, he gleaned a sly look and whispered, as if confiding in someone, "They's looking for the shiny rocks and pretty stones and old bones." He paused... "All togethers, all alones."

While he was speaking, a couple of times he inadvertently glanced toward the giant underground cavern west of us, in which the river disappeared. Then, suddenly, it was as if he realized he'd said too much. He clamped his mouth shut and brought his hands in close, wrapping his arms around his emaciated sides, and stared at the ground.

I glanced at my friends, who had been close enough to witness this.

Will curled a finger at me and drew me over. "I hate to sound like a mercenary, but what he just said sounded a lot like the description of a hoard of some sort."

I nodded.

Will continued. "There is no question that our guy has been wandering around this area for some time. I'm just wondering what he knows that we don't. We know this was a gold-and-gem-producing society, but we haven't seen much..." He offered that slippery smile of his, eyebrows bouncing. "That boy may be as mad as a bag of head lice, but if we were anywhere else, I'd be buying him a drink or two. Just to be sure..."

I turned to our new acquaintance. "How about another can of corned beef?"

Lord, what whores we were when it came to shiny things. Here we were, on the verge of extinction, stuck in the middle of a godforsaken South American jungle with a Venezuelan mobster looking to punch our clocks, and we were breathing heavy over the possibility — nothing more than the possibility — of a few pretty stones and some gleaming metal. Man, we were some sick puppies...

"You can stay with us, Slinka," said Will in his best, most convincing Spanish. "You are safe from the Painted Faces with us."

Which wasn't exactly true, because there was probably going to be a whole new group of Santiago's people coming in just about any time to try and whack us. But we decided not to overload the guy right away.

Cody broke up the party. "Okay everyone, you can damned well bet trouble is on its way, so we need some plans..." He looked around. "We can pretty much bet we're looking at helicopters or amphibians, so we need to draw them into us as they come. " He tapped the AT4 in his arms. "So...I can get one for sure. Then we'll probably have to play hide-and-seek with the remainder."

"Maybe not," Will said. He glanced around at us. "Where do you think Santiago is going to go first? I mean, like right away? What's the big draw for him other than our heads on pikes?"

I smiled. "The cave! I mean, he wants to kill us, but at the top of his list is probably going to be, 'are the gems still intact?'"

Cody glanced from me to Will, a degree of respect in his eyes. "Not bad, gentlemen. He may take a pass over us, but he's gonna have to know everything is good at the cave. And my guess is he's not going to want company. He's sure as hell not keen on sharing those stones, which will take him an hour or so to dig out of the walls. The ones he can reach, anyway." He paused for a moment, then glanced out into the jungle and at the natural sandstone cliffs that surrounded the city. "Like we said before, that cave lies right against those sandstone walls — actually, it goes into them."

Will nodded. "And two sticks of dynamite at the top of the cliff, above the entrance, and it would take a bulldozer a week to get to it."

"Not a nice death," I muttered.

"Not a nice man," countered Cody. "Sometimes, if we're not careful, we get what we deserve."

"So, we're guessing," I said. "But the plan is, we sucker at least one of those helicopters over us so Cody can, hopefully, take it out, and we have a team on the cliff with some dynamite in place to bury King Tut with his treasure." I brought up my hands theatrically. "And maybe we get to survive this!"

"There's still the small matter of getting home, señors," said Arturio.

"Well, you know, we might just be able to go home in Santiago's helicopter," I said with a smile. "That would really add insult to injury."

CHAPTER EIGHTEEN

We figured that Santiago would return with his two helicopters again and would probably bring along a couple more boys to finish the job, but what we saw coming in over the horizon was disappointing at best. Santiago's Bell 206 helicopter led the way, but behind him came two more copters clipping the tops of the jungle — probably fifteen or twenty card-carrying assassins on their way to visit us.

As soon as Slinka got a glimpse of the approaching helicopters, he ripped off the loosely bound ropes on his feet and was as gone as yesterday's breakfast.

"US-made MH-6s," muttered Cody angrily. "The boy's got connections."

Santiago wasn't taking any chances. Or maybe he was just really pissed off and wanted this over and done with. Regardless, we were screwed.

"Now I know exactly how Crockett felt at the Alamo," whispered Will.

"It's not over till they toss the dirt in your face," Cody muttered. He sat his Thompson down, brought up his AT4, and looked at us, his eyes hard as agates. "One of those is never going to touch the ground, so don't get all shaky and misty-eyed just yet."

We reviewed the battle plan again. It was a fairly good plan, but it was still the Alamo.

Will and I grabbed the dynamite and the cord for it, then tucked our pistols into our belts. For one final moment, we all stood there, monuments to courage and greed I suppose.

Cody broke the moment. "Get going," he growled. Then he offered the slightest touch of a grim smile. "When we're done, the one that's not bleeding has to buy the drinks."

In the next moment, Will and I were headed for the cave, Shadow right behind us. We were rolling the dice on Santiago's greed.

Cody and Arturio found an outcropping of sandstone at the edge of camp just into the mangroves. Cody pulled out a flare gun, held it up, and pulled the trigger. The flowering red flare drew the helicopters like dogs to a scent. The three black helicopters, packed with Santiago's soldiers, came sweeping in boldly. The lead copter had been fitted with a thirty-caliber machine gun on a universal mounting platform under its belly, and all the pilot/gunner saw was two men on the beach well ahead of him. His finger tightened on the trigger.

As the black birds closed, Cody waved Arturio off. "Get the hell out of here!" he yelled, pointing at the AK-47 they had picked up from Santiago's soldiers at the Cave of the Stars. "Find a safe place to annoy those sons of bitches with that rifle!" Then he brought the AT4 up to his shoulder.

Arturio, who was no stranger to uncommon courage, moved to the edge of the mangroves. He stood there for a moment, watching this new friend of his, who was poised in the dirty sand of the riverbank, feet spread, aiming his deadly weapon as the first bullets from the approaching helicopters began cutting rows toward him.

"Son a bitch got cantaloupes for *cojones!*" he muttered, as he crouched and began to fire rhythmic, three-second bursts.

Will and I cut through the jungle, then headed up onto the sandstone ridge, dynamite in hand. We were only a few hundred yards along the top of the ridge when we heard the report of the flare pistol. We paused just long enough to catch a glimpse of the helicopters as they turned and fell toward their prey. But sure enough, the rear bird broke away, toward the cave of precious stones.

Will offered a grim smile. "Ain't greed an amazing thing," he muttered.

Seconds later, as the other two copters fell below the tree line, there was a fierce explosion.

"I'm guessing that was Cody's little AT4 surprise," I said grimly.

Will nodded. "We can only hope."

Will and I found the perfect place, maybe a hundred feet above the entrance to the Cave of the Stars. There was a large rubber tree that had grown into the crest of the cliff, just off center from the top. About fifty feet from its trunk, along the cliff, was a large knot of roots that had tenaciously forced themselves through the sandstone in an unwieldy ball. It was there, almost above the entrance to the Cave of the Stars, that we buried the two sticks of dynamite and set a long, fifteen-foot fuse back to a huge pocket of roots under the monstrous rubber tree, where we could hide. I couldn't coax Shadow into the pocket with us, so I shooed him off. He'd be fine for the few minutes we were dealing with.

Only moments into our project, we watched Santiago's black helicopter roll across the top of the jungle, then come about and set down somewhere in the clearing outside the cave. But from our vantage point, we couldn't see the copter or who disembarked. From somewhere below I could definitely hear Santiago's harsh voice.

I looked at Will. "Showtime..." I whispered as I struck the lighter and he touched the fuse to the flame.

The fuse, which now draped down against the side of the cliff, indiscernible to anyone on top, began to hiss and burn in a steady, methodical fashion back toward the root ball where the dynamite was hidden. I risked one more look below, and could just see the aft rotor on the helicopter a fairly good distance from the cave. It looked like all was in place.

Carefully, quietly, we turned around in the huge root system and pulled ourselves out onto the top of the cliff again. There was no conversation. Neither of us was really happy about what we were doing. It was a little too cold for our style, but it wasn't just our lives we were preserving — we were also preserving a remarkable archaeological find.

We had just made it to our feet and were brushing off the dirt, ready to move away from the upcoming blast, when a voice — a familiar voice — from behind us whispered, "You know, I didn't expect to see you again, but here you are..."

Will and I jerked up, offering a quick, surprised glance at each

The Wild Road to Key West

other, then turned.

Passi!

After his initial shock, Will muttered, "The wanton witch of West Venezuela."

Passi ignored the remark, comfortable with the situation and in control. (Her large Indian friend had an Uzi.) "Why don't you and Will put your guns down and come over here," she said.

Both she and her accomplice were about fifteen feet from the sprawling root system where we had stashed the dynamite.

"We can hear you just fine from here," I said.

A burst from her accomplice's Uzi convinced us to drop our guns and move closer. I could smell the burning fuse now.

"Why aren't you down in the cave?" I asked, buying time, still not moving too close to her.

She shrugged. "Santiago wanted a moment alone with his treasure. 'The prize of a lifetime,' he calls it."

"Yeah," muttered Will sarcastically. "No question he'll be spending a lot of time with it..."

"So, we come up here to make sure we're alone." She shook her head. "And look what we find." Passi got an almost disappointed expression. She nodded toward her gunman. "You know, I almost don't like him to kill you. But some things, the stars decide."

"Actually, I think a lack of conscience makes most of your decisions," muttered Will, who was closer to her than I was.

The gunman was just bringing up his weapon when, from the darkness of the jungle behind him, there came a gray flash. Passi shouted a warning but she was a fraction too late. Shadow hit the gunman squarely in the chest, knocking him backward toward the cliff. The fellow took three staggered steps, trying to bring his weapon to bear, but his fourth step touched nothing but air. That was the last we heard of him. Well, there was the scream...

Our *bruja* was struggling with the pistol at her waist when there was a muffled roar and the cliff about fifteen feet to the right of her exploded in a maelstrom of dirt, rock, and smoke. The ground trembled like an earthquake as the top of the escarpment broke away and began, in almost slow motion, to crack out from the face of the surrounding bluffs, carrying the witch with it. Through the terror, the dust, and fire, the only thing that kept running through my head was, *Too much dynamite — way too much dynamite...*

The whole edge of the cliff that we were standing upon suddenly groaned, then cracked and pulled away, tumbling downward, exposing the huge, tangled root system of the rubber tree and taking Will and Passi with it. Somehow, I had managed to stumble backward a couple of steps in pure instinctual terror before tumbling to the ground, and that saved me. Shadow's reflexes saved him as well, as he danced back from the collapsing cliff.

When the trembling stopped, I realized that I was lying just inches from the edge of the decimated, newly rearranged cliff. Instantly, I glanced around, looking for Will, but through the dust and the haze of smoke, there was nothing to be seen.

"Will!" I yelled. "Will!"

Nothing...

I struggled to my knees and yelled again. The air was still so filled with dust it was almost impossible to see.

It was then that I heard my buddy's choking, gasping reply. "Here! Here!"

I looked out and there was nothing. I wiped my eyes with the back of my hand and crawled forward to the edge of the newly formed precipice.

"Here! Help!" cried a voice again, but it wasn't Will's this time.

I reached the edge and looked over. There, not three feet below me, grasping the mangled tentacles of the rubber tree's exposed root system, were Will and Passi, not two feet apart. They were covered with dust to the point that only their eyes were discernable. Below them was easily a hundred-foot drop into the jagged sandstone remains of the cliff. The entrance to what had been the Cave of the Stars was now buried under at least twenty feet of rock.

"Help me," cried Passi. "Save me...please..." she begged.

I could see the root she was holding was cracked and splintered — a very temporary situation...

Will hung helplessly next to her, his face cut and bleeding, the blood caked with dust, his eyes frightened. "Help me up, partner," he said. "I'm not having a good time here..."

Even as he spoke, the battered root he clutched gave and slid out another three inches from the cracked and pummeled sandstone.

There was no way I could save both of them. The naturally porous sandstone was losing its battle with the roots that it held. I laid myself flat on the ground and reached down as far as I could, both the people in front of me holding me with their eyes, begging silently. But at that moment Passi locked me with those copper eyes and began to speak softly, almost hypnotically.

"Save me..." she whispered, still holding me with her eyes, her voice slowly taking on a mesmerizing cadence. "Save me, Kansas," she cooed. "I can give you so much...I love you...you were the one all along..."

It was like I felt myself slipping into warm jelly — as if my will was separating from my logic. I wanted to stop. A part of me knew this was a snake-oil yarn, but my arms were reaching out.

"I can please you beyond your dreams..." she breathed heavily.

My hands were slipping over hers...

"Save me," she whispered again. "Pleasures you never imagined...my body, my lips, my mouth..."

"Well, she's got me there," moaned Will in that traditionally sarcastic manner of his, breaking the spell somewhat. "You're my good buddy, but I can't promise you any of those pleasures, dude."

He inadvertently tried to wave a hand and almost lost his grip for a moment, then groaned in resignation. "Okay, okay, maybe every once in a while, on really rare occasions, like your birthday. And backrubs. I can do backrubs," he grunted, staring up at me, his eyebrows bouncing.

I swear to God, even in a situation as absolutely dire as this, the damned guy could still drudge up the courage for levity. What an incredible character.

At that moment, I looked down at Passi and she saw the choice I'd made in my eyes. Her face went hard, her eyes cold, and she screamed at me vehemently in a language I had never heard before, her words bitter and sharp as knives. I was pretty sure it was a curse. Without another word, I let her go, as if I had a snake in my hands. And maybe I did...

CHAPTER NINETEEN

As my buddy and I sat at the edge of the precipice catching our breath, Shadow came over hesitantly, the hair on his back stiff and bristling. He was such an intelligent creature. He absolutely recognized the gravity of what had taken place. I put my arms around his neck. "It's okay, boy," I whispered. "You did good. It's okay, boy..."

Below us, we could see the jumbled remains of the cliff, which spread out in all directions over the now obliterated cave. Our guileful *bruja* lay in the rubble below, a twisted monument to deceit, lust, and greed. I turned away as if the sight itself was toxic.

The helicopter Santiago had come in on was just far enough from the cave to have survived, but there were no signs of Santiago or his crew. Our guess was the crew had taken positions in and around the cave entrance for security, just before the explosion.

Suddenly, the crackle of small-arms fire from the river brought us around. I turned to Will. "Cody and Arturio..."

In moments, we were up and moving.

While Will and I were dealing with dangling witches and exploding cliffs, two of the three black helicopters, packed with Santiago's civilian soldiers, were sweeping in on our friends at the river. All the pilot/gunner of the lead copter saw was three men on the beach well ahead of him. In moments, two of the men had disappeared into the mangroves, but one stood stubbornly in front of him, bringing up a black tube of some sort to his shoulder. The pilot was ex-police and had seen combat fighting insurgents in the jungles of Venezuela, and that was what saved him. As soon as he saw the burst of smoke from the rear of the tube he threw the bird over hard to the right. It was the best anyone could have done. But it wasn't quite enough.

The AT4 rocket screamed out, leaving a curling trail of smoke. It clipped the landing strut in an eruption of fire and smoke. The copter rolled to the port side from the explosion, tumbling through the air, its belly torn, the port strut gone. Somehow, over the screaming of the wounded and the loss of airstream control, the pilot managed to force his bird down onto the mangrove sand at the edge of the river. It hit hard, and the rotating blades bit into the heavy sand, twisting and snapping, pieces whistling away like deadly wasps. But by some miracle, everything came to a stop without an explosion.

The pilot of the second chopper instantly threw his craft away in a panic, dropping low and bringing it to a hasty landing several hundred yards down the beach. In moments, half a dozen of Santiago's soldiers were pouring out.

Cody watched all this without moving. He needed to know what his odds were. Only four of the men in the wounded copter got out before the spreading aviation gas found a hot spark plug and the machine went up in an explosion that sucked the oxygen from the air.

"Ten," Cody muttered, counting the six men from the other copter and four from the wounded/destroyed one. Ten against him and Arturio, with only a couple of magazines between them. And then there was still the other copter that had headed toward the cave with the gems…

Cody shrugged. "I've seen worse," he muttered. Then he was gone, into the jungle.

The bedraggled Slinka creature watched all this from the branch of a huge wild mango tree. He was terrified, wrapped up tightly in a ball, his back against the heavy trunk. "Ohooo, goblins and trolls! Goblins and trolls, and wraiths on wings! Dem strange peoples dat feed Slinka got lots of badness!"

As Will, Shadow, and I made our way back toward the beach, Cody and Arturio found each other at our designated spot where the mangroves began to turn into jungle. Moments later, we burst out of the brush.

Will glanced around, looking for our friends. "Where are they? You don't think they…"

"No, they didn't..." growled Cody as he stepped out from behind the trunk of a big ficus tree, followed by Arturio. "What took you so long?"

I exhaled. "We had an altercation with a wicked witch."

"And?" asked Arturio, who had been somewhat beguiled by her charms as well.

Will offered a cautious smile. "My guess, she's probably wearing a pointed hat and riding a tornado into Hell at this point."

"Cabrón!" muttered our friend, getting Will's drift.

"What about the rest of them — and Santiago?" asked Cody.

"It looks like everyone was inside the cave when the walls came down," I said.

Cody cocked his head. "Santiago too?"

"Yeah," Will replied. "Just before Passi…left us…she said he was inside the cave admiring his treasure."

Our friend offered a smile. "Works for me," he said.

The shouts of soldiers in the distance got our attention.

"Time to move," muttered Cody. "But we need to make a choice here. We either work our way into the jungle and try to lose them, and fight them guerrilla-style if we have to, or we put our backs to something, where they can't surround us, and see who cries 'uncle' first." He glanced back in the direction of the copters. "I don't think those boys planned on any kind of siege. Especially now, with no sign of their boss."

It was quiet for a moment, then Will spoke again. "We could maybe lose them in the jungle, but in that terrain, we won't know where they are at any given point." He wiped the sweat from his forehead with the back of his hand. "Hell, it's tough enough to know where we are. That makes me uncomfortable."

"Si," agreed Arturio with a sigh. "In this moment, I miss your

amigo, *de loco* Eddie, an' his fat pigeon."

"Goose," I muttered reflexively. I suddenly realized how much I missed that sixties-slang-spouting, one-eyed daredevil. I missed him a lot...

I'd been listening to the conversation, but I was also looking back, where the river was being swallowed by the gorge. I turned to my friends. "When Will and I saved the Goose from going over the subterranean falls, I saw something — a small stairway, cut into the rock, just inside the cave. It looked like it led to a cavern above. If we could get in there, we could hold off an army, and the enemy would have their backs to the light as they came in." I glanced around. "Bad for them, good for us."

I saw Cody nodding. "Not bad, amigo," he said. "I don't think many of those guys are real soldiers. They aren't going to do well in this situation for very long, especially when they can't find their boss."

"I don't think anyone's gonna find their boss for some time to come," Will muttered.

Unbeknownst to us, Slinka had slithered up a tree not fifty feet away, quiet as a spider, and was watching us intensely.

"I say we grab our packs and make a run for the river cavern," said Cody. "If we can find a way in, we can hold them until they get bored." He grinned mirthlessly, holding up his old Thompson 45. "And the ones that don't bore, we'll shoot. Then we'll fly Santiago's bird home." He grinned. "Damned poetic justice."

"Me gusta," replied Arturio, as he squatted, rubbing Shadow's furry neck. "Better than being shot at in a stinkin' jungle."

And so it was that the Hole in the Coral Wall Gang made a run for a mist-filled cavern that supposedly had a stairway to... someplace. Hopefully not Heaven. Or Hell.

Our competition soon figured out what we were up to and began a rapid pursuit. They could have easily taken us out with the helicopter, but after seeing what had happened to the first one, there were no volunteers for that ride. They didn't rush us either. They spread out and moved in slowly along the riverbank, figuring we were coming to a cul-de-sac where the river poured into the mouth of the cave.

We grabbed flashlights and extra ammunition from our campsite, then made a beeline for the opening of the descending cavern.

Misting plumes of water rose around us as we entered the encroaching dimness of the cavern. The roar of the river, descending furiously into the bowels of the earth, was an almost physical thing.

"Into de heart of darkness," muttered Arturio to no one in particular.

Close behind us, Slinka followed, not trying to remain unseen, but not exactly joining arms with us either.

"Theys goin' to da place..." he muttered. "Does they know?" He shook his head. "No, no! Only we's collects 'em, only we's hides 'em!" He eased out a shaky breath. "Shiny rocks, pretty stones, and old bones..."

We kept to the sides of the cliffs that had been carved out by the river over eons, but it wasn't long before we discovered a trail of sorts, cut from the rock centuries ago. Not long after that, I spotted the steps I had seen when Will and I were saving Eddie's Goose (literally). As we moved along, I could see Slinka following, closer now, sometimes paralleling us, taking frightened glances at the soldiers behind him. It looked like he had chosen sides. Shadow imitated his name the whole time, moving in and out from us, climbing above, then turning and working behind, curious, instinctively aware of the tension in the air and constantly alert and protective.

Where the trail began in earnest, there was a buttress of rock on both sides — obviously designed as a point of protection, but done in such a subtle fashion that it was difficult to tell it wasn't natural. Whoever had carved these walls so deftly, so long ago, had a remarkable understanding of stone.

With his binoculars, the leader of Santiago's men could make out his quarry two hundred yards ahead and moving toward the mouth of the monstrous cave. The jagged terrain hadn't offered much in the way of targets to this point. He needed to cut them off before they reached the interior of the cavern and the coming darkness became their friend, not his. As he studied the natural relief, the ex-soldier could just make out an animal trail several hundred yards away from the main path, but turning in toward it at the top. He called over one of his people. As the man squatted down in front of him, he pointed to the Remington model 700 sniper rifle the fellow had slung over his shoulder.

"Are you as good with that as they say?"

The man offered a caustic smile. "Better…"

"Good," the team leader said. "You're going to get a chance to prove it."

Cody Joe, long hair tied back in his traditional ponytail, eyes constantly moving, realized that this game could only have one ending. It was either the enemy or his people. He took one of the grenades we had purchased from Bobby Branch in the Keys (we still had two sticks of dynamite left, as well) and turned to us with a grim smile.

"You folks keep moving. Find some hiding places behind that promontory above. We're going to reduce the odds a little."

As we moved out, I watched Cody take some clear monofilament line from the breast pocket of his camouflage vest, then pull a second grenade from his belt. He tied one end of the line to the base of a hardy bush on one side of the trail and strung the line across the path, tying the end of the line to the pin on the grenade. Then he lifted the pin halfway out of its casing. Finally, he stretched the line further across the path and carefully wedged the grenade into a crook of hard sandstone. While Cody worked, Slinka quietly circumvented him and continued on, soon disappearing down a separate trail we hadn't even noticed.

When Cody Joe reached us, he had that hard, feral look in his eyes. It was exactly the same expression that longtime member of the Hole in the Coral Wall Gang, Travis Christian, would garner — just before he ripped someone a new asshole.

"Get up ahead, spread out a little more, and tuck yourselves into the rocks," Cody rumbled. "Weapons ready." He looked over at our Venezuelan buddy. "Arturio, you bring up the rear. Keep your eyes peeled, buddy."

"No problemo," replied Arturio, those strange gray orbs of his growing watchful again. As he fell back and found a cubbyhole, he eased out a sigh. "I think I spend too much more time with you gringos, an' Russian roulette gonna get boring. I thin' we gonna have to talk about upping my salary."

Will, a dozen feet above him and wedged into a crevice, humphed, "What salary?"

Arturio threw out his hands, palms up. "See? See what I mean?"

Santiago's men were moving at a steady pace, hoping to catch us before we reached the darkness of the inner cavern. Only a couple of them were actually ex-soldiers, and even they were in a hurry to get this over with. The lead man unknowingly tripped the wire while concentrating on the darkening path ahead. The pin slid from the grenade. He looked down and his eyes went wide. (Three seconds is just barely long enough to know you're dead.) The grenade detonated, killing the lead man and wounding two more.

At that point, Cody, Will, and I rose up from behind the buttress ahead and opened fire. Two more found their way to the devil.

It looked like our competition was down to three men, plus the pilot and a guard, both of whom had remained with the helicopter. I thought there was one more, but I couldn't spot him.

As another grenade bounced down the trail and exploded only a few yards from them, our pursuers realized these weren't the stupid *"gringo maricos"* that Santiago had described. And the money that their boss had promised didn't cover dying in a godforsaken stretch of the Venezuelan jungle. In moments, they were bolting back down the trail. None of them had progressed far enough to see the stairs that had caught our attention.

I turned to Cody, not looking forward to the answer but having to ask the question. "The helicopter? Do we go after them?"

"No need, if you're sure the other bird is waiting for us by the cave with the precious stones."

"I'm not sure of anything," I replied. "But it was there and empty when we blew the cliff, and after that there was no one left to ride in it."

At that moment, we heard the engine firing on the copter below, and the big blades beginning to whir.

Cody studied the retreating men for a moment, then spoke, almost to himself. "We don't have to worry about them. They were nothing more than hired help and they sure as hell know nothing about any treasure. They're all gonna go home and pretend this didn't happen." He sighed slightly. "We're good if we've got a chopper."

"Not to worry, the other copter will be there," Will chimed in. "Unless the monkeys learned to fly it in the last few hours." He paused and glanced up ahead, just into the mouth of the cave, where the strange rock staircase emerged from the grayish, mildewed stone. "Besides, I want to see where those go."

Almost 200 yards away, hidden in the jumble of an ancient rockslide, sat the sniper, who had deftly slipped away earlier and worked his way around both the pursuers and the pursued. He brought up his weapon and settled it against his shoulder, neck cocked, face leaning into the scope. He was carefully adjusting for range and what little wind there was, setting the crosshairs on the temple of the unsuspecting blond-haired man below, when he heard a strange, deep rumbling behind and above him. He paused. The sound continued, and suddenly, a heavy globule of saliva dropped onto his arm. The rumbling was growing in menace. He slowly lifted his eye from the scope just as another droplet struck him. The sniper barely had time to turn and scream as Shadow fell on him from the ledge just above his head.

The cry drew our attention to the rockslide just across from and above us, where the sniper's rifle banged and clanged its way down the mountainside. Shadow stood there, on a promontory of jumbled boulders, the remains of the shooter maybe fifty feet below him.

Cody glanced up at it all, shook his head, and turned to me. "That's one damned amazing dog you've got." He exhaled. "If you ever decide —"

"I won't," I said, interrupting him.

My friend offered a disappointed but understanding smile. "Yeah, I guess not." He glanced up at Shadow once more. "Freaking Rin Tin Tin with an attitude."

As we watched the chopper lift up and head southeast across the green expanse of jungle toward civilization, I was pleased on one hand and damned envious on the other. I wanted to get the hell out of there, and I knew I wasn't alone. And at that moment, I sorely missed Crazy Eddie. I suddenly realized that he was gone. I'd seen that guy cheat death so many times he made Lazarus look like a lazy huckster, and I could barely count the times that Eddie had saved our asses. Behind that one-eyed, wild-and-crazy persona was an extraordinarily savvy and courageous man. I kept thinking that the old Goose would be breaking the horizon at any moment. But he wasn't coming back for us this time…

When all the shooting was over and the copter was gone, we found ourselves just inside the cavern, the huge opening still providing enough light to see the river surging toward the underground falls. Mists were rising around us now, and the falling sun painted a rainbow at the mouth of the grotto. That same sun reached in and touched the strange steps just ahead of us, which had been hewn out of the hard sandstone centuries before and led into the darkening interior — a monument to man's continual need to conquer nature.

"Yeah, I want to see where those go," muttered Will again from behind me. "I'm telling you, nobody goes to that much trouble for nothing."

I shrugged. "It's not like we're on a schedule, is it?"

"You might as well please yourself, amigos," muttered Arturio, holding up an index finger and shaking it. "Because I can tell you this — Arturio is never coming back here. If I had a can of spray paint, I would write on da wall 'Arturio was never here!'" He huffed angrily. "At least when I play Russian roulette, I don' gotta tramp through hot damned jungles an' hide in caves." He wagged his finger again. "An' the only one tryin' to kill me is me!"

CHAPTER TWENTY

"Ooohh, tiny sweet crawlers!" Slinka whispered with relief as he crouched on a high perch just inside the cavern. "Dem nasty bad creatures is gone!" He paused and glanced ahead, into the darkening mists, wringing his hands. "But what does we do now? Does them others knows? How could they knows?"

As we stood at the base of the meticulously cut stairway, admittedly, part of me immediately wanted to return to the Cave of the Stars to make sure that damned helicopter was still there. Without that bird, anything we were doing now was just short of spitting in the wind. But there was something way down inside of me, which could only be explained as a combination of intuition and insight, that wouldn't allow me to leave without knowing.

I could see it in Will's eyes as well. It was a strange desire to plow ahead, to experience the unknown — a yearning to discover what exists at the core of the human creature. It was something that had developed over thousands of years. And I liked to believe it was often initiated by a power greater than our own meager instinct. I had to know where those stairs led. Just like every damned adventurer from Marco Polo and Columbus, to John Glenn and Jacques Cousteau, I had to see the things that others only dreamed of. I had to challenge the gods now and then — to have them reaffirm their omnipotence and reinforce my faith with an occasional, well-thrown bone.

With one final glance at each other, we slowly began to move up the ancient stairway.

As soon as we reached the top, the pathway leveled out above the river, which coursed along for several hundred yards before cascading into the bowels of the earth. It was darkening now. The light from the setting sun was fading and a soft, gray fog began to envelop everything. But the path was still clear, still ascending slightly, worn smooth by the footsteps of generations.

As we moved along, we turned on our flashlights. I reached out with my hand and touched the wall for balance. It was then that I noticed a smooth line in the rock to our right, maybe six inches wide and four feet off the ground, extending continuously along our path. All of a sudden, I was struck by a vision — a mental impression of thousands and thousands of people before me walking this path and running their hands along the wall — for balance — in the dim light of burning torches. Tens of thousands of people over and over again, for generations, their hands wearing a thin, smooth line in the rock.

We walked a couple hundred yards into the cavern. We were actually past where the river spilled into the earth, when the grotto suddenly narrowed. At the end, it abruptly spread out into a large circle about fifty yards across. The floor went from relatively worn to nearly smooth stone. The slightly domed ceiling was a lofty thirty feet above us. We glanced around, our flashlights throwing out their meager beams as we eagerly awaited the next act of this play.

It appeared that this particular place was a natural phenomenon, but it had also been augmented — smoothed and flattened in places to give it continuity. There were small holes along the wall about six feet above the flat stone floor, and some of them still contained the rotted wooden remnants of the torches they once held. Obviously, we were in some sort of communal meeting area — most likely something that was part of civil or religious ceremonies.

But it was the walls that caught our attention. They were one continuous, magnificent mural, carved into the sandstone and rising up a full six feet all the way around to where the mural blended into the smooth, domed ceiling. It took our breath away. I found myself imagining what it must have been like when all the torches around this gathering place threw out their light. What a glorious sight it must have been. There were beautifully carved renditions of courtyards, meeting places, homes, and places of faith. It was as if a common, agrarian hunter/collector society had been infused with a grander knowledge, and the story was told in those magnificent etchings. I began to take pictures.

As the story moved along, our flashlights showed that near the bottom of the stone history there were a few lines of a written language in an elegant calligraphy — dots, exotic slashes, and the most delicate, extraordinary curls, all in different sizes and depths. I was certain it held a message but I had no idea what it was. I was immediately drawn back to the identical writing at the Cave of the Stars and our theories regarding the people who had created that incredible monument to knowledge and celestial understanding. This flowing, exquisite calligraphy was not the product of Amazonian natives, but who these people were, or *what* they were, still remained a mystery.

The mural had obviously been a work in progress, but then, suddenly, it slowed and stopped, morphing from a magnificent, continuously carved description of the life of this tribe to carvings of the strange language for several, what I would call, paragraphs. Then the carvings went to what I was certain were names (and I would guess dates — because while the names would change, the line behind them changed only by one or two symbols). There were hundreds and hundreds of people, maybe thousands. And finally, the writing just stopped.

We all stared at this for a few moments, then Will spoke.

"It doesn't take a rocket scientist to figure this out. It looks like everything was rolling along, totally copasetic, for a long time. Then something happened, and people started dying." He paused for a moment, then spoke again, quietly. "I'm gonna take a stab at this, but I'll bet you dollars to donuts that this incredible history, and this tribe, ends just shortly after their visit from the German explorers Phillip Von Hutten and Bartholomeus Welser."

I nodded somberly. "This was obviously a ceremonial place of some importance. And when they all began to sicken and fade, they could do nothing but record the event — the extinction of their tribe and the physical recollection of a highly unique, dying race."

I paused and Will whispered, "Until there was no one left to record."

"I imagine there were some that survived," Cody added quietly. "Those few who saw the writing on the wall, so to speak, and got out with their families, into the jungles. But there weren't many." He paused and turned to us. "What I'd like to know is, what happened to the bodies? Have you all noticed that, for a fairly good-sized city possibly struck by a plague, we've found very few skeletons or remains?"

"It was a long time ago," I said. "And the jungle is a hungry creature."

While we offered conjectures, I noticed that Shadow, who hadn't left my side since we had entered the actual cavern, was uneasy. Every once in a while he'd offer a heavy rumble, glancing back toward where we had come from.

"It's okay, boy," I said gently, reaching down and rubbing the thick fur of his neck. "It's okay." The truth was, I just wanted it to be okay. We'd all had enough for one day.

Slinka, squatting in the shadows about fifty yards behind the strangers, was beside himself. "They's come!" he screeched silently to himself, clenched hands pressed against his temple. "Slinking searchers! Foul finders! They's come to the Place of Places! Oohhh, whirling wraiths, what does Slinka do if they…"

We noticed a small rectangular room extending out from the back of the cavern. It was cut from the rock in such a fashion as to almost be ambiguous. As we moved closer, I saw a fine line delineating a doorway, cut so perfectly that it blended into the stone in the slyest of fashions.

As we all began to walk over to it, the creature in the dark entranceway to the cavern, arms wrapped tightly around its skinny torso, hissed again. "Noooo! Noooo! All mine! All mine!"

My first thought was it looked like a ticket room or a coat-check at a ballroom. Also, this seemed to be a later addition, as the stone from which it was cut lacked the aged look of the mural that ran on both sides of it. The stone door in the center of the small structure was perfectly cut and displayed no handle of any sort, and fit extraordinarily tight against the stone frame.

Will (our team locksmith), stared at it for a moment, then began pressing against it in certain places, unfortunately without success. He exhaled angrily. "I'll bet you that it's pressure based, because the door, as heavy as it is, gives just slightly from the touch, but you've gotta know where and how."

For the next ten minutes, our friend pressed and popped and pulled. In the interim, Cody quietly backed his way into the shadows.

Slinka continued to curse quietly, fists clenched, tears running down his cheeks, promising retribution he had neither the courage nor the wherewithal to perform.

We were just about to give up when Will, in pure frustration, yelled, "Open up, you son of a bitch!" and kicked the door.

As he hopped back, holding his wounded foot and offering a few choice words about doors and bitches, I muttered sarcastically, "Yeah, that's great. When dealing with an ancient locking device that you can't open, kick it. Really skillful."

At that point, several things happened all at once. There was a shriek from the shadows near the entrance to the cavern, followed by a commotion involving some handpicked words from Cody, along with a continuing battery of screeches from the recently disappeared Slinka.

And…there was a sudden grating sound from the stubborn rock door, which suddenly seemed to be opening slowly.

Even through all the commotion and discomfort, Will looked at me and smiled. "When all else fails, kick it."

Cody dragged Slinka over and plopped him down on the stone

floor in front of the heavy door. Slinka was screaming about all the pretty rocks and shiny stones that "moon after moon, Slinka collect from da dead city!" being his.

"If that's true," Cody yelled back, "how in the hell did you figure out how to get this door open? Huh?"

The bedraggled little creature looked at him and shrugged. "Slinka kick it…"

That was a hard act to argue. It drew smiles from most of us. All except Cody, who was checking his scratches as if he'd been bitten by a rabid skunk.

After everyone calmed down, we made it clear that we didn't want anything that Slinka had found. That seemed to cool the little guy's jets somewhat. But ten minutes later, after we had examined his little "collection" with our flashlights, we were biting our tongues. Slinka had been a busy son of a bitch. He had a wide array of golden artifacts, many of which were adorned with emeralds and diamonds. It appeared that much of the upper populace wore the same golden, gem-encrusted neckbands that we had seen on the guardians with the elongated heads at the Cave of the Stars. Slinka had an impressive collection, along with a nice variety of small golden statues (oddly enough, all of the same design) and a couple of woven palm-frond containers of high-end mixed gemstones. The guy might have been a grubby little sucker here, but put him back in society with his "collection" and the boy was "Fifth Avenue" rich.

"No wonder we didn't find squat in the jungle city," muttered Will. "Marco Polo here has been scooping it up for years."

I couldn't help but chuckle. Damned if he wasn't right. But I was certain now that there was a good deal more to be found. Nonetheless, I found myself envious.

Indeed, Slinka had relaxed a little now that he realized we weren't after his collection. I think the trauma of this whole "abandonment and forced survival" had sort of driven him into a parallel world. It wasn't so much that his mind had snapped; rather, it had retreated to a level that allowed him to survive. And he had created a sidekick — Safren — someone to reassure him and ease his anxiety. Only time would tell about that. But there was no question that Slinka was relaxing, reacting much like an abandoned dog does when it suddenly finds it has been accepted into a new home; pleased but still slightly uncertain.

While we stood there trying to determine exactly what to do next, I saw it. I don't know why I hadn't seen it before (could have had something to do with the circus going on around me, I suppose). But there it was, in the center of the rear wall — subtle, slightly camouflaged from the dust of ages, but nonetheless, there was the outline, the indention, of a hand, exactly like the one in the Cave of the Stars.

Will and Arturio were talking about coming back to this area for a serious treasure-hunting expedition. Cody was kneeling, rubbing Shadow's neck. (He liked that "damned wolf in dog's fur," as he put it.) Slinka was standing off to the side, those big, dark eyes of his totally dedicated to watching all his stuff, still not quite convinced that no one wanted to steal his possessions.

None of them had noticed the hand. But I did.

I exhaled softly and slowly walked over to the wall. I stood there for a moment, somewhere between elation and disbelief lightly sprinkled with the awe of possibility. While my friends all seemed to be preoccupied and not paying attention to me, I reached up, put my hand in the indentation, and pushed slightly.

There was the same "give" as before in the rock around my fingers, and suddenly there was a low grinding noise — ancient gears responding, archaic mechanisms returning to life with obvious complaint. The wall I had been pressing against began to slide horizontally, ancient rock rollers moaning bitterly as the heavy stone drew itself to the side about two feet and introduced the darkness of another large cavern. I took a step back, lost to the magic of the ancients and the modern yearning of the adventurer.

"Whoa shit!" muttered Will.

Arturio crossed himself.

Cody, always the soldier, brought up his rifle.

Slinka just stood there, mouth agape, eyes like small, dark agates.

There was a moment of simple incredulousness, then we glanced around at each other.

"I don't know about you guys," whispered Will, "but I gotta have a look."

Once again, we forded the river of the ordinary and stepped into another world. It was a brilliant, extraordinary view, buttressed by remarkable wealth, but filled with an immense sadness. Only Slinka refused to enter. He was daunted by another door to the unknown. But most importantly, he wanted to watch over his "collection."

The cavern we stepped into was much like the others we had worked our way through. The whole affair was somewhat of a natural underground honeycomb. But where the cavern before was probably a common meeting/ceremonial place, this one had never been developed. It had been used for only one purpose. It was roughly rectangular, perhaps the size of a basketball court, with walls rising up into a natural domed ceiling. Again, there had once been torches on its sides that, at one point, must have lit the glittering sadness around them.

All across the rock floor were individual and family interment sites, the dead neatly laid out in what must have been their finest clothes with all that was most precious to them. This was the burial ground of the wealthy in the City of the Stars. It appeared there were families that the disease had taken one by one, the survivors carrying their kin on litters to be deposited with their loved ones and all that was precious to them....until there was no one left to carry the litters.

In the process of all this, I was struck by two things. The amount of wealth of gold and precious stones was remarkable, and the incredibly intricate artwork of jade and other precious stones and gems was absolutely stunning. But none of this was the product of a simple agrarian culture. There were gold mobiles that accurately displayed the solar system with precious stones and multiple statues of a *single* god. In addition, there was incredible but deteriorating artwork on treated animal hides, and remarkable carvings in mahogany and bone inlaid with precious metal. It was a wealth in archaeological value that was simply staggering. I was reminded of our Mayan find in Guatemala, only a couple of years earlier.

But this — this carried such a personal, intimate, incredibly sad story. There were the remains of children, lying next to their parents, who, as the last survivors of the family and probably already infected by the heinous disease, did all they could to prepare the mortal remains so the family's passing would be acceptable to spirit. And...I was surprised at the number of these people who bore the elongated skulls of what must have been a separate but assimilated race.

I sighed bitterly. I suspected the priests probably charged the richest, with their most precious belongings, to be interred in the safety of this sacred tomb. And yet I was amazed at what seemed to be the integrity of this dying culture. I couldn't find the panic and the ruthlessness that is usually seen at the end of a society. There was a decorum straight through to death, at least to some degree, with these people and their priests, and a clarity and integrity in their faith. I saw nothing that related to sacrifices or a preoccupation with brutality, as seen in so much of the early Central and South American cultures, and I had to wonder how much of this could be credited to the infusion of this strange second race and this simplicity of faith.

I knew, monetarily, that this was a huge find, but there was a part of me that struggled with my avaricious side. If this find could be preserved, I might feel more comfortable, but that wasn't really my choice. I was part of a pack of treasure-hunting wolves. The truth was, for now, none of this mattered. The treasure we had just discovered was safe for the time being. Right now, we needed to find that helicopter and get the hell out of there, so we wouldn't end up like our buddy Slinka.

CHAPTER TWENTY-ONE

The sun was gone and there would be little, if any, light left on the outside. It had been a long day and none of us felt like trekking out into the main cavern and working our way across the slippery rocks of the pathway with lanterns in the dark. So, we closed the door that led to the second, incredible find and moved out.

We set up a meager camp in the main cavern, ate dinner out of cans, and made it an early night. We were all awed, enthralled, and exhausted by the challenges and revelations of the last twenty-four hours. Slinka, obviously mending some psychologically, ate dinner with us (within eyesight), but slid off into the darkness after that.

Speaking of Slinka, we had a decision or two to make. Should we take him with us, or leave him there? And if we were to take him with us, how would we possibly care for him while in the midst of trying to extricate ourselves from the country? We no longer had an airplane, and we'd have to dump the helicopter right away to avoid being arrested by the authorities for theft.

Oddly enough, it was a decision we didn't have to make. By the time we awoke the following morning, Slinka was gone. It could be that he'd heard us talking about him — about taking him with us. But the truth was, Slinka was changing, relaxing. I think a large part of him had begun to remember the pleasure and safety of human company. I knew we hadn't seen the last of him.

Within the hour we had made it back to our base camp and picked up everything we absolutely needed, which wasn't much. Between the Indians and Slinka, I knew there wouldn't be much left when we returned.

It took us an hour to make it through the jungle and back to the Cave of the Stars (with Slinka cautiously following us once again, occasionally joining us in the jaunt). As we came up over the rise of jungle-covered, sandstone cliffs, I'll admit I was a little anxious, but I knew what I knew. I was just certain that damned helicopter was alive and well after the explosion.

The Wild Road to Key West

We cleared the jungle and trudged up to the edge of the cliff that Will and I had blown away with the dynamite, Shadow moving in, out, and around us, sensing the anxiousness we carried. Then we all stopped dead in our tracks. There was no helicopter below us.

We could all see the jumbled mass of sandstone rock that covered the Cave of the Stars completely, tumbling out into the clearing. But the helicopter that Will and I had seen earlier was gone.

After several vivid and definitive expressions regarding my memory and the bird we were supposed to fly away in, Cody turned to me. "Oh yeah, the copter's there. No problem."

I held out my hands. "I said it was there the last time I looked. That's the best I can do."

He skewered me with a stare. "Now we've got to wonder who got away…"

"Well, it wasn't Santiago," I replied hotly. "The *bruja* told me he was in the cave admiring his find just moments before the explosion. It was probably the pilot."

Arturio spat in the dirt and scrunched his mouth. "For the first time I have enough wealth to not worry about playing games that kill me, and I be stuck in a rat's-ass jungle where everythin' wants to kill me!" He looked at Will. "You don' got a revolver I can borrow, do you? I wanna spin the cylinder, just for fun…"

My partner offered up that goofy smile of his. "Okay, okay. It's not the end of the world. Let's head back to the river camp. We've got enough supplies to last us for a few days and we can shoot some game, catch a couple fish. Take some time off, get a suntan…"

Cody was already walking back the way we came.

"We could go by one of the local villages," Will continued, hands out. "Meet the neighbors. Have Slinka over for dinner…"

Cody was reaching for his pistol.

I grabbed Will. "Okay, George Carlin, that's enough."

Fortunately, Crazy Eddie, in his remarkable intuitiveness, had left a couple bottles of tequila stashed away on the Goose. They were put to good use that night. While in the process of sharing those bottles, I was reminded that tequila is a lot like duct tape. It fixes damned near anything...for a while.

The first part of the next day mostly involved recovery. The sun was too bright, everyone spoke too loud, and I wanted to gag just looking at the empty tequila bottles by the fire pit. No one had any motivation. Hell, what was there to get motivated about? We were stuck in a jungle in the middle of Hell's nowhere.

About halfway through the day, when we had recovered enough to make conversation beyond grunting and pointing, Slinka showed up again. We saw him sitting on a boulder near the river about fifty yards from us. It wasn't exactly "hi, buddies, how ya doing?" But for Slinka, it was a pretty big step.

Will pulled a can of beans and some corned beef from the supplies Eddie had left us, and warmed them on the campfire. The smell of food brought Slinka in another twenty-five yards. My friend fixed a plate for our "guest" and set it on a rock just outside the camp. Moments later, the plate was gone. Five minutes passed and suddenly, there was our jungle castaway, slowly easing into camp with his empty plate. He glanced around at us, still a little unsure.

"You got more for Slinka?" he asked cautiously.

"Food doesn't ask a lot of stupid questions or expect sublime answers," said Will with a smile. "Food understands..."

At that point, it appeared the dam of resistance with our little buddy had finally broken. In retrospect, I suppose he figured anyone who didn't steal his treasure and gave him food had to be okay.

We spent some of the day discussing our very limited possibilities. From the charts that we had, it appeared we were on a tributary of the Caroni River. The problem was, even if we could assemble some sort of raft, we would be bucking the current all the way up to any sort of civilization — and that word was used lightly — probably a hundred miles. It wasn't an encouraging situation.

On top of that, we had a second concern. Someone had gotten away in that helicopter…

The sun had just reached its zenith and started to fall, along with most of our hopes, when we all heard it — the steady, distant chugging of a diesel engine.

I looked up, then glanced over at Will. His mouth scrunched in a cautious fashion, but his blue eyes offered a glimmer of hope. Behind him, I could see Cody and Arturio instantly perk up. (They had found a deck of cards and were immersed in a lethargic game of poker under the branches of a large ficus, not twenty feet from the river.) Even Slinka perked up from his perch on a huge limb above us. As slow and deliberate as sleepwalkers, we all stood and turned toward the bend upstream and the sound of the engine.

"That sure sounds like…" muttered Will.

"Yeah, it does," said Cody, bringing himself together now and reaching down for his Thompson. The truth was, the only things that really flourished in the back jungle rivers of Venezuela were bandits and crocodiles.

In moments, a craft came around the distant bend. It was like something out of an old Bogart movie. The boat was probably forty feet from stem to stern and built with a shallow draft to negotiate the river's ever-changing sandbars. It was painted a sorely weathered puke green, and it had a big, aft-mounted diesel and a sizeable forecastle. Two men — Indian/Hispanic mongrels attired in dirty cotton pants, straw hats, and carrying heavy rifles — stood on the bow. There was another man in the wheelhouse, but the shade and the cracked glass windows made it tough to get a handle on him. I found myself sliding over to where I had set my Walther 9mm.

"I don't like this…" whispered Will, as he instinctively followed suit, reaching around to his belt for the reassuring feeling of his pistol.

The boat's engine stopped with a gurgle and a shudder, and she slid bow-first into the bank, about forty feet from us. One of the men threw out an anchor. The big craft responded to the current and came around, putting the men on the bow not thirty feet from us. Nobody had said a word yet. It was like one of those bad Westerns from the fifties.

"Be ready," whispered Cody harshly, bringing me from my reverie.

At that moment, I heard a raucous but familiar voice yell from the wheelhouse, "Ahoy, rapscallions! Your radical, prodigal brotha has returned!"

My jaw dropped. "I can't believe it," I muttered, as Crazy Eddie limped out from the forecastle door, his head wrapped in a large white bandage, his long hair spiked out from the sides of the dirty dressing, the patch over is bad eye slightly askew, one arm in a sling and the other hand holding a bottle of rum.

"Is life groovy or what?" he called as he moved toward us, accompanied now by the two guys who were on the bow.

Ten minutes later, we were sitting on the stern of the boat and Eddie was relating another tale that, as usual, should only be chronicled under the collective influence of some disposition-altering substance. Otherwise, it could only be considered a bald-faced lie.

Our friend explained that, after he crashed his airplane into the jungle (which by all rights should have killed him), he lay there, unconscious, for about a half hour. During that time, the local natives found him. They should have killed him right then and there and taken what he had, but for some reason, they thought Eddie, passed out and bloody in the cockpit, was already dead, so they ignored him and began taking anything of value.

While the Indians were at it, the foreman from the local diamond mining operation showed up with a couple of his people and their guns. He had watched Eddie's plane go down, ironically enough, only a few hundred yards off the road that led to his operation.

There was some argument as to who should make sure Eddie was dead and who should get his stuff. The boss of the diamond mining operation won. He and his people pulled Eddie out of the Goose to get at his belongings, only to find that he was still breathing.

The Wild Road to Key West

It was a hell of a lot of trouble to drag a gringo back to the mining operation when shooting him would have been much simpler, but the boss still had the remnants of a conscience. He decided to flip a coin. Heads, Eddie got to live. Tails, he was alligator bait.

Eddie won the most important coin toss of his life while still unconscious.

Sometimes, the gods, they throw you a bone...

When Eddie regained consciousness, there was some good news and some bad news. The good news was, he'd been patched up and it appeared that nothing had been broken, although he felt like, and looked like, he'd been attacked by sharks. The bad news, as explained by the foreman of the operation, was that bandits had gotten to his airplane and had pretty much stolen anything of value, from the instruments in the cockpit to all the gear Eddie had aboard.

Eddie was no fool. He knew what had happened. But he was alive and that was good; and secondly, he had secret places in that aircraft that a ferret on crack couldn't find. He smiled and thanked the mining operation boss, and drank his watery soup gratefully.

Two days later, with his cracked ribs and sprained shoulder securely taped, Edward Jackson Moorehouse rented a Jeep from the dredge boss and had a native take him to his demolished airplane. He spent an hour aboard the aircraft, then he had his driver take him to the river, where he found an unsavory but cooperative boat owner to whom he gave five hundred dollars, American, and promised a good deal more for a short journey downriver.

For thirty hours Eddie never closed his eyes. He sat in the small forward cabin with a pistol in his lap until the captain yelled out that he had come to "the place where the river fell toward a huge cavern," and he was "going no farther until he got his money."

An hour later, the captain was happy and so were we. Everyone was headed home. Everyone but Slinka. We tried everything we could think of, short of knocking him out and tying him up, but he wouldn't get on "that heavy floater." Every time I tried to talk him aboard, he moved away to the edge of the jungle. He had come a long way in identifying with his civilized half in the last few days, and I was certain he was "remembering" some of his other life, but it appeared that getting him on board that boat was simply a leap of faith he couldn't handle. Yet I could see, in his eyes, that he wanted to...

We left Slinka a can opener and most of our canned food, explaining that we would be back for him soon. For some reason, he was like a mongrel dog that you find and don't really want, but your conscience won't let you leave him be. It's like you just have to find the closest animal shelter or someone who will take him. Our problem was, we had immediate "situations" to deal with. Santiago was probably dead, but someone had gotten away in that helicopter. How much did they know about the cave? There was a part of me that just couldn't stand seeing that extraordinary find pillaged. Yet, I had no idea how to handle this.

The other side of the coin was admittedly more along a personal, if not narcissistic track. If someone found the Cave of the Stars and the lost city, it wouldn't be long before they ended up in that river cavern. Greed is an amazing damned thing. It's the fat, evil demon that lives inside most of us, and no matter how much we feed it, it's never quite enough...

That night, as the half-moon severed the dark clouds and cast shadows across the landscape, a ghostly creature slipped into the river and moved cautiously to the stern of our craft. It slithered up and over the stern railing like a centipede and disappeared.

CHAPTER TWENTY-TWO

It took two days of hot, sweaty, mind-numbing river travel (during which one of us was always awake) to put us within hiking distance of Icabaru. Our captain and his crew had proven to be reliable enough fellows, but I was quite sure they possessed their own fat, evil demons. Eddie paid them in gold coins (some of which we'd acquired during our last adventure in Guatemala, which he'd hidden in the Goose), and we went our separate ways. It was a long hike into town, and upon our arrival, we couldn't resist hitting a bar. We all needed a drink, we needed a vehicle, and most of all, we needed some information.

Well behind us, a shadowy wraith moved from tree to tree, silently blending in with the jungle, offering an occasional, cautious hiss.

Shadow parked himself by the door of the bar while we found seats inside. When the drinks were in our hands, Will turned to us and offered a toast.

"May your favorite liquor and the woman on the barstool next to you always possess your vision of perfection."

"Aaahh," muttered Arturio. "A quote that becomes more true as the night progresses."

After our second round, we were beginning to feel slightly more relaxed and Will struck up a conversation with a fellow next to us — tall, long dark hair, part Indian, hunched over his drink. The guy appeared to be a little above the average clientele, with his weathered but clean blue jeans and a fairly neat khaki shirt. My friend told him we needed a vehicle. The guy shrugged, saying there weren't many around and his wasn't for sale.

Will sat five of Eddie's gold coins on the bar and leaned in. "Are you sure?" he asked.

The fellow picked up a coin and hefted it in his palm, checking its weight. Then he brought the coin to his mouth and bit it with an incisor. He nodded agreeably and offered the closest thing to a smile. Ten minutes later, we owned a "vintage" Land

Rover with a bill of sale written on a napkin.

In the process, I asked, as casually as possible, if anyone had seen Santiago Talla lately. The man looked at me, then glanced at my friends, carefully weighing us. Slowly, he swept up his coins. Not looking at us, he muttered, "Word on the street is, Santiago Talla may have had an accident…" He shrugged. "But some say he is on his ranch. Who knows?" The fellow paused and squinted at us again. "You know, señors, now I don't like you as much as I did before." He suddenly picked up his coins and pocketed them. "I'm gonna go and pretend I never met you."

As the guy walked away, Will muttered, "Wrong question, I guess. But at least we have a vehicle now."

"I like de part about Santiago havin' an accident," said Arturio. "That make me feel all warm inside."

Cody exhaled, somewhere between grateful and hopeful. He held up his drink. "Yeah, I can live with that."

I nodded. "The truth is, man, I know what the witch said just moments before the cliff blew — that Talla was in the cave, admiring his new wealth."

Eddie nodded, already on his third drink. "Here's to scurvy rapscallions who get what they deserve!"

We found a table at the back of the bar and for the next hour or so began to lay out a plan. In one fashion or another, we had to go back to the lost city — if for no other reason than to bring out the emaciated castaway called Slinka. But nobody was fooling anybody here. While Slinka had a sizeable hunk of booty he'd collected — that was all his — it was our team who had found the extraordinary back cavern with its remarkable individual sanctums and all the wealth therein. Finders keepers…

The other issue was, if we brought out Slinka with all his wealth, it wouldn't take two weeks before most of what that guy had was in the possession of attorneys or hookers and the cavern on that river looked like Disney World. I wanted our little friend to be rescued and returned to his family, if we could find them. But honestly, I wasn't quite ready to let the rest of the world know about the mausoleum in the cavern and all its wealth, and I sure as hell didn't want the Cave of the Stars to be dug out and raped. The truth was, I had my own fat, evil demons, and they hadn't been fed lately.

Maybe there was a way of doing this where everyone won a little.

Travis Christian had just arrived home at his stilt house on the back-country side of Big Pine Key. He'd spent three glorious weeks in England with a blond bonny lass who had really pushed all of his buttons. But she was, of all things, a genetic biologist who worked hand-in-hand with the government. And he was an adventurer who played at being employed as a back-country fishing guide.

They had been doing this back-and-forth thing for a year or two now, but neither one of them was really ready to give up who they were or where they were for a full-time relationship. So it was what it was — grand entertainment that might accidently fall off the cliff and become something serious...someday...

After unpacking, Travis pulled a beer from the fridge and checked his answering machine, which had a couple of messages from his friend Kansas regarding a South American adventure and a missing friend of theirs by the name of Shane O'Neal.

Travis was a good friend of O'Neal's as well, and not being there for him struck a nail at the core of his being. He had been out of town once before, a couple of years ago, when an old friend had really needed him. His friend had died in a Guatemalan hellhole called Granja Penal de Pavón, and Travis never forgave himself. This was all too damned familiar.

Within moments he was on the phone to Shane. There was no answer. The big man eased out a hard breath and tried Kansas's number. Again, no answer. When he tried Will and couldn't get him either, he started to worry. Immediately, he placed a call to the office of the South Florida Drug Enforcement Agency in Key West. It was there, through one of his friends, that he learned the scenario — that Shane O'Neal was under protection in an undisclosed place for the time being, and that Will, Eddie, and Kansas were in Venezuela on an undisclosed adventure — that they were somewhere in or near a couple of jungle holes — Santa Elena de Uairén or possibly Icabaru.

Travis sat there for a moment, weighing it all. Then he reached for the phone and called Bobby Branch on Cudjoe.

"Hey, man," he said. "Travis Christian, here." He nodded. "Yeah, you too. It's been a while." After a moment or two of catch-up, he paused. "Listen, I'm gonna need some stuff, Bobby..."

Travis began to list off a few items of minor destruction. Afterwards, he paused. "Bobby," he said with that heavy growl of his. "You've been selling stuff to cowboys for a long time. When was the last time you got to *be* the cowboy?"

During the day, while picking up supplies for the retreat back to Santa Elena de Uairén, we carefully inquired again about Santiago Talla. The answer was the same. No one had seen him. The consensus was that he was either at his ranch, where his people were in the process of branding calves, or he was out of town.

"Son of a bitch is out of town, all right," muttered Eddie. "Playin' poker with the devil."

"Got to hope you're right," said Cody. "But I'm gonna tell you the truth." He paused and glanced around at us. "I need to know..."

We rented rooms at the boarding house in town. Given all that we'd heard regarding Santiago, I felt we'd be safe — at least overnight. That evening, I dressed Eddie's wounds again. The truth was, although he refused to admit it, he was in pretty sad shape. He needed a day off and we needed to find out for certain about our nemesis, Santiago Talla.

The Wild Road to Key West

It was midmorning the next day when Will, Cody, and I headed out on the road to Santiago's ranch. It took some doing, but we managed to talk Eddie into staying in the room he was sharing with Arturio. We left Arturio and Shadow with him.

We knew now that Talla owned 300 acres just west of Icabaru. He had cleared the property and turned it into pasture, the rich jungle soil making good grassland. Santiago raised prime Venezuelan beef in what was, strangely enough, a serious hobby of his.

"I guess you can only steal so many diamonds and shoot so many people before you feel the need for a diversion," muttered Will as we made our way along the road toward the ranch once again.

Fortunately, the compound, as we had learned from our last experience with Santiago, was only about a mile out of town. We had also learned from our DEA friend Shane O'Neal that Santiago had a special crew of *rancheros* — a battery of soldiers and exceptional ranch help he had molded into a living version of the Old West — a constant working version of the American ranch, loyal to him only, like Caesar's praetorian guard dressed as cowboys. They were a living interpretation of Santiago's overactive imagination — the men who managed his cattle, rode horses, and wore six-shooters.

We were also aware, after our last visit, that there was a gate and a guard on the road that led into Santiago's compound. We pulled off on a side road about a quarter mile from the gate. Everyone checked their weapons. The plan was to take the guard or guards at the gate by surprise and get the information we needed — specifically, was Santiago alive or dead? If we didn't get what we needed there, we'd have to work our way into the compound.

We were barely out of our newly purchased Land Rover and organizing our gear when a gruff voice shouted in Spanish, "Halt! One move and you're all dead!" In the next few seconds, we found ourselves surrounded by a half-dozen *rancheros*. One of them, apparently the leader, stepped forward and spoke in passable

English.

"Aaahh, de gringos *mi jefe* is looking for," he said. He smiled — not pretty. "You should be more careful about who you talk to in the cantina."

Cody issued a brief but poignant expletive about overpriced trucks and assholes, then he glanced around and realized the futility of any resistance. Our friend reluctantly dropped his Thompson, then pulled out his .45 and let that fall to the ground. We followed suit. There was no percentage in heroism here, at this moment.

Will looked at me, eyebrows raised. "Santiago?" he mouthed. "Shit! He's alive!"

Ten minutes later, our hands were bound tightly behind our backs and we were being marched into the *jefe's* compound. I could see that the large corrals, some distance from the house, were filled with cattle and the branding pits off to the side had heavy irons stuffed into the glowing coals. Talla's *rancheros* were hard at work. It was a scene straight out of a Clint Eastwood Western.

As we reached the hacienda, we were drawn away from the spectacle by a dark voice that sounded like gravel crunching under a boot. There was Santiago, far too alive to suit my taste, standing on his walk-around veranda. He was dressed in slightly soiled blue jeans, boots, a sweat-stained khaki shirt, and a cowboy hat. He was, evidently, a "working rancher," which I couldn't help but find admirable. His trusty Colt .45 was holstered at his waist — the pistol, we had heard, that he practiced with almost daily.

"You know," he said with a wave of his hand, "you people have become aggravating to me." He pointed out at the branding pits. "I have things to do."

I saw Cody tense up next to me. I stepped on the toe of his boot and he eased up.

Santiago lit the *cigarillo* he had in his hand and blew out a cloud of smoke with a satisfied sigh, then turned back to us. "It is not good for my image, all this running around after you," he grumbled. "Normally, I would just kill you and be done with it, and hang your bodies in a conspicuous place to make my point." He paused. "But it seems, from what my sources tell me, you are somewhat well connected — you and that amigo of yours, the former DEA captain, O'Neal. In my position, this...business of bright stones...I have to maintain a certain decorum with the authorities. Killing connected *Americanos* is not generally good for business."

But at that moment the demeanor fell off and those dark eyes went hard as diamonds. "But I can let no one — *no one* — get away with what you did, trying to kill me," he whispered heavily. "It would be bad for my image."

I thought that he had missed the most salient point — that he had already been trying to kill us. In the blink of an eye, Santiago drew his pistol and put three rounds at our feet, inches from our boots. I hated to admit it, but that was impressive. The guy was fast.

"I would like to kill you," Santiago muttered. He turned for a moment toward the branding pits in the distance, where his *rancheros* were hard at work, then came back to us. "But instead, today you are going to learn a lesson. One that you will remember for the rest of your lives."

I didn't like the sound of that at all.

Cody, as always, was still undefeated. He looked at Santiago. "How did you do it? How did you survive the dynamite and the cave? And how'd you manage to get back?"

Santiago couldn't resist a smile as he holstered his gun. "The priests would tell me that God turned His back for a moment." He shrugged. "I think it's more like the devil saw an opportunity to preserve one of his own. When I got into the cave, I realized I had forgotten my camera. I went back to the helicopter to get it and the cliff fell."

"Your pilot was with you?" I asked.

The diamond boss shook his head. "No, he was inside the cave."

I brought up my hands. "But how did you get back — the helicopter..."

Santiago offered another grim smile. "A long time ago I realized that every person you depend on for your survival makes you weaker. I can fly helicopters. I just like having a pilot." He took one more draw on his *cigarillo*, flipped it into the yard, and turned to us. "And just so you know, I'm going back for what is in that cave. It is mine, gringos, mine!"

Will was listening, but he was caught up in Santiago's previous implication and was staring out at the branding pits. The diamond boss caught him.

"Yes, my friend, you are right," he said with a mirthless stare. "A punishment you can never forget is only fitting in this situation. Something you will wear forever." He offered an ugly grin when Will flinched, realizing for certain what our nemesis had in mind.

"The pain, which is excruciating, is only the first part of it," the diamond boss said. "But the degradation, the shame, is so much more rewarding to me than simply killing you." He paused and glanced again at the branding pits, where his people had just pulled down a heifer and tied her legs. The animal was bawling in fear. The smell of burnt flesh already filled the air as one of the wranglers pulled a red-hot iron brand from the fire — a circle with an "S" in the center.

"You'd be better off to kill me," growled the indomitable Cody. "Because — "

Santiago waved him off. "Yes, yes, I've heard it all before. And yet, here I am." He sighed dramatically. "And here you are, preparing to wear my Circle S brand forever." Then his face went hard as stone. "It is the price you pay!" he cried bitterly. "And you should be on your knees thankful, gringo, that this is the only price!" He exhaled hard and put his hand on the Colt .45 at his side. "Trust me, if it wasn't for your law enforcement connections in the U.S., this would have ended differently."

That afternoon was one of the most painful, humiliating, and shameful moments in my entire life. They took Will first. He tried to be strong and not fight, but in the end, when Santiago's men forced him to the ground and ripped down his pants, exposing his buttocks, he began to yell and twist — not just in fear, but in an anger that rose from the depths of his soul. Nonetheless, they held him firmly, their eyes, and Santiago's eyes, alight with a sadistic, almost carnal delight. When the fiery hot brand touched my friend's flesh, he screamed in fear and pain. I could hear the sizzle for a moment and see the waft of smoke rise...and I can't remember seeing anything more horrible, or macabre, on so many levels.

When they grabbed me, I did no better. I fought and screamed and bawled like a calf as the burning iron ate into my flesh.

True to character, the only one they couldn't break was Cody. He didn't struggle much when they took him over and forced him down to the ground. As hard as it was for him, he knew this was going to happen, regardless of his struggles. The more he fought, the more damage he'd receive, and the less capable he'd be to exact revenge.

As the fiery metal seared him, he groaned in misery, grinding his teeth, but the entire time he stared up at Santiago. And in the end, it was the diamond overlord who broke the stare.

"You Americans," huffed Santiago, standing over us in all our misery. "So arrogant. Sometimes you just have to be brought down a notch or two." He offered an ugly smile. "'Seared' by reality." He brought his head up and threw out a hand dramatically in the direction of the compound gate. "Go now, and don't come back to this country again. Or I *will* kill you!"

At the time the whole thing seemed a bit overdone, and then I realized why...

I caught a few words as he turned to his man and whispered harshly in Spanish, "Take them to their vehicle, then kill them in the jungle. Make it look like a robbery."

I suddenly realized that the last announcement, about letting us leave alive, was just theater. Santiago was simply covering his ass in case the American authorities came back this way. A yard full of witnesses would see us leave alive.

The two men dragged us over to an old pickup and threw us in the back. The pain of even the slightest movement was excruciating and the drive back to our Land Rover was straight out of Dante's Inferno. At that point, Santiago's men unceremoniously pulled us out by our feet and dumped us on the ground. One of them kicked Cody in the back, just because.

There was a part of me that felt like I could just lie there and die. The waves of fiery pain were absolutely inundating. But there was another part of me that was filled with anger, hate…and fear. Fear is one hell of a motivator.

Cody had curled up in a ball on the ground, his hands tucked against his waist, begging not to be killed — oddly out of character for my friend. But it drew one of the guards over — a fairly large man with a pistol tucked into his waist and shoulder-length, Indian-black hair. I knew, at this point, that Cody was going for broke. The man pulled his pistol as he grabbed Cody by the front of his shirt to turn him around before he shot him. But at that moment, even through the excruciating waves of pain he was experiencing, Cody's right hand swept around to his spine where he religiously kept a small stiletto. In a millisecond, he buried it in the throat of his assailant and slashed.

I immediately screamed as loud as I could. It drew the other assassin's attention for a fraction of a second. That was all Cody needed. As the man in front of him dropped to his knees, the life fading from his eyes, Cody snatched the fellow's pistol from his hand and shot the other bandito in the chest three times.

In no time, our incredible friend was on his knees, crawling slowly, painfully, trying to reach the door handle of the Rover. But they had ground the fiery brand into him until it started to cool, and it didn't sear off all the blood vessels. After all the movement, he was bleeding badly. Will was crawling over to him. We were in rough shape, the pain so heinous, it curled around us in suffocating, nearly paralyzing waves.

But at that moment I heard it — the soft hissing sound that Slinka made when he was frightened. At first, I blew it off. It wasn't possible. But there it was again. I glanced around and suddenly flinched. There was Slinka, crouching in the darkness of the jungle about fifteen feet away, those big eyes staring, filled with fright.

I exhaled with relief, shocked by the impossibility of our little buddy showing up here. We didn't need any more bad surprises right now. "Slinka," I whispered. "Help..."

I thought he was going to bolt, and in fact he did, for a couple dozen feet. Then he stopped and turned, sitting on his haunches, as if perhaps seeking out, unearthing, that human part of his being again.

Finally, slowly, he came back to me in that slithering, cautious crouch of his, as my friends watched with incredulousness and hope.

"Water," I whispered, looking over at Cody. "Get the canteens — the water holders, out of the truck."

Our wild friend hesitated, glancing about at the Rover and the dead men, then at the woods, muttering gibberish, his hands moving with fearful jitters. Just when I was sure he was going to run, he turned and went to the cab. Moments later, Slinka had the water. I pulled myself over to Cody and turned him onto his side. I tore off my shirt and soaked it with water. My brave friend gasped in agony as I pulled down his pants and washed his wound, removing as much of the blood as I could.

Will, reaching down and finding that remarkable courage he always possessed, crawled to the vehicle. Slinka followed and helped him pull out our medical kit. We were able to give Cody a shot for pain, then get some antiseptic cream on our friend's wound and cover it with a large adhesive bandage. From there, I went to work on Will, using the same process, grinding my teeth in misery, wanting to throw up from the smell of my own burnt flesh. Most surprisingly, Slinka stayed and helped. He muttered gibberish feverishly, and his hands shook, but he held on.

Finally, Will turned me on my side and dressed my wound in the same fashion. "You're gonna have a big S on your ass for the rest of your life," he muttered, offering a bitter smile. The codeine from his pain shot was starting to come home. "If you're just mildly good in bed, your nickname with the women has gotta be 'Superman' from now on."

"Back at you," I whispered through gritted teeth.

I turned to Slinka, who had performed incredibly well through this. "How did you find us?"

Our little friend, sitting on his haunches in that typical style of so many wild simians, looked at us. "Slinka just follow road." He did that shrug again. "Slinka smell you."

"Whatever works," muttered Will with a smile. "Glad to have you aboard, little buddy."

CHAPTER TWENTY-THREE

There was no staying in town any longer. It wasn't going to take Santiago long to figure out that our demise didn't go the way he had planned. We drove back to the boarding house and got Eddie and Arturio, and, of course, Shadow. The smart thing would probably have been to head back to Santa Elena de Uairén, where we might have a chance of getting out of Venezuela in one piece. But pride and anger are the archenemies of good judgment.

There was a burning in us that couldn't be assuaged by pain cream and Percocet. The more I thought about the shame and the indignity, and recalled that bastard's arrogant smile, the more I wanted to go back. I knew it was stupid, and damned close to suicidal, but I couldn't help it. There are things that keep a man awake at night, and near to the top of the list is a failing courage when it really counted. And I knew I wasn't alone. Besides, we didn't really have to kill his couple dozen employees. We just had to take the head of the snake.

We all wanted payback, no question, but this had been a monster for Cody. A man with his level of pride simply doesn't handle a situation like this well. He could barely walk, and we had to physically stop him from going back immediately.

"Nobody brands me like a goddamned steer!" Cody growled. "Then throws me my hat and tells me to leave. Not now, not ever!"

"We'll make him pay, Cody," I said bitterly. We had all gathered in the late-afternoon shade of the big gumbo-limbo tree just outside the boarding house. "But right now we've got to get out of sight and find someplace safe for the night."

Will stepped in at that moment and reminded us that we had hidden some additional camping gear in the jungle, at our old campsite by the river where we had kept the Goose while looking for the Cave of the Stars. (At the time, we were trying to keep the weight down in the Goose while we did our air search.) It was far enough away to be out of Santiago's sensible search pattern for us (if he was searching) and it would give us a day to recuperate. If we were lucky, our spare radio and the motorcycles might still be there.

It seemed like a good plan...

We had, of course, acquired Slinka in the process — or he had acquired us. I wasn't actually sure how that had fallen. He sat, hunkered down by the Land Rover, nervous to hives but holding on. Nonetheless, he had somehow followed us and had been there to help when we really needed him. As far as I was concerned, that earned him a berth on this wayward voyage. The fact that he had secretly come with us (apparently stowing away in the engine room while eating the last of our canned food, then following us on land), then ultimately helped us in our time of need, was a huge improvement over the edgy, distrustful creature we had first encountered. He was gradually recovering and recalling — becoming human again.

At some point, I was looking forward to finding out who our strange companion actually was, but there was a lot of heavy lifting we had to wade through first.

"Let's be smart for now," I said. "Let's heal for a day so we can do this right and live to tell about it. Let's take a drive and see if any of our equipment is left at the campsite by the river." I held up a finger. "Remember, this isn't just about us; this is about protecting Shane and his family, and our lives, in the future. Don't think for a moment Santiago is gonna forget or forgive." I paused and glanced around at my friends. "This is 'last man standing' shit."

"Okay, okay," said Eddie. "But you know damned well that Santiago's going to move on the Cave of the Stars soon."

I nodded. "Yeah, that might be true. But he's got a problem with that gig — a whole hillside of dirt that he sure can't move himself." I held up a finger. "And if he brings in a team to dig it out, then he's got a brand new problem. I'm guessing he thinks it's safe where it is, for the moment, especially if he thinks we're dead."

Cody nodded, not happy about the decision but aware that it

made sense. He looked at us. "Yeah, but this thing about us being dead is a small window..."

We couldn't have known, but timing was on our side. Santiago was caught up in his yearly branding and the sale of his cattle that were ready for market. He was anxious to get back to the Cave of Stars, but he was the only one, besides the gringos he had branded (and, he assumed, killed) who knew about it. But he hadn't heard from the two men who were supposed to have killed the gringos. That made him a little uncomfortable.

We had Arturio go to the local tack and hardware store and purchase a few blankets and some canned food for us and Shadow — just enough stuff to get us by for a day or so. After that, we'd either be on our way out of there, or we wouldn't be needing any more supplies...

It was a miserably painful ride back to the river, given our seared rear ends. In fact, sitting anywhere was torture. As soon as we parked our Rover by the river, Shadow was out of the door and checking the perimeter, nose up, taking in all the smells, ears perked, listening with the acumen of a war dog. I'd never seen anything quite like him.

Cody caught it too. "Damn, what a fine animal." He looked at me with a slight grin. "You know, I hate to be repetitive, but if you ever..."

I shook my head and couldn't help but smile. "Would you sell your child?"

Cody shook his head. "No, but I've known children who deserved to be sold."

The gods had smiled on us. The equipment we had left hidden near our original campsite was still there. It was the next best thing to a miracle, given what scavengers the local natives were, and we accepted it gratefully. Especially surprising was the fact that our motorcycles were still there, as well. Altogether, we had enough blankets to get our sore asses off the damp ground, and plenty of food to get us by. Along with our medical supplies in the Land

Rover, we could get through the night. Tomorrow, however, was another story. We weren't even sure at this point exactly what we were going to do. All I knew for sure was, we just couldn't walk away.

We spent the last of the day setting up camp and making something to eat. Slinka, surprisingly enough, was beginning to settle down. He helped with firewood and didn't manage a solid freeze when Shadow came over to check him out.

I spent a few minutes speaking with Slinka while we ate some canned stew, and for the first time, he became somewhat communicative. It came in short, tight sentences, as if it was both difficult and painful for him to remember, but he actually spoke of the plane crash — "Big dragon fall out of sky, me in belly, fire and smoke and pain!" Then he suddenly became agitated. "Safren! Safren!" His eyes shut tight and he began to shake.

I did the only thing I could think of. I reached over and put my arms around him. Again, I thought he was going to bolt, with all the trembling he was doing and his eyes darting back and forth. But somehow, the trembling slowed and he began to calm.

"Safren..." he whispered again as I held him. "Safren..."

It was a long night and no one slept well — certainly not with the prospect of going to battle against a vicious jungle warlord and his horde of bandits. But, you know, it was like Cody said: "This ain't the Alamo. The only one who has a genuine vested interest in turning our guts into garters is Santiago Talla. The rest are just paid help." He paused and glanced around at us. "Cut the head off the snake..."

The following day, our branding wounds were starting to scab. Will passed out a couple of pain pills for each of us, and the horrible misery began to abate.

Crazy Eddie caught a glance at me while I was changing my dressing. He took one look at my butt and muttered, "Whoa shit, man! I mean, whooo dang! That's an ugly bitch!" He couldn't help it and laughed at his own joke. "You dudes are serious 'bad-asses.'"

As we gathered around a small breakfast fire, Cody got out our maps and studied them for a few minutes. I saw the corners of his mouth turn up in a slight smile. I knew that smile. It wasn't comforting.

Our friend with the long blond hair, blue eyes, and a cobalt-hard need for revenge, spread out the map on the ground and called us all over.

"I don't think we can go through the front door again with Santiago," he said. "We've played that ace."

Will snorted. "You're right there. That tune ain't on the jukebox anymore."

Cody couldn't help a small grin. He held up a finger. "But I've got an idea. Having studied this map, I see that the river we came in on curves around Icabaru and comes through the back side of Santiago Talla's ranch." He paused for a moment, glancing around at us. "It looks to me like Talla is up to his eyeballs in branding and getting cattle ready for market. His ranch is barely a couple miles downriver from Icabaru. If we could find a boat, we could come in quietly from behind. We keep some straw hats pulled down, dress like the help…" Again he looked at us. "I'm betting we can get close enough to cause a distraction with the last of our dynamite, then put the boy down."

Arturio looked around at us. "This is stupid dangerous, amigos." He paused and a small smile touched his lips. "But I am somewhat fond of stupid and dangerous, eh?"

"You only live once at a time," said Eddie, with a smile of his own.

"There's a small wharf not a quarter mile outside the town," Will said. "I remember seeing a handful of boats there as we came in…"

My buddy glanced over at me and his eyebrows did that Groucho Marx bounce.

Cody glanced around at all of us questioningly. One by one, we nodded.

"Once more, into the fray," I muttered.

CHAPTER TWENTY-FOUR

I sat Slinka down and explained to him that we had to take care of some things; that it was not possible for him to come, but that we would be back before the sun went to sleep. He stared at me and there was a strange new look in his eyes. For the first time, I saw trust in those large, dark orbs — and hope. He still dealt with his demons — at night I could hear him moaning and rambling pitifully, and there was still fear and pain, as well — but he was growing, coming back from the dark place that had claimed him for so long.

He squatted in front of me, looking up like a faithful dog. "You not leave Slinka, please…" he whispered, and there were tears in his eyes. "Not like Safren…"

My eyes welled with tears. He had broken through. He had connected with life again, but in the process, he was remembering and the pain was enormous. If it had been any other situation, I would have stayed with him, but our lives, and his life, were on the line.

I reached out and touched my small, emaciated friend on his arm, and he didn't pull away or run. Slowly, so slowly, his other hand came across and grasped mine, and our eyes held.

"I'll be back for you, my friend," I whispered, emotion choking me. "I promise."

Just before we left, I tied Shadow off to a tree, giving him twenty feet of line. Then I spoke to Slinka once more, telling him to untie Shadow after sunset. To let him be free if for some reason we weren't back…

An hour later, at what was considered the docks of Icabaru, we lucked out and found a crusty-looking old Warao Indian fisherman with a battered but well-maintained twenty-foot-long line boat. He thought two hundred dollars, American, was just right for a day's rental. As the fellow loaded his most precious gear in the back of an ancient pickup and drove away, we went to work. We cautiously unloaded our weapons, which were wrapped in

The Wild Road to Key West

blankets. We had two sticks of dynamite left. Cody had his Colt .45 pistol and an extra magazine. He would have preferred the automatic Thompson, but in this situation, it was impossible to hide.

Will and I still had our 9mm Walther pistols, and Eddie, even with all he'd been through, had preserved his Mossberg short-barreled semi-automatic shotgun. With his shirt out, he could just stuff that down a pants leg.

Arturio had taken a .38 revolver and ammo from one of Santiago's men (who was supposed to have killed us after we'd been branded). All of us were wearing low-attention clothes — cotton shirts and heavy pants or jeans, like the typical ranch worker, and thick-brimmed hats. (The fellow who owned the boat had pointed us to a provisions store in town.)

We pulled out about midafternoon after firing up the old converted Chevy 283 engine — Will at the tiller and the rest of us getting as comfortable as possible on the stained and weathered deck. Neither Will, Cody, nor I could actually sit comfortably, given the painful branding. It was more a matter of leaning to one side.

I could feel the tension in the air and was reminded of a few words by our incredible friend Travis Christian. "Don't let anyone fool you," Travis would say. "Very few people go into a combat situation smiling and eager. Only crazy people are really comfortable with people shooting at them. The only time it's ever tolerable is afterward, with beer."

We got about three-quarters of the way downriver to Santiago's place and pulled up on the shoreline under some big mangroves. They offered shade, but enough airflow to keep the mosquitoes down. We wanted to go in just before sunset, when everyone at the ranch was tired and at a low ebb of attention.

Crazy Eddie leaned back against the gunwale and pulled out the remains of a battered joint. He lit it, took a puff "to steady his tiller," then offered it around. Arturio was his only taker, who took a hit, exhaled heavily, and passed it back. In a few minutes, Eddie, chin on his chest, was snoring.

Cody looked over and shook his head. "We should all be so lucky," he muttered enviously.

Two hours later, it was time. The sun was dropping at the horizon and the shadows were growing lazy and long. We motored the last couple of miles, and when we could see the outbuildings of the ranch, Will took the boat into a small mangrove channel with high ground on the side of the ranch. Ten minutes later, with our sun-browned faces and the hats that we had taken a moment or two to "weather" with a couple of stomps, we were just a handful of Venezuelan *rancheros* working our way back into the ranch compound.

My eyes were instinctively drawn to the branding pits as we entered the actual compound from the pasture side. I still hurt like hell, but right now, pain was taking second place to survival. I also noticed that the main gate to the ranch was open. With the branding and sale of cattle going on, it was obviously too damned inconvenient to have it constantly closed.

Our timing was excellent. Five minutes later, I picked out Santiago, on horseback, coming in from the main pasture. When he reached the hacienda's black, wrought-iron gate and fence, he dismounted. One of his men grabbed the reins and walked the horse back to a hitching post in front of the barn, maybe a hundred yards from the house. There were six or seven saddled horses already tied to the rail.

Cody studied the large open area, which was much like a town square, in front of the hacienda and its components. He glanced at a tack shed on the far side of the square, a little over a hundred yards from the ranch house. It looked like it was closed for the day.

"That would be a good place for an attention-getter," he whispered to Will, glancing at the cotton bag I held with the dynamite in it, then back to Will. "Do you think you can handle that?"

My friend nodded. All of a sudden it had gone serious and he didn't trust his voice not to crack.

"Set about a ten-minute fuse on one stick of dynamite," Cody muttered, not looking at us, his eyes casually surveying the compound, already taking in the weak and strong spots to defend. "That should draw Santiago out and give me a shot at him." He looked at us. "If, for some reason, I don't get that opportunity, feel free to kill the bastard."

He turned to Arturio. "You take a stick of dynamite now, as well. As soon as Santiago is down, you light a very short fuse on that stick of 'bang' and casually throw it somewhere." He smiled savagely. "Confusion is our friend at that point." Cody glanced over at the horses by the barn, then came back to us. "Listen, the idea is to survive this. Once Santiago is down, if it's confusing enough, we can either beat a casual retreat to the boat or take those horses and ride straight out the gate." He turned to Eddie. "You get comfortable over by the barn. Keep an eye on our transportation out that way. We're just covering bases here, because there's a real good chance that nothing will go the way we've planned it."

As I gave Arturio a stick of dynamite stuffed with a small piece of fuse, Cody offered another of those savage smiles. "Just remember who is on your side, and if we all get separated, try to regroup near the front gate, when we've run out of people to shoot or things to blow up, okay?"

One last time my friend turned to Will. I'll always remember him the way he was at that moment — invincible, audacious, and late-night movie brave.

"Now, Will," Cody whispered. "Go set your 'stick of bang' in the tack room and light the fuse — remember, a ten-minute fuse. We'll all wait around here until you come back. Then we'll spread out and prepare for a little mayhem."

If I wasn't nervous before, I was now. I shot a glance at my buddy Will. His eyes mimicked his words. "Be careful, amigo..."

Ultimately, I was amazed by how invisible we were. There were at least fifty people moving in and out of the five-acre compound — *rancheros* finishing up from working and branding cattle (who also doubled as protection), the heavy security (maybe ten to fifteen men) mostly at the front gate and by the back road to the river (which we had stayed away from), and some household staff running errands. Fortunately, most of the little limestone rock cottages for the help were set well away from the functioning part of the compound. Santiago's stately residence was set behind a wrought-iron fence, also about a hundred yards from the actual working compound. We pulled our hats down and tried to remain inconspicuous.

We separated some near the center of the homestead compound but far enough from the tack room to keep from getting splinters when the dynamite blew.

I was trying to stay close enough to Cody to be of help when things got hot. I could still see Arturio, perhaps fifty yards off to my left, looking for a good place to make mayhem with his stick. Eddie was moving toward the barn.

Cody was cautiously moving along the street on the far side of the palisade area, head down, perhaps seventy-five yards from the front of Santiago's home, trying to find a suitable place for a clear shot at his arch enemy, when Santiago stepped out onto his porch and moved casually to the wooden rail, lighting a *cigarillo* and staring out at the low mountains in the distance. It was his custom about this time of the day, although we couldn't have known…

That long blond hair of Cody's stood out, rolling down to his shoulders, even with the hat. Santiago cocked his head and watched for a moment, exhaling smoke through his nostrils like a dragon. In a second his eyes changed — surprised, then hard. His hand instinctively went to the pistol at his side. He turned quickly, slipped back into the house, and grabbed the handset of his two-way radio communications system off the table in the foyer.

A few moments later, Cody Joe was casually turning into an alleyway off the plaza when two big men appeared in front of him. He was already reaching for his pistol when someone stepped up behind him and the lights went out. By the time I turned into the alley, all I caught was a glimpse of Cody being lugged away.

The tack store was already closed for the day, but Will had managed to jiggle the lock and light his "attention-getter" with a ten-minute fuse. He was headed back toward the barn and corral when he saw two big guys dragging an unconscious Cody across the compound toward Santiago's ranch house.

"Shit," he whispered, instinctively pulling back against the wall of a blacksmith shop. "This is not good." He exhaled hard. "Damn, damn, damn," he hissed. "I should have listened to my mother. I could have been a rich dentist, fixing people's teeth instead of knocking them out!" He quickly glanced around, but none of his team was in sight. Suddenly, he saw Arturio, standing beside a small dry goods store for the *rancheros.* Arturio's eyes said that he, too, had seen what happened. They casually drifted toward each other.

Eddie, the most innocuous of us all — his long hair, bandaged arm, and straw hat giving the impression of an old, down-on-his-luck cattleman — had avoided any attention. He was down by the barn, but he could see that something was going on. Many of the security people in the compound were moving in the direction of Santiago's place. "That ain't good," he muttered, as he reached down and felt the reassuring solidness of his sawed-off shotgun inside his pants leg.

Cody awoke to a painful buzzing in his head. It took him a moment to realize that he was laid out on the wide front porch of a large home. The bandit diamond boss was standing over him, accompanied by a couple of his well-armed men. One of the men bent down and slapped Cody across the face a couple of times. That got his attention. Our friend was just getting his bearings when Santiago eased over and squatted in front of him. He patted Cody on the cheek.

"Who are you?" he said. "You have destroyed my property, killed my men, and even when I send my people to kill you, here you are again and they are gone." He held up a finger. "I don' like this. Are you American law enforcement, like that annoying Señor O'Neal?"

Cody didn't see much point in lying. "No, we're not. We're just people who don't like you. We don't like anyone who tries to steal what we have, or kill us."

The big man kneeling over Cody chuckled darkly. "You would not be the first to dislike me." He paused. "What is your name? I always like to know the name of someone I'm going to kill."

Again, Cody saw no gain in lying. "Cody. William Cody."

Santiago's eyebrows furrowed. "Cody…hmmmm, Cody… Is that not the name of a famous western *Americano* gunman?" he asked. Before our friend could reply, Santiago said, "Yes, William Cody — a renowned gunman and buffalo hunter…"

Cody nodded, "Yeah…okay…" he said as he eased himself into a sitting position.

"Aahhh," muttered Santiago, appearing somewhat pleased with this revelation. "A distant relative of an *Americano* Western gunman…" He pursed his lips, then slapped the Colt .45 he wore on his hip. "Perhaps you have used a Western six-gun, huh, amigo?"

Cody shrugged. He didn't see the need to mention that he was quite good with a six-gun.

"Well," announced the diamond lord. "I am going to take that as a yes." He paused for a moment, then shook a finger at Cody. "By all rights, I would just kill you now, because you have caused me too much trouble. But I say, I will give you a chance." He paused and smiled. "How about we have an American Western gunfight? You and me? If you win and shoot me, I give you your life. I will tell my men not to kill you." There was a brief exchange of words in a local Indian language between Santiago and the half-dozen well-armed men on the porch. But from the looks in their eyes, Cody was pretty damned certain there was no real clemency in that conversation.

"But if I win…" Santiago held out his hands, palms up, the conclusion being obvious.

"Better than a sharp stick in the eye," said Cody, with a sense of grim humor.

"Hah!" chuckled the Venezuelan gangster. "I like that! I will use it after you're gone!" Then he turned to one of his men and rattled off a few words in the local language again. The guy went into the house, and a moment later, returned with a holster and a six-gun. Santiago took the gun, opened the cylinder, and punched out four of the six rounds. He looked up at Cody. "I want you to have a chance — but I don't want you shooting too much. Two bullets should be enough for a man named Cody."

Santiago slid the gun into the holster and tossed it to Cody. Then he smiled. "This should be interesting, no, amigo?"

CHAPTER TWENTY-FIVE

I stood among the growing audience outside the diamond lord's wrought-iron fence, my hand on the Walther 9mm in my belt. Santiago's men began forcing the crowd back out into the plaza to make room for the gunfight. As we were being shuffled away from the fence, I could see Will working his way through the crowd toward me, and Cody buckling on a holster on Santiago's front porch.

As my friend eased up next to me, I asked, "You're okay, huh?"

He nodded.

"The big bang at the tack shop is still on schedule?"

Will nodded nervously once more. "Yeah, it's on." He pointed toward the main house, where we could see Santiago and Cody surrounded by a number of nasty-looking folks. "What's happening here?"

"A gunfight, I think."

"Should we interrupt it?" Will asked.

I shrugged. "I don't know yet. We'll play it by ear. One thing is for damned sure; if this turns out to be a genuine gunfight, we're going to try to keep it fair."

As the sun began to slip across the horizon, casting brilliant yellows and reds into the pale-blue evening sky, the two contestants rose and marched out through the courtyard just beyond the wrought-iron fence. They stopped and nodded harshly, then began to back away from each other, their eyes locked in an ancient ritual as old as time — an amalgam of courage, enmity, and power, to be sealed in blood. It was, like it or not, the nexus of our planet's most basic element — the right and the transfer of power. It applied to everything on earth, from hummingbirds to elephants, and it came down to four words: *Only the strongest survive.*

They slowed and stopped about thirty feet apart, as if by some intuitive command.

The Wild Road to Key West

Santiago offered a nervous smile. "It is time, gringo," he growled. Then, without another word, he drew surprisingly fast.

Cody flinched as Santiago's round clipped his right earlobe, but Santiago was knocked backward by the impact of Cody's bullet to his chest. (Our buddy had done this far more times than he let on.) The bandito dropped to his knees, gasping, his gun falling from his hands and tumbling into the dirt. But the first thing we all noticed was the lack of blood. The jungle gangster had just taken a round to the chest...and he wasn't bleeding. Cody, who had shot this man before (without the desired effect), figured it out immediately. Santiago had donned his bulletproof vest earlier in the day, just in case...

A couple of Santiago's men drew their weapons. But before either Will or I could get our guns up, there was the brutal roar of a shotgun. The two bandits were slammed backward by the blast, and there were screams and yells from the surrounding crowd as they fell back in panic.

There stood Eddie, his bandaged head held high, the barrel of his Mossberg still smoking.

I looked at Will and we stepped forward, our weapons drawn, covering our friend.

A split second before Cody pulled the trigger again, Santiago, still on his knees, screamed, "No! Stop!" He stared at Cody and slowly brought out his hands. "You can't shoot me — an unarmed man..." The bandit, still gasping from the pain of being slammed by a high-caliber bullet, drew a breath. "An unarmed man!" he cried again, nodding at his gun in the dirt next to him. "It's against your code — the code of the Old West!"

Cody paused just a fraction at those words, and I could see a bold, crafty light ignite in Santiago's eyes. Given this degree of encouragement, he almost smiled.

"You can't shoot a man without a weapon..." Then he suddenly turned to his men in the torch-lit crowd. "Kill him!" he cried. "Shoot him!"

At that moment, the air went heavy and everything fell quiet. The truth was, not many of Santiago's men really liked him (except for some of his *rancheros*) and more than one of them had been lightly branded for transgressions.

"Kill him!" yelled Santiago again, an octave higher.

But now, even the diamond lord's few bodyguards hesitated.

Finally, one stepped forward and drew his weapon. Arturio, who had cleverly come up from behind and to the side, shot him. I nailed the one that came up from behind Arturio. That pretty much did away with the opposition's enthusiasm. The remainder of Santiago's men were shifting uncomfortably in the torchlight. Even though they outnumbered us, they had begun pulling back into the shadows, their eyes bouncing nervously from side to side, no longer certain how many of us there were or whether this situation was worth dying for.

Cody stared at his adversary for a moment and his hand holding the gun seemed to falter, the barrel lowering slightly.

The diamond boss exhaled the breath he'd been holding. Still kneeling, he whispered, "You see? You can't..."

His eyes shifted for a millisecond to the pistol by his leg.

"Go ahead," said Cody. "It's the best deal you're gonna get."

But at that moment there was the sound of weapons discharging, horses thundering, and men shouting. I looked up to see about twenty of Santiago's *rancheros* charging into the complex. This was the group of soldiers that the diamond lord had molded into a living version of the Old West — loyal to him only. These were the extraordinary men who managed his cattle, rode horses, wore six-guns, and satisfied Santiago's slightly twisted imagination. I knew then that Santiago must have contacted them by radio when he first spotted Cody in the compound.

The gunshots and confusion drew Cody's attention for a fraction of a second. The eyes of the big man in front of him went bright and hard as he snatched at the gun.

Cody brought his pistol up and pulled the trigger. But as he did, a round from one of the rancheros clipped him in the ball of his shoulder. It knocked him back and his bullet slammed the dust where Santiago had just been.

The charge of the *rancheros* put Santiago's people back on

their feet. The tide was turning. Nobody wanted to end up on their boss's bad side. They'd seen that movie. Besides, it looked like there were only a handful of gringos.

Somehow, through the smoke and the dust, we all managed to find each other. But it wasn't looking good. Eddie was already beat to hell from previous engagements with crashed airplanes. Arturio had been nicked in the thigh and was bleeding more than he liked (with no money being at stake). Cody, Will, and I had torn open our branding wounds, and the backs of our pants were red with blood, and now Cody had a superficial shoulder wound. Nonetheless, Cody Joe yelled at us like an old sergeant in a beach assault, waving at us to follow him.

We needed to get out of the courtyard complex and among the smaller buildings that served as storage and shops for the people in Santiago's employ. With the reinforcement of the *rancheros*, the last of Santiago's personal guards had grown bolder. Bullets were zinging off the lime plaster of the small buildings as we ducked and rushed through the narrow alleyways. I looked up for a moment and saw the tack shop, about seventy-five yards in front and to the right of us, on the main artery of the compound.

Will, only a few yards away, saw me glance at the mass of *rancheros* and bodyguards charging into the honeycomb of small structures, spreading out in a half-circle and headed our way. At the lead was Santiago.

In the other direction, I could see two pickup trucks full of armed men coming into the compound. They must have been outer perimeter security. Now, it really felt like the Alamo.

Our only chance was to try to make it to the jungle that surrounded the back side of the compound, but that was beginning to look like a fool's errand as well.

At this point, as we huddled against the wall of a small cantina, Arturio pulled out our final stick of dynamite and a match. He turned to us. "Go!" he cried. "Go! All of you! Run through the alleyways for the jungle!" He exhaled hard, then offered us a grim smile. "I will stay…and discourage them for a few moments…buy a little time…"

Bullets were slapping the white plaster around us — the limestone shrapnel stinging our flesh like angry bees. We could hear the shouts of our pursuers growing closer and we were all nearly out of ammo.

"Just light the damned thing and throw it at them," shouted Cody over the din. "You're part of the team and we're not leaving you behind. We're not leaving anyone behind!"

Arturio paused for a moment, staring at Cody. There was a strange look on his face.

"Damned right!" Eddie cried over the noise. "You're one of the 'Hole in the Coral Wall Gang' now! We don't leave our people!"

At that moment, for perhaps the first time since I'd known him, I saw the lights come on in Arturio's eyes. It always seemed as if he was simply floating in the stream with no real connection. It wasn't that he didn't do what he had to do, but there just wasn't a lot of commitment. Nothing to win, nothing to lose... But suddenly, I saw a small flame of passion, of connection in his gray eyes, as if maybe he finally belonged to something more than a smoky barroom, a bottle of tequila, and a pistol.

"I be right back," he said, as he struck the match on the wall next to him and lit the short fuse on the dynamite stick in his hand.

There was no stopping him. With a final smile and a soft, *"Adios, amigos,"* Arturio turned and bolted toward the enemy trucks coming into the compound. Using the buildings for protection at first, then zigzagging wildly in the open as he tried to get within throwing range, he danced through the fusillade of bullets slapping the dirt around him like a quarterback going for the winning touchdown. At the last minute, he threw the deadly red stick at the approaching pickups. But I saw him recoil then as a round hit him, and he collapsed.

The driver in the lead truck realized what was happening and tried to swerve away, but he was too late. The explosion threw the vehicle onto its side, tossing its occupants out like ragdolls. The other truck screeched to a halt, its occupants tumbling out but not altogether anxious to take on a group that was throwing dynamite sticks.

In the next moment, Will was headed toward Arturio at a run. I don't know why, but I suddenly found myself behind him while bullets zinged by us like angry wasps. In moments we had Arturio up, his arms over our shoulders, and we were stumbling back toward our friends — whose situation, truthfully, offered very little improvement over our own.

We careened back to the whitewashed stucco walls of our cantina enclave and quickly checked Arturio's injuries. At that point, I was beginning to think the guy possessed some sort of serious juju. For all the firing at him, he had only taken a single wound to the shoulder — the one that knocked him off his feet. But he was bleeding badly.

"This is seriously harshin' my mellow," muttered Eddie, as he pushed his last rounds into his Mossberg. "I could be home, tellin' lies and gettin' high." He huffed angrily.

I glanced at Will as we all crouched against the stucco walls, and somehow, my old buddy managed a smile. "It's not an adventure worth telling if there aren't any dragons," he whispered with a battered grin. "Imagine the wonder in the barmaid's eyes when we're telling this story…"

A few rounds struck the corner of the building just above our heads, bringing us back to the vivid present. We ducked, and Arturio, sitting with his back against the wall, blood running down his chest, wheezed and held up a forefinger.

"I'm getting paid extra for this," he grunted. "I just want you to know ahead of time."

The enemy was moving down from Santiago's residence and the surviving men from the trucks had grouped together. They, too, were headed our way from the other direction.

We were trapped and everyone knew it.

A moment later, I ran out of ammunition, and seconds after that, I heard Eddie toss his shotgun aside with a brief expletive and pull out his pistol. Will was already out of ammo. Cody was down to a few rounds in his pistol.

"I'm not gonna wait here while they come to shoot me," he

huffed. William J. Cody stood and stared at us, those cobalt eyes of his on fire. "It's been a pleasure, my friends, and an honor..."

But as my friend turned and we stumbled to our feet to go with him, the strangest thing happened. I heard the sound of rotor blades... And only seconds behind that, the gruff roar of a big machine gun.

At that moment, a helicopter rolled over us and chewed up the territory our assailants were holding in front of our position. I couldn't help it. I staggered out into the street with Cody right behind me. And there was one of the most beautiful sights I've ever seen. It was a Huey — the old American standby for several unpleasant wars. Given the situation, it might as well have been an angel. The side doors were open, and inside was an older, Vietnam version of a tripod-mounted M-60 machine gun, roaring away, those heavy rounds making mincemeat of our pursuers. As the helicopter banked, the guy behind the gun spotted us and waved.

"Son of a bitch," muttered Eddie. "That's Bobby Branch, from Cudjoe Key!" He held up a clenched fist. "Freakin' rapturous, man! Totally radical!"

Santiago couldn't believe it. He had the gringos cornered like mice and at the last minute, this bat from hell appears! He and his remaining men ran for the cover of the closest building — the tack shop — using the roof for cover, pressing their backs against its walls as they reloaded.

We watched what was happening through the smoke and dust, crouched down against the wall of a battered, bullet-pocked storage building of some sort. I glanced at the tack shop down the street, then turned to Will and raised an eyebrow, my palms out. "I thought you said ten minutes?"

He shrugged. "Ten minutes, twelve minutes — it's not exactly a science," he whispered harshly. "Anytime now, I would imagine."

It was then, as if the gods had heard his words, that the walls of the tack shop suddenly seemed to puff out and disintegrate in an oxygen-sucking explosion. At the same time, the roof rose, then collapsed in a fiery blast. The last image I remember of Santiago Talla was that of a very surprised and disappointed man...

A few moments later, after Santiago and the better part of his henchmen had ridden off to Hell, we brushed the powdered lime dust off of ourselves and I heard Will whisper, "There will always be a special place in my heart for dynamite."

Will's well-placed explosion and the helicopter above us (which was sawing up the last of the resistance) pretty much put a cap on the party. The few *rancheros* that were left had begun to make a run for the jungle. Everyone else had long since fled the inner compound and locked themselves inside their homes.

Five minutes later, as the helicopter was setting down, I finally got a look at the pilot — the big shoulders, the long dark hair...

"Travis Christian," I muttered somewhere between awe and disbelief. "Travis freaking Christian!" I shook my head. "This just doesn't happen in real life," I whispered incredulously. "It's like in the freakin' movies!"

Will got quiet for a moment and his eyes caught a strange glint. He held up a finger, his lips pursed in a small, curious smile. "We've had this conversation before," he said. "But I'm gonna say it again, because it deserves to be said." My friend took a breath. "The gods don't always smile on everyone all the time, but some of us are simply card-carrying members of 'the good luck club.'" He shrugged. "Maybe we did a few things right when they needed to be done in some other time and place, and we're getting interest on that investment now. I don't know for sure. But I do know that fortune is a capricious but wonderful bitch on occasion."

Will paused and looked at me. "Kansas, have you forgotten how many times the Big Guy upstairs has touched us? There's no bloody reason in this world why we should even be here, but we are! Let me tell you something once again...three-quarters of the people in the world would listen to this conversation and say it's bullshit. That things like this just don't happen; that it's B-movie stuff. But one-quarter — the incredibly lucky, the right-timers who cautiously stepped out of foxholes still alive when all the blood had been spent; the pilots who crashed airplanes and walked away without a bruise; the sailors who watched their ships hammered to death on coral reefs and somehow floated into shore on a shattered mast — they would listen to this and smile." He held up his finger again. "Because they know that there's somebody above all this madness who throws those damned bones!" Will got that big grin of his. "Now, let's go over and greet our buddies like the freakin' gift from the gods that they are!"

A few moments later, Travis Christian and Bobby Branch had dropped their winged chariot into the remains of Santiago's plaza and we were hugging our guardian angels like the winning team at the World Series.

Finally, I stepped back. "How? How in God's name did you find us?"

The smart thing to do would have been to hold that question until we were a few miles away, but I couldn't help myself.

Travis glanced around at the cobblestone square and the buildings surrounding it — all absolutely devoid of life. There was simply no resistance left and there probably wasn't a living antagonist for a quarter-mile radius. It wasn't the smart thing to do, but we were all riding an adrenalin high at that point — we were kings of the moment.

Our big friend pointed to a small cantina across the street, which still seemed to be intact. "I could use a drink," he said. "Let's get out of the open, just in case there's any of the opposition left about. We'll dress our wounds and I'll explain. Then we're out of here."

We found a table and Will found some beers. Travis got that rare, wry grin of his, and began his story, with Bobby Branch interjecting the parts that Travis probably wouldn't have mentioned.

In a nutshell, Travis explained that when he realized the situation while he was back in the Keys, and thanks to his contact at the DEA, he called a buddy of his out of Miami who served as one of the major liaison officers for humanitarian aid to South America via U.S. military donations — most of it done through large cargo aircraft on fairly regular flights out of Homestead Air Force Base, and generally into U.S. military installations within South America. Travis explained the rather unusual situation to his friend and the officer agreed to help him.

What Travis didn't bother to mention was that his liaison officer friend, Colonel Max Trand, had done a stint in Vietnam about fifteen years earlier. He was a young lieutenant then, who found himself, and what was left of his squad, lost in the jungle and pursued by a company of North Vietnamese regulars. He had run out of tricks and half of his men were wounded. Just when he was sure that his time on this planet had come to an end, an angel appeared in the sky just above the treetops in the form of a Huey (HU-1A) helicopter, and his radio squawked.

"This is Captain Travis Christian," the angel said. "It looks like you could use a ride home. A quarter click due east of your position, there's a clearing. Get your ass over there. I'll annoy Charlie while you make your way."

The damned guy in that helicopter and his gunner took on the pursuing NVA company, chewing them up and forcing them to dig in for a few precious minutes while Lieutenant Trand and his men made it to the landing zone. Then the angel named Travis Christian dropped in next to them, the falling sun creating misty beams of light through the nearly fifty bullet holes in the helicopter, and took them home.

If Travis Christian needed a ride on one of his aircraft, you could damned well bet he could have it. Anytime. Anywhere.

Travis reminded his old friend that he knew this effort was a non-authorized rescue mission, and he would understand completely if it was out of the colonel's ability.

"Yeah, yeah," said the colonel, waving him off. "Take a break, smoke a cigarette. I'll see what I can do."

Two hours later, Colonel Trand had lined up a ride on a McDonnell Douglas C-9 headed out of Homestead AFB for Caracas the following day.

From there, it just got better.

When Travis and his buddy, Bobby Branch, landed in

Caracas, an American captain in a military Jeep was waiting for them. With a minimal amount of conversation, he took them to a small, American-controlled air facility about twenty miles from the airport. An hour later, a somewhat weathered but very serviceable Huey helicopter landed. The pilot shut it down, disembarked, and walked over to Travis.

"The keys are in the ignition," he said with a wry smile. "I know your reputation. Try to bring it back in one piece, okay?" Then he turned and walked away.

Bobby Branch stood there, open-mouthed, as the guy walked to the parking lot and got into a nondescript black car, which immediately drove away. He glanced over to the big copter with the M-60 mounted just inside the cabin door. He turned to Travis. "Who the hell are you?"

CHAPTER TWENTY-SIX

Needless to say, it was a joyous reunion, and we had a few more questions, but we had wounds to take care of. Cody needed a couple of butterfly bandages for the bullet slice on his shoulder. Arturio had been winged in his thigh, just barely into the flesh, but he had also taken a through-and-through just above his collarbone while throwing dynamite at the pickup trucks. Neither was life-threatening, but they would make for a miserable couple weeks of healing. Eddie wasn't shot, but he was bruised, banged up, and worn out, and we had to clean and rebandage his airplane-crash injuries.

Will, Cody, and I all needed attention for our branding wounds, which had lost most of their scabbing and were bleeding again.

In the interim, Bobby and Travis gave us more details about their trip, explaining that it was the DEA that had given Christian the co-ordinates to Santiago Talla's property, as well as some aerial photos of the layout of the ranch and the hamlet around it. Without that, and the magically appearing helicopter, none of this would have happened.

One thing was for sure — Travis Christian had some serious friends…

Before darkness set in completely, I glanced around at my companions, then turned to Travis. "How about a lift?" I said. "I have a dog and a…friend…I have to pick up."

We quickly dismantled the machine gun and stowed it on the inside of the helicopter. It would have been a bit intimidating for any civilian business. Then we all piled in and headed back to our camp by the river, well to the west of town.

Travis found a sandbar by the river on which to land, and when the blades quit rotating, I was out the doors, calling. But there was no answer. Shadow had developed this loud, deep whine when he saw me or wanted my attention. I listened carefully as I splashed through the shallow water from the sandbar to the shore, but there was nothing.

Then I called for Slinka.

Still nothing...

By the time I reached our camp, I was freaking out. I knew it had been a gamble to leave them, but I didn't have any choice. Neither of them would have done well in the turmoil of what we'd just been through. Perhaps Shadow might have been okay, but someone would just as likely have shot him.

Unfortunately, now both of them were gone.

When the others found me, I was nearing full-fledged panic. I suddenly realized that I was really attached to that dog, and damned if I hadn't come to find an odd appreciation for that strange little creature who had suffered some sort of major trauma and had managed to rise above it enough to help us when we needed it. He was gradually returning to being human again.

We began to spread out and call. I took the battered road toward town. I had only been walking for a few minutes, already beginning to imagine the scenarios that come to mind, when I spied a figure in the distance coming toward me through the darkening river mists. It was moving slowly, carefully, crouched slightly — thin and angular with disheveled hair. Slinka!

I broke into a smile and cried out to him. Immediately, I saw him relax and begin to move more quickly in my direction. When Slinka reached me, he did the strangest thing. He knelt and put his arms around my legs. "Ooohooo..." he muttered. "Slinka so glad you come back for him." He looked up at me, his huge eyes rimmed with tears. "Slinka don' wanna be alone anymore..."

I knelt down and held that fragile, thin frame of his, pulling him in against me. "You'll never be alone again, Slinka," I whispered, realizing I was committing myself to making his life okay. And somehow, it seemed right to do so.

But at that moment, I heard something else coming down the trail — fast. The dark silhouette burned through the mist ahead, and after these last few weeks, my first instinct was to reach for my pistol.

Then I recognized that shape — that large head and full chest, those lean haunches... Shadow!

My boy hardly slowed down as he screeched up to us, throwing himself up at me as I knelt, his paws against my chest, his muzzle burying into my neck.

I had forgotten. After all these years without the company of a friend like him, I had forgotten. I had cast aside the memory of what it was like to feel the honest affection of a creature who had nothing to gain from your company but the pleasure of the experience, and wanted nothing tangible back but the love he or she traded for yours.

There were tears in my eyes as I knelt and held my dog, and he made that little whine in his throat while that heavy, wet tongue found my face and neck. I was suddenly reminded of the expression by the great writer and humorist, Will Rogers: *"If there are no dogs in Heaven, then when I die, I want to go where they went."*

We knew it wouldn't be long before the authorities picked up on this whole affair. In twenty-four hours this place would be crawling with Venezuelan law enforcement. We decided to make a run for Santa Elena de Uairén. We could hole up there for a day and get organized, then Travis could fly us into Caracas, return his helicopter, and we could catch our collective breath in one of the small outer towns, like Cuidad Caribia or Maiquetía, for a few days, find a doctor, and lick our wounds.

Needless to say, it was somewhat of a challenge getting Slinka on a helicopter. There was a lot of yelling and thrashing in the beginning, but our little friend, feet tied, finally accepted his fate, muttering viciously about being swallowed by a "giant whirlybug." Other than that, the trip to Santa Elena went smoothly. The little town was just as we had left it. In fact, when we set the copter down and the blades quit turning, there was the same grubby little guy and his gorilla-like buddy, asking if we wanted them to watch the helicopter overnight "for a very reasonable price."

I explained that we had used their services before. Travis glared at both of them. (Even the gorilla wilted under my friend's hard, green eyes).

Finally, Travis shrugged. "See you tomorrow morning," he said, then turned and walked off.

We followed.

It had been a long few days. We had a couple of drinks at Arturio's favorite bar. There were no takers that night for Russian roulette, thank God. (We'd seen all the shooting and blood we could deal with for a while.) An hour later, we were in our respective rooms and were sound asleep. Shadow bunked with me.

We made it to Caracas by noon the following day and rented a seven-passenger van. Then, Travis returned his helicopter. There was still some of our collective blood on the floor and a few bullet holes here and there.

"Once a cowboy, always a cowboy," muttered the taciturn officer who had given our friend the copter. He shrugged. "Actually, given all I've heard about you, it's in better shape than I expected."

We spent the afternoon at a doctor's office, getting inspected, injected, sewed, and patched. Then Cody found a motel, we all found rooms, and slept for twelve hours.

The following day, we realized there were some things we needed to resolve, not the least of which was our strange little companion, Slinka. The first thing I did was get him a bath and a haircut. Then Will and I went out and bought him some clothes, which he donned with a degree of uncertainty but cautious appreciation. Surprisingly enough, under all that dirt and matted long hair was a fairly good-looking guy, although he was somewhat emaciated. He still carried that cautious crouch and his eyes still constantly shifted.

Will saw me looking at my small friend apprehensively.

"Some things take time," he said, and put his hand on my

shoulder.

I guessed Slinka's age at about nineteen or twenty. There was no way to determine how long he'd been in the jungle. When I asked, he just shrugged.

"Sun go up, sun go down. Sun go up, sun go down..."

The next thing I did was find the largest newspaper in Caracas. Then Will and I paid a visit to the managing editor. I explained our situation to him and needless to say, he was fascinated by it. (Primarily because it represented a great human-interest article — a guy survives alone in the middle of the jungle for God knows how many years...)

Pablo, the editor, had been with the paper for quite a while, and he vaguely remembered the disappearance of an aircraft the better part of seven years ago. We spent the next hour researching their old papers for stories about airplane crashes. Sure enough, Pablo found it. In 1982, there was a flight from Boa Vista, in Northern Brazil, to Caracas, that disappeared in a vicious summer storm. Pablo was a true newspaper man — he loved a great story. He became like a terrier after a rat. From his archives, he found the papers from that time and the related articles.

Once we were pretty sure we had the flight, Pablo called the Venezuelan FAA office and had a manifest faxed over.

As it turned out, there were eighteen people on the DC3 that left from Boa Vista, the capital of the Brazilian state of Roraima, in the northwestern quarter of the country. I estimated Slinka's age at about twenty. Doing a little rough calculating, I figured there were only two people on Flight 703 in that age group — a fifteen-year-old and a seventeen-year-old. They were brothers. The boys, Slinkan and Safren Losado, were flying into Caracas, then on to the island of Aruba off the coast of Venezuela to spend a few weeks with a rich uncle who lived there.

"*Slinkan!*" Will muttered incredulously, staring at me.

"*Slinkan!*" I repeated.

We had found him! My God! The kid was only fifteen years old when the plane crashed. Somehow, only God knows, he survived the crash. I'd heard of things like this happening — a single survivor in the right place at the right moment, or just simply held in the hands of a greater power. Who knew? Nonetheless, it was true. Also, from the article it appeared that the search authorities had incorrectly estimated the flight path of the plane in the storm, way too far to the west, and that hadn't helped rescue efforts.

Apparently, Slinkan's brother had either died in the crash or shortly thereafter. It was all just too much for a fifteen-year-old, slightly pampered child to handle, and reality eventually slipped away. It was a miracle that he survived at all. But I suspected that the native who helped us — the one whose son Cody had saved — or someone like him, might have been influential because I had heard Slinkan mumbling from time to time about the one "painted face" who left him food.

We couldn't have known, but it was Tabo who found the battered and totally distraught child hiding in a cave, just inside the "Forbidden City." For no other reason than good people come in all colors and social dispositions, Tabo brought him food in the beginning — lizards and monkeys baked on coals, and fruit. But that was Tabo's secret, because the priests saw the crash — the falling sky demon — as a sign of evil. And by the sheerest of remarkable coincidence, it was forbidden to enter the old ruins. The legends told of an evil that killed all who had lived in the canyon city.

So, Slinkan Losado didn't exactly prosper, but he did manage to survive. The only real casualty was his mind...and it wasn't long before his brother began to visit him.

All that aside, the one thing we knew for certain now was that Slinkan Losado had a family somewhere in Brazil who was in for a wonderful surprise.

I promised the editor an exclusive on the story and asked for one final favor — we needed the address and phone number of the Losado family in Boa Vista, Brazil.

My phone call to the Losado family was met with disbelief and some umbrage. The family was fairly wealthy. They owned a small rum distillery and raised sugarcane. Over the years, and especially in the beginning, they had dealt with numerous people trying to extort money, claiming to know the location of their son, and commercial psychics assuring them that they could "see" their lost child.

They tried working with some at first, but it always proved futile, and their disappointment eventually morphed into bitterness. It was only when I put Slinkan on the phone that everything changed. The family immediately chartered an aircraft and five hours later, we met with them.

We were in the lobby of our motel. Slinkan was standing by the desk, Will and I next to him, when a well-dressed but definitely apprehensive man and woman entered.

It began with disbelief because Slinkan had changed greatly after enduring six years of jungle survival. He was thin as a rail, gaunt, his posture was bent, and he bore scars from the crash and the mistakes he'd made. His hair, although trimmed, was still unmanageable, his eyes frightened and wide. But it was his mother who slowly stepped forward and whispered his name, as if it was a magical, impossible plea to the gods. She stared at him, and it was then that the world stopped turning for a moment.

"Slinkan?" she asked, wanting more than anything for this dream not to end; to not wake up breathless and crying again. She stood there for another moment, then held out her arms and whispered again, "Slinkan…"

Suddenly, the lights seemed to come on in the young man's eyes. Tears welled and he choked on the emotion rising within him as the shattered memories began to flood back. He took a ragged, uncertain breath and stepped forward, then took another step. "Mama?" he croaked. "Mama…"

In the next second, the family was embracing, sobbing with joy and struggling to accept the impossible, but thanking God for the gift.

There were tears in Will's eyes, as well as mine.

"There's a serious bone from the gods," my friend croaked.

I could only nod, afraid that my voice would crack.

The reunited family embraced each other for a few moments,

the parents muttering words of endearment and assuredness, and Slinkan struggling to digest it all. Finally, when the passion ebbed, Slinkan gently pulled away and turned to Will and me. Slowly, he walked over to us, then he lifted his arms and came into ours. No words were necessary. We just held each other for a few moments, tears in our eyes. Finally, our little friend whispered, "Slinka never forget…never forget…"

At that moment, we let him slip from our arms. I stammered that Will and I would be back in a few minutes, and we left the family to their own private miracle.

EPILOGUE

Within a week, Slinkan had made incredible strides. At our request, his family found a motel and spent some time getting to know their son again. I know it wasn't my place, but I felt somewhat responsible for the strange little guy. I wanted to be certain that he was going to be well cared for and accepted, and that he was happy. I needed to know who his parents were and what they were like, for more reasons than one. Slinkan had a fortune in gold and gems hidden in that cavern in the jungle, and I didn't want him to be taken advantage of at any point. Toward that end, we had a private detective run a report on the young man's parents.

They came back solid — they had lots of money, were well respected in their community, and appeared to be head-over-heels happy about having their son back.

Speaking of fortunes, we had decided to leave the huge mausoleum find in the cavern by the river where it was for now. The gold, gems, and artifacts were completely safe for the time being. All the bad people involved in our pursuit were dead. Besides, we weren't really equipped for an extraction of that nature at this time. We were all in rough shape from our recent adventures. And, as far as that particular find went, we all felt that there was a huge amount of important archaeological and societal value there. Imagine a tribe of Indians who were somehow infused by a group of people that offered them a unique understanding of life, death, the distant stars, and God (not *gods*). At some point, with the right professional people, that unique cemetery might offer some significant insights.

And the truth was, collectively, we'd had all the adventure we could handle for a while. None of us were hurting for money, except for Arturio. So, I had some money wired from my bank in Key West and gave our buddy twenty thousand dollars to keep him out of trouble during our stay in Caracas, and to help set him up in the Keys. We had all agreed to take Arturio back to Key

West with us. We had hopes it might offer him a new perspective on life. (Other than bars, tequila, and revolvers…)

Will chuckled at that. "The only difference between Key West and Santa Elena de Uairén is that in Key West it's not legal to shoot yourself," he muttered with a smile. "Everything else is up for grabs."

As for Slinkan and the very valuable collection of artifacts he had accrued over the years, we would have to come back in the immediate future and collect those for him. He found them, they were his, and we had no right to keep them from him.

But the truth was, I didn't want him returning to the cavern again. We would come back soon, gather up his collection of artifacts from his secret room by the river, and bring them to him and his parents. But after that, I wanted him to begin to put all of his time in the jungle, including his memory of that experience, in the far back of his mind. The more it became surreal, like a dream, the safer everyone would be. There was, of course, hardly any way in hell he could find his way back to the cavern. And, in fact, he had never even entered the remarkable mausoleum portion that we had found.

During our final week in Caracas, I had seen our little friend Slinkan begin to find himself, which was an extraordinary accomplishment. He was back in the world again. He was safe and he had found those who loved him.

The one suffering the most from this displacement was probably Shadow. Motel rooms and walks in the park for a quick pee in the bushes just wasn't his style. I could see that he missed the open spaces — the wind, the jungle, and the water.

So did I. It was time for us to go.

KEY WEST, THREE WEEKS LATER…

We were all gathered around a dockside table at Schooner Wharf in Key West — the full membership of the Hole in the Coral Wall Gang. Even Shane O'Neal and his wife had joined us for dinner to celebrate survival and success. The air was filled with the scent of orange blossoms and hibiscus, and the salty rich smells of the sea. The background stereo was piping out an old Jimmy Buffett tune, and I could hear our boy crooning about a white sports coat and a pink crustacean. All this blended with the savory aroma of fresh boiled shrimp, broiled lobster, and the culinary trademark of the Keys, conch fritters.

Everyone was pleasantly glazed, although Crazy Eddie might have been a little ahead of us in the race toward inebriation thanks to the killer pot he'd been nipping on. Shadow was contentedly curled up at my feet. When we had settled into our seats, a smallish, wafer-thin waiter in an oversized Hawaiian shirt had come over and taken our drink orders. He glanced down at Shadow, who was almost under the table, and looked at me with a touch of disdain.

"We don't allow...*animals*...in the restaurant, sir," he said.

"Then tell him to leave," I said.

Shadow looked up at him as if he understood every word (he probably did) and offered a low growl, heavy and menacing.

The skinny fellow's fingers did a nervous little dance and he stepped back, flustered. This was above his pay grade.

I handed him twenty dollars. "It's okay," I whispered confidentially. "He only eats bad guys, and you wouldn't even be a snack."

Amid the laughter, I could see that all of us had finally begun to relax. It had been a harrowing and damned exciting few weeks, with lost treasure, cowboy diamond bosses, *brujas,* bandits, boats, and planes. Great barroom stories, as Eddie would say. But it felt really nice now to wake up in the morning and not have to worry about someone wanting to kill you or steal from you.

We were, of course, already looking for a new Goose for Eddie. (It was probably the third or fourth. I had begun to lose count.) Arturio was doing well. He had found a nice little apartment off Front Street and had purchased a used but stylish Mustang, like mine. He was rapidly sliding into the Key West lifestyle — which wasn't all that dissimilar to Santa Elena de Uairén. But here, you weren't required to kill yourself if you lost at a game of cards.

All in all, everyone was quite content. We had survived the nearly impossible once again, and in another week or so, we were preparing to return for Slinka's treasure. Once we had given Slinka what he had collected over the years, and perhaps had taken a handful of relics from the adjoined mausoleum — for expenses — we could put that all behind us. For the time being...

Well, that is to say, we could put *most* of it behind us. There was, of course, the bewildering, paradoxical, but thoroughly buried Cave of the Stars, with its social and scientific implications.

After a good deal of thought, we all came to the conclusion that some things are better off left undiscovered. Man is a confused enough creature as it is — no point in discouraging or confounding him further regarding his faith and his origins. In these troubled times, our belief in a greater power is like a secret, wonderful weapon that protects and guides us — from our mores and codes, to our tolerance and benevolence. It works for me and my companions, I know that.

Over the years, and thanks to friends like Will, Travis, Eddie, Cody, and Rufus, I've learned that life is really nothing more than a series of lessons. No one requires that you learn them, but you're tested periodically, regardless, to see how you're doing.

Intertwined in all of this is the gift of faith. It's a mercurial essence that seems to slip away at times, then returns when you least expect it, like an old friend knocking at your door. While it's most often associated with spirit, faith is really an all-encompassing principle that includes friends, family, and a deep, elemental confidence in ourselves regarding what is good and right. It is also the harbinger and nurturer of courage. The most fortunate of us are those who accept our faith as a partner in life and have come to the understanding that we are simply not alone on this remarkable journey.

Sail on, my friends. Sail on...

I hope you have enjoyed this novel. If you would like to be added to my mailing list (to stay apprised of new novels and to receive bimonthly updates and my newspaper columns), email me at: reisig@ipa.net

—*Michael Reisig*

And…be sure to read the rest of
Michael Reisig's best-selling

ROAD TO KEY WEST SERIES

THE ROAD TO KEY WEST

The Road to Key West is an adventurous, humorous sojourn that cavorts its way through the 1970s Caribbean, from Key West and the Bahamas to Cuba and Central America—a Caribbean brew of part-time pirates, heartless larcenists, wily women, voodoo bokors, drug smugglers, and a wacky Jamaican soothsayer.

Kindle Book only $3.99

To Preview or Purchase this book on amazon.com, use this link:
http://www.amazon.com/dp/B004RPMYF8

BACK ON THE ROAD TO KEY WEST
The Golden Scepter—Book II

An ancient map and a lost pirate treasure, a larcenous Bahamian scoundrel with his gang of cutthroats, a wild-and-crazy journey into South America in search of a magical antediluvian device, and perilous, hilarious encounters with outlandish villains and zany friends will keep you locked to your seat and giggling maniacally.

Kindle Book only $3.99

To Preview or Purchase this book on amazon.com, use this link: http://www.amazon.com/dp/B00FC9D94I

ALONG THE ROAD TO KEY WEST
The Truthmaker—Book III

Fast-paced humor and adventure with wacky pilots, quirky con men, mad villains, bold women, and a gadget to die for. Florida Keys adventurers Kansas Stamps and Will Bell find their lives turned upside down when they discover a truth device hidden in the temple of an ancient civilization. Enthralled by the virtue of personally dispensing truth and justice with this unique tool, they soon discover that everyone wants what they have—from the government to the Vatican.

Kindle Book only $3.99

To Preview or Purchase this book on amazon.com, use this link: http://www.amazon.com/dp/B00G5B3HEY

SOMEWHERE ON THE ROAD TO KEY WEST
The Emerald Cave—Book IV

The captivating diary of an amateur archaeologist sends our intrepid explorers on a journey into the heart of the Panamanian jungle in search of *La cueva de Esmeralda* (the Emerald Cave), and a lost Spanish treasure. But local brigand Tu Phat Shong and his gang of cutthroats are searching for the same treasure. If that wasn't enough, one of the Caribbean's nastiest drug lords has a score to settle with our reluctant heroes.

Kindle Book only $3.99

To Preview or Purchase this book on amazon.com, use this link: http://www.amazon.com/dp/B00NOABMKA

DOWN THE ROAD TO KEY WEST
Pancho Villa's Gold—Book V

If you're looking for clever fun with zany characters and electric high adventure, this one's for you! Reisig's newest offering is guaranteed to keep you locked to your seat and slapping at the pages while burbling up a giggle or two. In the fifth book of this series, our reluctant Caribbean heroes find themselves competing for the affections of a beautiful antiquities dealer and searching for the lost treasure of Mexico's most renowned desperado.

Kindle Book only $3.99

To Preview or Purchase this book on amazon.com, use this link: http://www.amazon.com/dp/B01EPI6XY4

BEYOND THE ROAD TO KEY WEST
Mayan Gold—Book VI

First, the reader is drawn back over 400 years to the magnificent Mayan empire — to the intrigue of powerful rulers, Spanish invasion, and an adventure/love story that survives the challenge of time. Moving forward several centuries, Kansas and Will stumble upon a collection of ancient writings and the tale of a treasure that was cached by the great Mayan ruler, Nachán Can...

If you're looking for remarkable characters, high adventure, enduring romance, and absolutely bizarre situations, come follow Will and Kansas in *Beyond The Road To Key West.*

Kindle Book only $3.99

To Preview or Purchase this book on amazon.com, use this link: http://www.amazon.com/dp/B01M293NDP

A FAR ROAD TO KEY WEST
Emeralds and Lies—Book VII

In the seventh book of Michael Reisig's best-selling *Road To Key West* series, Kansas Stamps, Will Bell, and the "Hole in the Coral Wall Gang" face their greatest challenges ever. They return to the Guatemalan jungle to retrieve the remainder of a Mayan king's incredible treasure, but in the process find themselves engaged in a grassroots revolution, pursued by a vengeful colonel in the Guatemalan military, and immersed in the intrigue of a World War II Nazi treasure. Then, there's the beautiful sister of a revolutionary, the golden Swiss francs, and the greatest challenge of all — *Granja Penal de Pavón* — the most terrifying prison in all of Central America. Wrap all this around factual historic and modern-day circumstances, and you've got a zinger called *A Far Road To Key West.*

Kindle Book only $3.99

To Preview or Purchase this book on amazon.com, use this link: http://www.amazon.com/dp/B072VRR2VY

Also, be sure to read...

CARIBBEAN GOLD
THE TREASURE OF TORTUGA

In 1668, Englishman Trevor Holte and the audacious freebooter Clevin Greymore sail from the Port of London for the West Indies. They set out in search of adventure and wealth, but the challenges they encounter are beyond their wildest dreams—the brutal Spanish, ruthless buccaneers, a pirate king, the lure of Havana, and the women, as fierce in their desires as Caribbean storms.

And then, there was the gold—wealth beyond imagination. But some treasures outlive the men who bury them...

Kindle Book only $3.99

To Preview or Purchase this book on amazon.com, use this link: http://www.amazon.com/dp/B00S8SR0WW

CARIBBEAN GOLD
THE TREASURE OF TIME

In the spring of 1980, three adventurers set out from Key West in search of a lost treasure on the Isle of Tortuga, off the coast of Haiti. Equipped with an ancient parchment and a handful of clues, they embark on a journey that carries them back across time, challenging their courage and their imaginations, presenting them with remarkable allies and pitting them against an amalgam of unrelenting enemies. In the process, they uncover far more than a treasure. They discover the power of friendship and faith, the unflagging capacity of spirit, and come to realize that some things are forever...

Kindle Book only $3.99

To Preview or Purchase this book on amazon.com, use this link:
http://www.amazon.com/dp/B00S8SR0WW

And...

CARIBBEAN GOLD
THE TREASURE OF MARGARITA

The Treasure of Margarita spans three centuries of high adventure. Beginning in 1692, in the pirate stronghold of Port Royal, it carries the reader across the Southern Hemisphere in a collage of rip-roaring escapades. Then it soars forward five generations, into modern-day intrigue and romance in Key West and the Caribbean.

A staggering fortune of Spanish black pearls and a 300-year-old letter with a handful of clues set the course that Travis Christian and William Cody embark upon. But it's not an easy sail. Seasoned with remarkable women and bizarre villains (including a Barbadian treasure-hunting gangster, a duo of persistent South Florida scoundrels, and last but not least, the Russian mob), the adventure ricochets from one precarious situation to the next.

Kindle Book only $3.99

To Preview or Purchase this book on amazon.com, use this link: http://www.amazon.com/dp/B00X1E2X2K

Made in the USA
Las Vegas, NV
26 April 2022